Harry Brett is a pseudon[...] the author of nine pre[...] *Criminal World* and *Get Me Out Of Here*. He also co-authored the DS Jack Frost novel, *First Frost*, under the pseudonym James Henry. His work has been translated into many languages. His fifth novel, *Kids' Stuff*, received an Arts Council Writers' Award in 2002, and became a long-running stage play in Riga, Latvia.

He has judged numerous literary prizes, including the John Lewellyn Rhys Prize and the Theakstons Old Peculier Crime Novel of the Year. He has been the Literary Editor of *Esquire* magazine and the Books Editor of the *Daily Mirror*. He teaches Creative Writing at the University of East Anglia, where he is a Senior Lecturer and the director of the new Creative Writing MA Crime Fiction.

He lives in Norwich with his family.

The Goodwins by Harry Brett:

Time to Win
Red Hot Front

Praise for *Time to Win*:

'*The Godfather* in Great Yarmouth' Ian Rankin

'A tale of family and power and mayhem, Harry Brett's *Time to Win* is a winner on all counts' Megan Abbott

'An atmospheric and riveting tale' *Guardian*

'*Time to Win* is fearsomely good: doomy and atmospheric' Nicci French

'* * * * * – dark and gritty' *The Sun*

'A heart-pounding thriller for our time . . . A 21st century *Long Good Friday*' Tony Parsons

'Darkly brooding and atmospheric . . . Noir at its best' M.J. McGrath

'Harry Brett writes a fun plot with witty elegance' *The Times*

'Gritty and stark, with a skilful evocation of the down-at-hell, bleak seaside town' *Sunday Mirror*

Time to Win

Harry Brett

corsair

CORSAIR

First published in Great Britain in 2017 by Corsair
This paperback edition published in 2018 by Corsair

1 3 5 7 9 10 8 6 4 2

A CIP catalogue record for this book
is available from the British Library.

PB ISBN: 978-1-4721-5265-7

Typeset in Granjon LT by Hewer Text UK Ltd, Edinburgh
Printed and bound in Great Britain by Clays Ltd, St Ives plc

Papers used by Corsair are from well-managed forests
and other responsible sources.

MIX
Paper from
responsible sources
FSC® C104740

Corsair
An imprint of
Little, Brown Book Group
Carmelite House
50 Victoria Embankment
London EC4Y 0DZ

An Hachette UK Company
www.hachette.co.uk

www.littlebrown.co.uk

To Rachel

The quay was deserted, glowing black. What light there was, from the distant street lamps and warehouse security lights, was creeping out onto the water with the steady drizzle.

Across the river more lights rose up into the low night sky, which was pressing down hard on the world. He knew what he was looking for on the other side, but he couldn't narrow his focus. It was a struggle keeping his eyes open. There was this sharp buzzing pain on one side of his head as well. He wanted the pain to go away. The voices too.

Shut up, he thought he said. But no one listened. It was too late. Get off me, he could have added, because it felt as if someone was stretching across him, playing with the centre console, positioning his feet around the pedals, though all the wrong way round. He couldn't uncross his legs for the life of him. He was not in control. There was a pain in his chest now also. It felt like he was fighting, bursting to be let go, but he also knew how weak he had become. A fat useless fuck. His words, or words he was hearing.

A breeze had developed, even though he was still in the car. Perhaps the window was open, the door, but it was becoming even harder to feel, to see ahead, which was wrong. There was no ahead this way. Someone was telling him, again and again, that he was going to die. It was all his fault. Hearing, does that go last, he thought? If so he could have sworn he then heard a soft, Goodbye. A different voice. Female.

But there was another sound, after finally going over the edge. It was the sound of water, as clear as perfectly polished glass.

There was a time when the sound of rain was comforting, calming. Now it pissed her off. It was autumn already, she remembered. September 1. It was not her favourite month. She let the patter swirl around her head for another few minutes, realising she was listening out for something else. Breathing, snoring. But it wasn't there. She lifted her head, opening her eyes. Propped herself on her elbows. Rich wasn't there.

Tatty flung back her side of the duvet and climbed out onto the soft carpet, peering through the gloom for her dressing gown. She got to the blinds before spotting it in its own silky puddle, having slipped off the back of the chaise longue. Rich was forever castigating her for leaving her clothes lying around, clothes he'd spent a lot of money on.

She opened the blinds, taking in the wet grey slapping against the huge French doors. In only her nightie, short, also silk, she had an urge to open the doors, step out onto the balcony and feel the wet and cold on her skin. She needed to wake up, shake the Zimovane from her system. Looking out across the stretch of wide, dull grass that made up the top of Gorleston's tired esplanade to a short stretch of gunmetal grey sea, which all too rapidly merged with sky, she thought better of it. She reached down for her dressing gown, stood, noticing a couple of figures, directly across Marine Parade.

They were not facing her way, not moving either, but hunched together on the pavement by the entrance to the last car park on the front, like the world they hated owed them everything. They were wearing scum gear, as Rich would call it. Hoodies, tracksuit bottoms, cheap trainers. None of which, she suspected, had ever been near a washing machine, or paid for. Smoke began swirling around their covered heads. A car, a long, light brown Lexus, rolled from the car park, seemingly nudging them out of the way, and they set off, in an absurd loping gait, towards Yarmouth, from where no doubt they had come.

Relieved, Tatty stepped back from the French doors and slipped her gown on, realising how dim the bedroom still was. Lights, she needed lights, warmth, on this most dull of early autumn mornings. She made her way straight to the en-suite, pressing the control panel as she entered. With a ceiling of halogen beating down on her she keyed the shower buttons, and caught herself in the mirror as the water gained heat. Her tan was fading fast. The air in this part of the world stripped you like sulphuric acid. Sun rarely happened.

Rich had said she shouldn't bother coming back with him from Ibiza. She could spend another month by the pool. No, she couldn't. There was the Smokehouse project nearing completion, her elder children to see, the house to get ready for Zach's return, before he was off again. 'You'll not be seeing much of me, sweetheart,' Rich had said.

'We're that close to getting the Americans on board. And I expect I'll have to be in Athens at some point soon.' He always wanted her out of the way. She never saw much of him. He hadn't even come home last night. It wasn't the first time.

Slowly the shower restored some feeling, some clarity. Stepping out, wrapping the towel around her paling body, she felt a tired, dull anger growing. He could have rung. He could have left a message. 'I didn't want to disturb you, sweetheart. Not in the middle of the night. I don't know where the time went. But we made great progress. It'll be signed within days.' Those would be his shady words, when he did show up, she could imagine all too well. He rarely surprised her.

To check once more she walked back through to the bedroom, to her bedside table, the mobile on it. No texts or voicemails from Rich. Or email, not that that was his style. He never emailed her. He emailed his kids, but not her. She wasn't sure he even knew her email address. Wrapped in a towel, she picked up the phone, shook it, as if that might somehow refresh the apps. Nothing changed. She wasn't going to ring him.

Throwing it on the mound of duvet in the middle of the bed, she then picked up her watch, which until recently was his watch – a heavy white gold Rolex. He now had an Apple Watch, the 18-carat rose gold one, which he barely knew how to use. It was just past nine. Late for her, but she was still on holiday time. She put the chunky Rolex on and, edging towards the French window, she thought about what she was going to wear today. What could you wear to protect yourself against that? Not some shitty tracksuit, for sure. Oilskins. The word came to her, as if from another country. Another century anyway. Did people still wear oilskins? Did they still exist?

The scum were not in sight, anywhere up Marine Parade, but someone was at the door. The front door. She could hear the bell, ding-donging away downstairs. That sound was from another century, because the bell had been there when they'd bought the place, nearly thirty years ago now. It was the only thing they hadn't changed. Rich thought it quaint.

Who the hell could be ringing it at this time? Her mind was now clear enough to process information, to think more rationally. It was too early for the post or a parcel delivery. It was not the kids, having forgotten their keys, which used to be such a common occurrence, because Sam and Ben were in London, where they'd been all summer, and Zach was in the Atlantic. Could Rich somehow have forgotten or lost his? It had never happened before. Besides, he wouldn't use the bell, he'd thump on the door, and shout when no one came quick enough.

She was out of the bedroom and hurrying along the landing when she realised she was still wrapped in nothing more than a towel. But it was a far more modest piece of cloth than her dressing gown. She continued down the wide, softly carpeted stairs and along the hard oak floor of the hallway, lit only by the poor natural light seeping through the smoked security glass panel at the top of the door. She thought she could make out a head, in a hood.

Just before she reached the door she felt something shift deep inside her. A small tremor.

She had a sudden, terrible urge to confront life, full on, sod any precautions that Rich was always so insistent upon. She flung open the door, not thinking whether the security chain was in place, anger and aggression coursing through. She knew it was not going to be good news. It never was when people visited them out of the blue. 'Hello?' she said, though faintly, short of breath.

'Mrs Goodwin?' A woman stepped forward.

She was shorter than Tatty, rounder and far paler, and stuffed into a too-tight dark waterproof. That's what people wore now, waterproofs, made from high-tech synthetic fabrics. Zach had loads. 'Yes?' Tatty said.

'I'm Detective Sergeant Julie Spiros, family liaison officer for Norfolk Constabulary, West Yarmouth branch, and this is Detective Inspector Peter Leonard.' She was holding out her ID. Scum of a different sort.

The man next to her nodded, his lips shut tight in a grimace. His waterproof was hanging off him by the hood. He was tall and skeletal. He was not holding out his ID. He didn't need to.

'May we come in?' Spiros said, stepping closer. 'Perhaps we can go somewhere where you can sit down. Is anyone else in the house?'

Tatty must have nodded a yes, and then shook a no, her confidence already shot, because she found herself walking backwards with the two police officers. A chunk of cold wet cloud came inside with them. Their wet shoes squeaked on the oak flooring, and Tatty was pleased Rich wasn't there because he would have been livid with them for not wiping their feet properly.

'Would you like to put some clothes on?' Spiros said. 'I can come with you.'

Tatty looked down at the white towel. She was still damp from her shower. The air in the hall was now damp too, and cold. She would like to get dressed. But it was never quick. She was not going to let someone she didn't know come with her either. 'No,' she said. 'I'm OK.'

At the end of the large hall, to the left of the staircase, tucking the towel tighter around her, she didn't know which way to go, into the sitting room, or the kitchen. Would they want tea, coffee? Was she meant to make them a drink? Rich had always treated the police with as much courtesy as he could muster. She thought she needed a coffee at least. It was the right time in the morning, so she led them that way.

In the huge kitchen, which once upon a time had been a double garage, she made straight for the marble-topped island, reached out for its thick, firm edge, turned to face her unexpected visitors, realising she was not going to make any coffee until they told her why they were there. They knew it too.

'Would you like to sit down?' said Spiros, glancing around the cold airy place, at the acres of glass looking out onto thick drizzle.

There were bar stools around the island, and over in a corner the glass-topped dining table, around which stood some steel chairs. It was not a comfortable kitchen. It was rarely warm, despite the under-floor heating. 'Why are you here?' Tatty said, a voice, her voice coming back.

'I'm sorry, but we have some bad news,' said Spiros. 'Please, sit down.' The man, Leonard, had still to say a word.

'No,' Tatty said. Not sure whether she was saying no to the idea of bad news, or no to the order to sit down. Her mind flashed to her children. Ben would be at work, in the City. Sam would be at work, down the road in Holborn. Zach would be being tossed around in the Bay of Biscay. It could get very rough, so she'd been told. Even at this time of the year. Had the boat capsized? Sunk? How would anyone know, so soon? An emergency signal set off? A tiny beacon in monstrous waves, Zach clinging to a life raft. He was a strong, tough kid.

'There's been a fatal incident,' said Leonard.

So he did speak, when it mattered. And Tatty felt like she was in a bad TV show. She shook her head, found she was still clinging, not to a life raft but the marble top of the kitchen island. His voice was as thin and grave as his stature.

'A car, your husband's car, went into the river by Fish Wharf, the back of his offices,' Leonard continued.

'I'm afraid your husband's body was found in the car this morning, by police divers,' said Spiros.

'Oh,' said Tatty. 'Oh.'

'An operation is underway to retrieve the vehicle,' said Leonard.

'What about him – Rich?' said Tatty. 'Where's he?'

'The body has been recovered from the water,' said Spiros, her face colouring. 'There was nothing anyone could do. I'm so sorry.'

'How? How did it happen?' Tatty said. She found she'd let go of the marble top. She also found she could breathe. Zach's boat had not sunk. He had not drowned. Rich had drowned.

'We don't know yet,' said Leonard. 'Obviously we'll be doing everything we can to get to the bottom of what happened. Have you found any notes?'

'Notes?' said Tatty, feeling her mouth move in ways she knew were not appropriate.

'Explaining perhaps why he might wish to take his life?'

'You think he committed suicide?' She almost laughed.

'We'll need to look at everything,' Leonard continued. 'There'll be a post-mortem.'

'It's definitely him, is it?' Tatty said, quite calmly.

'We believe so,' said Spiros. 'If you'd like to see the body, we can arrange that.'

'Yes,' said Tatty. That was the thing to do, wasn't it? She looked down once more at her towel, at her shins, her feet poking out and now looking rather brown against the white marble. She tried harder not to smile. 'When?'

'We'll make the arrangements, and let you know.' Spiros again. 'Is there anyone you'd like to call, who you'd like to be here with you, this morning? Can we call anyone for you?'

There was, but Tatty was not going to say who. She felt her heart rushing forward.

'I'm afraid,' said Leonard, 'that given who your husband was, we're not sure how long his death will remain out of the media.'

8

'We urge you,' chipped in Spiros, 'to contact family members, friends, those people who need to know, as soon possible.'

There weren't many. Ben, Sam, Megan perhaps, Nina too – she'd be upset. 'But Zach's in the middle of the Atlantic,' she said. 'His phone won't be working.'

'Can I make you a cup of tea?' said Spiros.

Tatty hadn't noticed her accent before.

2

'Where the hell's Simon?' said Frank, swerving across South Quay and into the parking bay at the front of Goodwin House. He was on the hands-free, talking to Sian, Rich's PA, who was in Goodwin House, a few metres away.

'Amsterdam,' she said. 'He's coming straight back.'

'When did he go to Amsterdam?'

'Yesterday evening. He was on his way to Las Vegas.'

'Vegas?' Frank didn't know anything about that. 'Without Rich?'

'It was pretty much last minute. Their surveyors are still not happy – something to do with contaminated land by the old oil depot. He was going with Amit, Amit Sharma, and that scientist woman from the university. Rich was meant to be in Athens early next week, so he couldn't have gone, but . . .' Her voice tailed off.

Frank didn't see the swarm of police, the tape, the vehicles, the fire brigade and an ambulance too, until he'd edged his Range Rover into the parking space at the side of the building, his usual spot. There was a dirty yellow crane on a barge rising out of the Yare. He had no idea how they could have got that bit of equipment there so swiftly. Had

Rich's Merc been retrieved already? He couldn't see it on the quay. Though there were too many vehicles and people for him to see everything.

Rather than walk round the rest of the building and onto the jammed river frontage, he turned back towards the main entrance. He was not prepared for the police, this much rain. Besides, no one seemed to have noticed him. He pressed his card against the pad and the glass double front doors parted slowly with a shaky whirr. They were going to give out one day soon. They weren't built for this climate. The lobby was empty, it was always empty, and he made straight for the stairs. The lift was as flimsy as the doors. He needed solid ground under his feet this morning. Not that the stairs were particularly firm.

It was a squat, three-storey building, previously occupied by Halliburton. It wasn't built to attract attention, or last. Its best asset was the position. Rich and Simon had been talking about knocking it down and putting up something with more flair. Simon anyway. Reaching the first floor, Frank wondered whether that would ever happen now. He couldn't believe Rich was dead. He'd worked for him for twenty years, on and off. Rich was the only person who'd consistently treated him with any respect. But it hadn't only been about respect of course.

He pushed through to Sian's office, which also doubled as the reception area. The black leather furniture had never looked right.

Sian was on the phone, another call. She looked up and waved sadly. She hadn't been working there for more than a year. Her father owned the North Beach Holiday Park.

She was his youngest, and he wasn't busy enough to employ her as well as her siblings. She was too small to be pretty. Feeling stiff and damp, Frank went to the nearest chair and slumped down. The leather creaked. He got out his phone, but no one had called or messaged him since Sian, thirty minutes or so ago. The news was the same – more illegal immigrants, traffickers and terrorists having a field day, no end to the Brexit negotiations – so he tilted his head back and looked up at the greying ceiling tiles. The building was riddled with asbestos.

Rich liked the odd drink, and cigar, a good plate of food too. He was a big man. But he was only fifty-two. He had only been fifty-two, Frank corrected himself. Too young to go over the edge of a quay in a new Merc with dynamic stability control. What the fuck had really happened? Frank looked at Sian. She was still on the phone, no longer looking his way. The police could be all over this building. He knew he should do something, but he worked for Rich, had worked for Rich, not Simon.

'Frank,' said Sian, putting the receiver down, 'I don't know what to say.'

She was never short of words, normally. 'What happened?' he said, getting up now. He walked towards her desk. 'What do you know?' He was conscious of his own size, how he was looming over her. He knew people found him intimidating. That was the point of him, Rich used to laugh.

'When I got here this morning, the police, and, you know, the fire service and the lifeboat people, were out the back. Loads of them.'

'They're still there,' said Frank.

'They wouldn't let me go anywhere near. I didn't think . . . I didn't think it had anything to do with Rich, but one of the ships further down or something . . . that someone had fallen in. Does happen.'

Much of this side of the river was owned and controlled by the Port Authority. A few wind-farm support vessels and North Sea rig supply ships hired spots along the quay-side. Other cargo and survey ships dotted the port, though none directly out the back of Goodwin House. There was a kink in the River Yare that made mooring anything normal size or above out of the question. This was one of the reasons Rich bought the building. Free river frontage. Goodwin House's land ended ten metres from the edge.

'What made them go there?'

'I don't know,' Sian said. 'Like I said, they were there when I got here this morning. Somebody must have seen something, and reported it.'

'So when did you find out it was Rich's car?'

'It was weird. They rang, the police, asking for Rich, and then they started asking about his car.'

'The car's registered here, to the business,' said Frank, more to himself.

'Then they came round. They weren't here long. It's not as if people don't know who Rich is – was.' She sucked in air, perhaps for effect. 'He was a good man, all that he did for this town. They said I wasn't to go anywhere, and that they'd be back.'

Frank looked over his shoulder at the taut, black-and-chrome office furniture, and through the glass to the other offices on this floor. They were empty. 'Where is everybody?'

'Celine's ill. She's been ill all week. And I texted Mark, told him not to come in.'

'So he knows about Rich?' He didn't like Mark. Didn't trust him. He was too good-looking, too well presented – for Great Yarmouth.

Sian coloured. 'I rang you first.'

'They told you his body was found in the car?' Frank said. Things seemed to have moved fast. The police blundering around, opening their big mouths.

Sian nodded. 'There'd been a fatal incident, they said, involving Richard Goodwin.'

Frank exhaled air. He needed a cigarette, but he hadn't smoked for years. 'The offices, were they locked when you got here, first thing?'

'Yes, all seemed normal – apart from what was going on out the back. Everything was locked up and the alarm was on.'

'What time did Rich leave yesterday evening?' said Frank. It was a stupid question. Rich didn't keep regular hours. Frank had always struggled to keep track of him when he wasn't needed.

'He was here when I left,' said Sian. 'Him and Simon. The accountant, Amit Sharma, had been in earlier in the afternoon. But he'd gone, before me. To get ready for the trip – I guess.'

'Mark, the others?'

'The only people left past five were Rich and Simon.'

'When was this decision made to go to Las Vegas?'

'Earlier in the week. Tuesday?'

It was only Thursday today. Thursday the first of September, Frank thought. Rich's birthday was in early September, next week, the seventh. He didn't want to think how young he would have been.

'They were going through all the paperwork and drawings yet again yesterday afternoon,' said Sian.

Frank hadn't been into the office since last Friday, before the bank holiday weekend, almost a week ago. He wasn't expected to be in every day. That was never the arrangement. He had other things to keep an eye on, stuff that Rich couldn't be seen to be involved with. Frank hadn't spoken to Rich for a few days either. They called each other when necessary. Frank was always ready to come running when needed. 'Do you know if Rich had been in contact with Will Keene yesterday, or the day before?' Keene was the company lawyer, and an old friend of Rich's. He'd also been fielding the HMRC enquiries, which were becoming personal. They'd been going on for months. Didn't seem like there was any urgency. Rich hadn't been overly anxious, this time.

'Probably,' Sian said. 'You know what they were like. They spoke all the time. But there wasn't a meeting or anything. Not that I was aware of.'

'What time was Simon's flight?'

'Ten past eight,' Sian said. 'Norwich–Amsterdam.'

Frank turned, opened the door to the empty office space at the back of the building. He walked through the cheaply partitioned room, avoiding the neat desks, to the windows stretched across the rear. The venetian blinds were down, they were always down, but the dusty slats were as horizontal as they got. Without having to angle them he could see through clear enough. He could see more than he wanted from up here.

The yellow crane on the back of the barge was lifting the car. Or had been. The car, Rich's months-old silver Mercedes CLS coupé, was half in and half out of the River Yare. Dirty red straps were attached front and back. The car was emerging rear first. Except there was no movement that Frank could discern. Had something jammed? The rain was coming down harder, and the wind was streaking across the river, ripples turning to white caps. An orange-and-white supply vessel, covered in rust like a bad rash, was over to the right. The mooring space in front of it was vacant.

Frank looked down again, at the squat capstans, not spaced close enough to stop a car, at the authorities, dolled up as if their lives depended on it. All show. Who was he meant to protect now, he wondered.

The car began to move, as he looked, further out of the water, but it was still tipped forward. Rich had never liked that car; he'd wanted the new S-Class, but there was a supply issue. It must have got stuck on something in the drink, otherwise the tide would have shifted it. Frank didn't want to see Rich's body, and presumed they must have already removed it from the vehicle and taken it to the morgue. A clutch of police divers had gathered over by a rubber inflatable, which was sitting on the quay. There was no ambulance, no black undertaker's van, among the many vehicles and all the equipment. Everything was dripping.

Directly across the river, perched on Ferry Hill, was a sleek grey box. The wide, tall windows were reflecting the low grey sky, while the long balconies were sheltered behind more glass, which was reflecting more of the sky, and the dark, fast-flowing river. Even in such weather the building stood out, shiny in the gloom. Simon said he had spent a million on it – cheap for what he got. A shitload of money for a concrete box was what Rich had said about it, pissed off that Simon, and his fancy London architect, had grabbed the view from Goodwin House.

3

She couldn't wait any longer. Besides the house was suddenly too crowded. 'Sam, Ben,' Tatty shouted quietly, 'I'm going for a walk.' She didn't intend for them to hear and hurried to the closet, where she started rifling through the coats, the anoraks, the waterproofs. It wasn't raining hard, but it was always blowy on the front. Blowy was the word Nina the cleaner used. 'It's blowy out, Mrs Goodwin,' she'd say. *Mrs Goodwin, Mrs Goodwin*. It was never Tatty, or Tatiana. Tatty had long given up urging Nina to call her by her first name.

Nina's mum had come with the house. Then Nina had inherited the job when her mum became too decrepit. Nina was born in Gorleston, like her mother. Had never lived anywhere else. She was exactly Tatty's age, though Tatty had lived elsewhere once. Not that she ever tried to think about it.

Tatty found something that seemed to fit. It was a horrible shade of green. She looked down at her feet, her pumps. Where were her trainers? Her phone she knew was safely in her jeans pocket. She spotted her old trainers in a corner, next to a pair of Rich's, still bright purple and white. She wasn't sure he'd ever worn them. The only

18

exercise he ever took was fucking. He was particularly proud of that.

She backed out of the closet, in the horrible green jacket and her old trainers, desperate to get out of the house before anyone noticed. She wasn't used to creeping around at home. That was Rich. And the kids, when they were younger anyway.

'Mum?' came Sam's voice, as she was thinking of her.

A couple of steps short of the front door, Tatty turned to see her daughter rushing down the stairs.

'Where are you going?'

'For a walk, love. I need some air.'

Sam looked perplexed. 'Out there? You never go for a walk.'

'Sam, I need to get out.'

'I'm coming. You shouldn't be on your own.'

'I want to be on my own.'

'Since when have you ever wanted to be on your own?'

'Oh, for God's sake, Sam.' She could feel her phone trill, a message coming in. She knew who it would be from. Longing immediately gave way to irritation. She'd had enough impatience, she realised, for a lifetime.

'Mum, I'm coming too. We've barely spoken. Please. He was my father.'

Rich's determination was in Sam's eyes. Fortunately, she had her mother's face and physique, or so everyone said. 'When I get back, we'll sit down,' Tatty said. 'You're not even dressed. You don't want to go out there. It's blowy.' When Tatty said blowy she still didn't feel like a local, even after all these years. She felt like a fraud. She swung round, strode towards the front door, let herself out. Sam might have been in the dark about many things, but so was she.

As she stepped from the shelter of the porch the wind slapped her right in the face. She eyed her car, taking up space for two on the forecourt. Rich would have had something to say about that. She didn't have the keys with her and immediately forgot about driving off in warm, quiet German luxury. She was going to walk. As Sam said, she never went for a walk.

She reached the edge of the property, glanced back at the house, which had grown over the years with the children. But unlike the children, the house was out of proportion, ugly. It was never meant to have got so big. She suddenly hated all the frilly, decorative bits of plastic too. Perhaps she'd knock it down, start again. Put up something new and stark, like Simon and Jess's place. Or move.

She crossed the road, took the tired tarmac footpath straight across the grass to the upper esplanade. There were a few people and dogs about, but nobody near. The sea was shuddering below, waiting for the smallest of excuses to explode. She opted to stick to the upper esplanade and set off towards Yarmouth, the onshore wind keeping her from straying too near the edge. Up ahead the cranes and vast struts of the outer harbour dominated the skyline.

When they first moved here the outer harbour didn't exist. Many of the locals thought it still shouldn't exist. The project appeared to have been misconceived from the beginning, the harbour's original purpose far from being realised. It had cost millions, a large chunk coming from EU funds, now forgotten. Rich had been involved from the beginning, as chair of the Great Yarmouth Regeneration Board. He'd made enough out of it, as had others, which further enhanced his standing. As ever, he'd brushed aside any grumblings when the new harbour had lain idle for so long, and didn't mind too much that Lowestoft had now secured huge state backing to redevelop its port to serve the wind farms. He'd thought his super casino plans were even more crucial to Yarmouth's future.

One strange thing the outer harbour had done was push a load of sand towards Gorleston beach. Nearing the old harbour mouth, Tatty looked down at the acres of dull, golden beach, the lifeguard hut flying a lonely yellow flag. But all the sand was largely wasted. Few ventured across it. It was always too fucking blowy. Perhaps she'd move to the Mediterranean for more than a month a year. She pulled the zip up, though the jacket was no tighter. It was far too big for her. Was it Ben's? Funny, his dress sense was as bad as Rich's had been. Sam had style, as did Zach, when he could be bothered.

Ben had eventually got a message to Zach by a scratchy signal when the boat was sailing close to the French mainland – apparently the satellite equipment was playing up, though Ben had been convinced Zach had given them the wrong number for some reason. Not that Zach could get back any quicker. Not that he'd want to get back any quicker, Tatty thought. Sam was Rich's favourite.

Tatty looked towards the old harbour, with the new harbour, which did seem to be a bit busier nowadays, towering behind it. A small forest of cranes and girders, erected with the cushion of extraordinary backhanders, protection rackets and fraud, at least where Rich was involved.

Who was complaining? No one had ever dared to complain to Rich's face. He was too big, too powerful, too vital.

Sam had gone with her, late yesterday afternoon, when she went to check if it really was Rich who'd died. It had seemed the correct thing to do. The Greek Cypriot police family liaison officer, Spiros, led them into the mortuary, a quiet wing of the James Paget Hospital. At least they hadn't had to go far. And then he was suddenly there – but not. A pale bulk, even more bloated than normal, beached on a massive metal tray. They only pulled the sheet back as far as his bare chest. The room was freezing, and far too bright. Tatty saw the bruise on his temple before anyone said anything. No one had warned them.

'What's happened to his face?' Sam had said.

'There would have been considerable force as the car crashed over the edge and hit the water,' said Spiros, hesitantly.

'What happened to the air bags?' said Tatty. 'I thought they were meant to stop that sort of thing.' A large, shiny Merc, the least you would expect. Not that they would have been able to keep the car afloat, she supposed.

'We're looking into everything,' Spiros had said. 'There will be a full post-mortem as soon as possible. But the pathologists are stretched at the moment. The county council has slashed the pathology budget.'

Tatty felt her phone buzz again. She sighed, deciding she'd walk to the end of the upper esplanade before she took the device out of her pocket. There was no need to hurry any more. To hide. To fear. She was going to have all the time in the world to do exactly what she wanted, do things her way.

It appeared that Rich had drowned, they'd phoned to tell her earlier this morning. An initial post-mortem had found water in his lungs, river muck in his mouth. However, further tests were to be conducted. The police didn't elaborate as to why.

Tatty wondered whether their suspicions had been great enough to hurry up the initial report. She could still see that bump on his head. Considered whether they'd yet extracted his brain — not that they would ever find out what had really gone on in it. Richard Goodwin had done so much for Great Yarmouth. So he'd liked to think. So he'd liked to convince people. But there were those who saw his practices as not such a fucking good thing. You could never be that successful and have no enemies. 'Comes with the territory,' Rich used to brag.

Reaching the last bench, she sat, pulling the phone from her pocket. She twisted her body away from the sea, read the misting screen, sighed once more, when she should have smiled. Ties, more ties, when it was only ever meant to have been a bit of escapism with someone who came on to her persistently, relentlessly, like he cared. Someone who was smart and sophisticated, fit and attractive. She shook her head. She didn't need this, now. She was going to have to map her new territory carefully.

4

'What are you doing?' Ben had been wondering what the scrabbling noise was. He'd considered vermin, rats. He was a London boy now.

'I'm looking for a coat,' Sam said, not turning round in the tight closet.

'Why?'

'I'm going out.'

'Are you taking Mum's car?' They'd both come down by train yesterday, Sam some hours ahead of him. He'd waited until he'd finished work. He wasn't going to hurry any more than he had to.

'Hadn't thought about that.' Her arms dropped to her sides. She shuffled to face him. 'Can't see anything suitable. I was going to walk.'

'Where? It's horrible out.'

'I don't know. Along the front?'

'Why?'

'To see where Mum went?' She shrugged. 'She's not back yet. She left ages ago.'

Ben's mind was still elsewhere.

'Where have you been?' Sam walked out of the closet.

Ben took a step back. Sam's face was taut. 'I was in Dad's study.'

'Doing what?'

'Just being in there.' He glanced over his shoulder. Took a breath, shrugged. 'Looking. It was weird.' He hadn't been in the room for years, and hardly ever on his own. As children they were never allowed, unless they were being bollocked. As adults, well, he for one kept clear. He didn't know what he'd find. He didn't want to know. He wished he hadn't seen what he had: torn wood, busted locks on the drawers. Nothing inside the drawers appeared disturbed, however. But he'd been too nervous to look properly. His mother hadn't said anything. 'Where do you think Mum is then?'

'I don't know. She was being weird. She didn't want me to go with her.'

'She walked off in the rain?' He'd watched her leave the house from upstairs. Saw her head across the grass to the upper walkway, turn towards Yarmouth. He didn't want Sam to think he'd been watching, waiting for an opportunity to do some digging in his father's study.

'Yeah.'

'It's all weird, isn't it?' he said, his dad's desk sticking in his mind. No one had said anything about a burglary, and nothing else in the study looked like it had been disturbed. He'd have to have another look, wait for the right moment. But that room still gave him the creeps.

'I can't work out what she's thinking,' said Sam. 'What she really feels.'

'When have you ever?' Ben shook his head, wanting things to fit together. But they never had. 'He wasn't very nice to her, was he?'

'That's not fair,' said Sam, looking at the front door. 'He spent enough money on her anyway.'

'Fuck's sake, Sam! I can't believe you of all people would think that that's something to shout about.'

His sister flushed. 'What I meant was, he supported all her projects happily enough. The latest one, that old smoke-house, how much is that all costing? They should have pulled it down, with half of Yarmouth.'

Ben didn't say anything. He'd forgotten about it. Forgotten that his mother did work, if work was the right word, occasionally.

'He supported you as well, didn't he?' Sam continued. 'You wouldn't be living in such a fancy flat on your salary alone. Not in King's Cross.'

'You don't know what I earn.'

She spluttered. 'Not that much.'

'He supported all of us, one way or another. But there were reasons why he did anything, and they weren't totally magnanimous.' Ben knew he could be a pompous prick sometimes. Certainly his dad used to tell him as much.

'No one's totally magnanimous.' Sam began heading for the front door, saying over her shoulder, 'He was my father, and I loved him. So did Mum. She stuck with him, for all these years.'

Ben looked beyond Sam to the front door. The bare light oak with the strip of thick smoked glass at the top. He wondered what sort of options his mother actually had. It was practically impossible to do anything his father didn't want you to do. So she'd gone for a walk, finally. 'Sam, don't go running after her. If she wants to be on her own, let her. She'll be all right.'

Sam stopped before she got to the door. Ben knew she wouldn't go any further. She wasn't wearing the correct clothing. He stepped towards her, across the cold, echoey hallway. It was not a comfortable home, never had been, despite the additions and the gadgets, the luxury furnishings and fabrics. She turned round, and he could see her eyes glistening.

She sniffed drily. 'I'm trying to care. Our dad's died. We're never going to see him again. Hear him.' Another dry sniff. 'Or get any of those stupid texts and emails. But it all feels sort of flat. I don't think I feel enough. What's wrong with me?'

'Sam, nothing's wrong with you. Look, I feel the same. Let's have a coffee.' He took her arm gently and pulled her towards the oversized, over-equipped kitchen. 'He was fucking difficult.' Other, more accurate, words were coming to mind.

'No, that's not it,' Sam said, walking beside him. 'I don't think I ever really knew him.'

'Well, you were his favourite,' Ben said.

'That's what makes it worse.'

Ben moved over to the coffee machine and fiddled about while Sam went to stare out of the window at the drizzle falling on the sheltered back garden. Even from where he was he could see that the garden was still meticulously maintained. He had no idea who the gardener or gardeners were now. His thoughts shifted to Nina the cleaner. He knew she was still coming, because he hadn't heard otherwise, and he would have. She was part of the family, more or less. She wouldn't have broken into his dad's desk. She was beyond loyal, wasn't she?

He went to the fridge and was surprised to see four bottles of champagne in the wine rack. His mother hardly ever drank, while his dad had only ever drunk red wine and brandy, except for the odd occasion when the champagne came out and he was obliged to have a glass. He always complained about the bubbles; there were either too many, or too few. Ben then remembered it would have been his father's birthday next week. Had his mother been planning something? A surprise dinner? He would have hated that. His father had never liked surprises.

'Do you think he did it on purpose?' Sam said, still staring out at the garden.

'What?'

'Drove over the edge.'

'You mean kill himself?'

'Yeah.' Her voice was her mother's. Tired. Exasperated. 'That's what the police are suggesting.'

'No, not for a minute. Well, OK, it did occur to me, for a few seconds. But he was Dad. Suicide? No way.'

'They found him behind the steering wheel.'

'That doesn't mean it wasn't an accident – that he'd meant to drive in.'

'He had a big lump, sort of here.' She pointed to her temple. 'It was horrible. The airbags hadn't deployed.'

'Maybe it wasn't going fast enough.'

'Odd sort of accident, then,' said Sam.

'Yeah – odd sort of accident. Look, why don't we let the police do their thing? They'll tell us when they know for sure.'

'You trust them to get it right?'

'You know any better?'

'I am a lawyer, Ben.'

'You're a corporate lawyer, Sam. How long have you even been qualified?'

'Do you have any idea what sort of training we do? Besides, I work for a big firm. It's not all corporate.' Sam was back by the kitchen island, looking at the new coffee machine. 'How does this work?'

Ben pressed a button and a hiss of steam escaped from a gleaming metal pipe. 'It probably needs to warm up.' He stood back, added, 'I think Dad was killed, murdered.' Saying it aloud, he realised, made the idea surprisingly exciting. He wasn't so boring after all. His dad, murdered – what the fuck would they think of him at the office, once it got out?

Sam reached for a coffee cup, placed it under the machine, pressed another button, as if she did know what she was doing, more than him. Coffee sounded like it was being made. Dark liquid began to trickle into the cup.

'If he was killed, I don't see how it could have happened,' she said. 'So, like, someone put the car into drive, and leapt out at the last moment? Dad would have had to have been incapacitated first. Unconscious or something. Otherwise, why wouldn't he have got out? Or tried to climb out once it was in the water? People do get out of sinking cars. I suppose it could have been pushed in – but wouldn't there be some evidence of that? Skid marks? Who would go to such lengths anyway, and risk being seen? Why wouldn't they just shoot him?'

'Dad knew a lot of very stupid people.'

'And some very smart ones.' She lifted the coffee cup from the tray. Put it on the counter. Reloaded the machine. Got another cup. 'I can't believe they don't have a coffee maker that does more than one cup at a time. Look at the size of this thing.'

'There was mostly ever only one person here,' Ben said. 'It probably does more than one cup anyway. You don't know how it works properly.'

'Who'd want to kill him?' she said.

'Fuck's sake, Sam – could be any number of people,' Ben said. 'We have no idea what Dad was involved with. Or the sort of people he worked with.' Ben thought once more of his father's desk. Thought back to all the conversations he'd never had.

Sam turned, walked towards the doorway. 'He did a lot for that fucking town. All the business, the money he brought in. People should be more than grateful.' She opened the door into the hollow hallway.

'Don't kid yourself,' said Ben.

'He'd never been in any serious trouble, not with the police, the authorities, or anyone else that I knew of, for that matter,' Sam shouted.

'That's not quite true,' Ben shouted after her. 'Hey, don't leave me with this thing.' He looked at the machine, not knowing how to stop the water trickling through the system, and into his cup. The liquid was paling. 'Sam, come back.' He hated weak coffee. Wasn't sure why he was drinking it at this hour anyway. Alcohol would have been more appropriate. He'd always been too fucking uptight and restrained.

He pulled the cup away and was watching the water splutter onto the tray when he heard the front door open and voices in the hall.

5

'Frank,' said Simon, 'we've got some work to do.'

Simon was behind his desk in a crisp blue shirt and dark brown leather jacket. His feet weren't on the table, but up, on the wastepaper basket to the side. He was wearing black jeans and black leather trainers, clearly expensive, designer. He was leaning back. His office chair had a lot of give. He was trimmer than Rich had been, much fitter, and younger.

'It's Saturday morning,' was all Frank could say. He wasn't pleased he'd been called in by Simon. He'd spent yesterday in his garden, toying with the shrubs, spreading some shingle, tweaking the borders, thinking.

'Look, Frank, I know you and Rich went back a long way. I know you were fond of him. Believe me, so was I. He was my brother. I loved him. I'm truly fucking devastated. The whole family's in pieces. But life moves on. We owe it to them, to Tatty and Ben and Sam, and young Zach. Hey, sit down, will you?'

Frank looked around. There were two big leather armchairs in front of the desk. Different models to those down in the reception area, Sian's outpost. These were older, softer, lower, on purpose. Frank wasn't feeling like being talked down to. 'I'm fine standing,' he said.

'We need to move some papers, some computers, before the police get more interested in this place.'

Frank shook his head. 'I worked for Rich, you know that.'

'Rich was pretty good to you, wasn't he, Frank? He always supported you, always made sure you were all right. Kept you out of trouble.' Simon smiled.

'I worked for Rich,' Frank repeated, feeling something slipping inside him.

'Rich is dead,' Simon said. 'So now we've got to do the best we can for those he's left behind. He'd want you to do that, Frank.'

Frank wasn't sure. He didn't think he'd ever understood Rich's relationship with Tatty, with his kids, but he supposed Rich had always supported them, given them what they'd wanted, never left them. He was loyal like that, though not in other ways. 'What's going to happen, Simon, here, with the business?' He glanced over to the bank of windows, the opened venetian blinds. Where did the business really begin, or end? The bits that Simon might have been involved with. It was bright outside. The sun had made an appearance earlier. No hint of rain. There was a fresh wind. Even inside Goodwin House there was a tang of oil and fish.

'We're going to carry on.'

Frank looked at Simon, and Simon met his gaze, straight on. But it was impossible to see beyond those dark eyes. 'I worked for Rich for over twenty years,' Frank said. 'You've only been involved for what, the last three, four? Rich built it up. It's all his doing.'

Simon coughed. Swept back his thick, dark hair. Women loved him, but not as much as he thought. 'Not sure what you mean, Frank. But I'll tell you, things have changed a lot recently. We're in a much better place than we were three years ago. The deal with Prime – that could end up being worth a hundred million alone.'

'I thought that wasn't sealed yet.'

'Oh, it will be.' Simon pulled his feet from their rest, stood. Walked over to the window. 'As long as we keep a careful eye on things here. Now, I'm not saying we need to remove everything. We don't want to look like we're panicking. And it might not get to the stage where police are crawling around the place, but Rich . . . well, you know, he wasn't himself recently, and he might have been a little sloppy. We need to be prepared.'

Frank walked over to the window, keeping his distance from Simon. The barge had gone, as had all the emergency vehicles. Though some blue-and-white police tape still marked off a wide area – four capstan lengths' worth. It was fluttering in the stiff breeze, playing with the unusual brightness. 'Rich was always careful,' he said.

'Frank, you knew him better than anyone – practically. Are you telling me you didn't notice anything? His behaviour recently? You think he was behaving normally these last few weeks, and months? He was my brother. OK, we weren't always so close, but I could tell something wasn't right. We talked about it – as much as you could ever get Rich to talk about things that weren't going his way. He'd been under a huge amount of strain, Frank. It wasn't only the Prime deal but all the trouble he was having with the Greek hauliers, plus his tax problems. That alone could have scuppered everything. The fucking Revenue – hate them. You know what the Americans are like. They're obsessed with due diligence.'

'The ones you're dealing with, from Vegas? You've got to be kidding.'

'Oh, they like to know exactly who they're going into business with. They have their ways of getting information. And, well, you knew Rich, things weren't brilliant at home. I don't want to go into that now. Tatty deserves some space, some respect at this dark time.'

'Who did it?' said Frank, still focusing outside, on the gap Rich's car went through. There was a metal barrier, the sort that divides a motorway, but it was ten metres or so inland, at the back of Goodwin House. You had to drive a hundred metres downriver to get on the other side. It was how contractors and suppliers accessed the ships. Rich's car must have left its parking space outside the office, driven that distance, returned to the back of the building, but on the other side of the barrier. Then it must have lined up, facing the river, and gone over the edge. Some spot. Some planning. Whose?

'Who did it?' said Simon. He was looking out of the window as well. He stayed looking out of the window. 'I know what you're thinking, Frank. It's hard to take. We all know what Rich was like. A real force of nature. But he hadn't been himself.'

'You were with him on Wednesday evening, here, until when?'

'Not late. Six or so. I was booked on the ten past eight flight from Norwich to Schiphol.'

'What sort of mood was Rich in?'

'He was bloody pleased he didn't have to go all the way to Vegas, I can tell you that. He seemed tired. Really tired.'

'He was meant to be going to Greece, though. Athens – next week? Is that right?'

'Yeah. There's a stall on some lifting equipment, because of the switch in hauliers.'

'I know,' said Frank. *Lifting equipment!* Once upon a time it was fruit and veg. All lies.

'Reliable hauliers aren't easy to find, in this market. They've all got too much business.' Simon was looking at Frank now.

Frank glanced out of the window again, catching a glint off Simon's bright boxy home straight across the river. He shook his head. 'Rich could handle the Greeks. He'd been doing it long enough.'

'They're not so easy to deal with these days. The competition has picked up. The Eastern Europeans are all over the place now, calling the shots. Not just the Albanians, the fucking Lithuanians too. You think the Turks, the Syrians, have any say?'

'Rich never backed away from something because it was difficult. If he wanted something to work, he made it work.'

'Maybe he didn't want that bit of business any more.

Who could blame him? Maybe his heart wasn't in it. I don't know.'

'You left him here at six, so you say. On his own?'

'If I thought he was going to do something stupid like fucking kill himself, I wouldn't have left him and flown off to Amsterdam, would I?' Simon said.

'I don't suppose you happened to see anything from your balcony, Wednesday evening, before you left? You would have had a perfect view.'

'I went straight from here. I wasn't going to stop to say goodbye to Jess – you know what I mean. That girl.' He almost whistled.

Jess had some front all right. Frank understood all too well where she was coming from and where she was hoping to go. He only wished she'd focused on someone other than Rich. Or maybe it was the other way round. 'Someone must have seen something,' he said.

'I don't think the police have any idea what time the car went in,' Simon said. 'It wasn't spotted until the morning.'

'Some CCTV must have caught something,' Frank said, an idea forming.

Simon sighed, returned to the seat behind his desk. Sat heavily. 'Let's hope they don't start sniffing around too hard – for all our sakes – and stick with the obvious.'

'Which is what exactly?'

'That the poor sod fucking killed himself.'

No one had yet found a note, not that Frank knew about. 'I'm having a problem with the location. Right across the river from your fancy new house?'

'He did it in front of his business. Think of it that way. The business he'd built up for so many years. It was his life.'

'Do you think he regretted getting you involved?'

'You don't have any brothers or sisters, do you, Frank?'

Frank shook his head. He'd been fostered at three.

'Rich and I had a complicated relationship, I can't deny that. But mostly we got on well. Look at the way this place has expanded since I've been around.' Smiling smugly, Simon got up once more. Moved back towards the window.

Frank knew about the tensions. He knew about other things as well. He wanted this conversation to end. What did Rich call Simon? 'A right slippery little shit.' He used to say people fell for Simon's good looks, his polish, especially the Americans. 'That's why I brought him in, Frank. He's useful.' Too useful? Rich might not have had the looks, the polish, but he had the fucking nerve.

'Rich loved Yarmouth,' Simon continued. 'He devoted most of his working life to the town. But he felt let down. Can you blame him? They were trying to get him off the Regeneration Board altogether, and I'm not sure he ever got over no longer being chair of the Commerce Committee. The casino licence could have been revoked at any time, and the contaminated land issue wasn't going away. He could see that he might just be the biggest problem to Yarmouth getting a super casino, the thing he'd battled for so long. And, as you know, HMRC were closing in again.'

Simon cleared his throat. He didn't smoke, but he had a habit of clearing his throat. Slippery? He lectured people, that was for sure; unlike Rich, who had always talked to him as an equal. Frank could never work for Simon. 'This doesn't add up, and you fucking know it.'

'There were issues with Tatty as well, Frank. They'd been married for nearly thirty years. Thirty fucking years, Frank. He didn't want that to fall apart after all this time. He loved the idea of being a family man, thought it looked good on his CV. But he couldn't help himself, could he?'

'You think I don't know what was going on there?'

Simon looked at him, but didn't smile this time. 'You might have been close to Rich, but no, you didn't know everything.'

Neither did you, Frank didn't say. Instead he said, 'None of this makes sense. You honestly think Frank drove over the edge?'

'Maybe he did want to make a point to me. I'll have to deal with that. But he'd become the liability, and he knew it. Rich didn't do failure.'

Frank's eyes swept around Simon's office. He saw nothing but plans, ambition, expansion, and a man willing to do anything to get to the top. Rich should never have got his younger brother involved. But, as Simon said, Rich was a family man. 'Where do we start?' He didn't want Simon removing stuff without him. He didn't want Simon shifting everything in his favour. He had to protect Rich, Rich's memory. Tatty and the kids too. Simon didn't give a shit about them.

'Rich's office,' Simon said cheerfully, heading towards the door. 'I've got an issue with the fucking password on his computer. I'm sure you know what it is, Frank. Rich always told me that if anything ever happened to him, you knew all the answers.'

A fat chunk of brightness was still hovering on the other side of the windows. It shouldn't have been there.

6

Tatty pressed the end call button, feeling cold and hot at the same time. 'It was Simon,' she said.

'We heard,' said Sam, behind her. 'So he wants what?'

'He wants to come over.'

'Again?' said Ben.

Ben was next to her, in the front passenger seat, his legs relaxing into the plush footwell. He'd been tall for so long. Taller than Rich. 'He wants to see me,' she said.

'Yeah, well he could have waited yesterday,' said Sam.

'Simon gets awkward around us,' Tatty said. 'I've always felt that. He doesn't like hanging about.'

'What's he meant to say?' said Ben. 'He probably feels embarrassed. Knows too much.'

Tatty wasn't going to comment. She didn't have to.

'I wouldn't like to work with Simon,' Sam said, then took a large gulp of air. 'I've always found him a total slime ball. Poor Dad.' It wheezed out of her mouth.

'Dad couldn't have been easy,' Ben said.

'He wasn't slimy like that,' said Sam.

Tatty put the car into reverse, accelerated without looking over her shoulder, while turning the wheel. She then flicked the car into drive, swung it round and motored across the front yard, barely slowing before moving straight out and onto Marine Parade. The wide road was empty except for parked cars. The bright weekend weather hadn't brought the hordes. It hadn't for decades.

'You in a rush, Mum?' Ben said.

'I don't know. I guess.'

'What about Simon, coming over?' Sam said.

'We had to get out, didn't we?' Tatty said. They had reached the end of Marine Parade and she followed the road round onto Avondale, the large Edwardian terraces now mostly all spruced up, but still characterless. It was like they'd been refurbished and then gone back to sleep.

The High Street was busy. Slow traffic, slower pedestrians. Everyone was so old. Mobility scooters were everywhere. When Rich persuaded Tatty to move to Gorleston she was barely twenty. It hadn't seemed so bad, given where she had been living, and despite the fact that everyone else was in their eighties. The age gap had closed terribly.

She peered up at the sky, a mash of blue and white, then back at the dark crowded road, splattered with yellow and red lines. Except Rich was never going to get that old now, just her. She was angry. Couldn't believe she'd gone along so easily with his plan to stuff her in a big detached house, impregnate her, again and then again. The way he bought all those clothes, jewellery, gadgets, extensions, projects – silence. She fell for it all.

Reaching the end of the High Street, the messy junction onto Southtown Road, with not a peep from Ben and Sam for minutes, she wondered whether she might have killed him, had he not killed himself. Lately she'd been having the most violent thoughts, at night, emerging from another restless dream, and now during the day as well. Would her temper have got the better of her? Maybe it was the menopause, or the amitriptyline. Or Nathan – she was only now learning to use his name quietly to herself.

Rich hadn't killed himself, though, had he? She couldn't believe that he had.

There was a jam on Bridge Road, backing up past the huge grey Matalan outlet. There was always a jam on Bridge Road, as people approached one of the few entrances to the long spit of land that was Great Yarmouth. Why so many people continually tried to get into the town was another unexplained story.

The sun came out again, as they neared the bridge, and the sun hit the cars and trucks ahead and the open red-and-white striped barriers, and the first bridge operator's stone building to the left. The bridge rarely opened. But they'd spent enough money recently making sure it still could. As they crawled up onto the bridge they all looked right, down the River Yare, at the sun glinting on the dirty ripples.

Tatty's eyes swept along South Quay, catching the restored green steamer sitting redundantly on Hall Quay, and a couple of chunky supply vessels further along towards Fish Wharf. The traffic was now moving and she didn't catch Goodwin House sticking out on its shallow bend.

'Fucking idiot,' Tatty found herself mumbling. Though she didn't know whether she was addressing Rich, for getting himself killed, or herself for having stuck with him for so long.

'Mum, please,' Sam said from the back.

Her voice was wavering, and Tatty wondered whether Sam was getting teary again. She sighed, knowing she didn't see enough of her children any more. She hoped that would change now. They were all she had, all that she properly cared about anyway. 'Guys, we're going to have to help each other through this. I want us to stick together. We've got some difficult times ahead.'

'Mum,' said Ben, 'weren't we going to get some flowers?'

'Flowers? Shit, yes. But I couldn't stop outside the florist. You can never bloody park anywhere near there.' She'd forgotten.

They were now stuck at the lights on the Yarmouth side of the bridge. Barclays Bank, one of Rich's banks, was directly ahead. The Star Hotel was a little further on, shy behind its smudged mock Tudor façade. She didn't think there had been anything starry about it for decades. Rich nevertheless had loved it. Said it was an institution that couldn't be allowed to fail. He'd wanted to buy it, some years ago, until he fixed on the land by the Pleasure Beach, and persuaded himself that the future could only be brand new. He'd leave Tatty to involve herself with the odd restoration project, if she so wished. She did. She'd always needed roots, she was coming to realise.

They were moving at last, merging onto South Quay, the *Welcome to* signs pre-labelling the district *Historic*, by the grand Victorian town hall. Rich was proud of his time there as chair of the Commerce Committee, and then heading up the Regeneration Board. Both roles part-time, both roles a doddle for him. There'd been no opposition. Who was going to object to the sort of money he helped bring in? No one kept a close eye. No one dared ask too many questions. What would they be asking now?

'There are no shops down here, are there?' said Sam, 'unless things have changed.'

'No,' said Tatty. 'Well, yes, things have changed, but there are no proper shops, certainly no florists. When were you last in Yarmouth?' The traffic was suddenly sparse and flowing, and they sped by the historic buildings on their left and an empty stretch of newly cobbled quay on the other side. Few tourists came down here, despite all the intentions, the grants.

'You know what, I haven't been to Yarmouth, this part of town anyway, for a couple of years at least,' said Ben. 'How weird is that?'

'Me neither,' said Sam. 'I find it strange to think Dad still worked here.'

'To be honest, I never knew what he saw in the place,' said Ben.

'Money,' whispered Tatty. 'Come on.'

A long block of low-rise 1950s residential accommodation, council, neglectfully brought to an end the old port architecture. And then the warehouses began, on both sides of the road. Scruffy, more than a few were abandoned. The others firmly shut up because it was the weekend. There was even less traffic and no pedestrians, and the sun had gone in. The pavements petered out in the dim clouded shade.

'It's bloody difficult to see,' said Ben, loudly, 'where the money might be around here.'

'That's why he liked it,' said Tatty. 'As he used to say, nothing better than a bit of wasteland for making a profit. He knew how to work the system, where the subsidies were, the tax incentives, the loopholes. Loved how no one expected anything to come back to life. They just let him get on with it. It was only when Simon got involved that people started looking a tad more closely. He likes to make a statement. Look at his house. He's far too vain.' For a moment Tatty thought of someone else, another vain man. Nathan. Except when Nathan fixed you with his eyes, he didn't let up.

'It's not only that, Mum,' Ben said. 'The culture's changing. All anyone talks about now is accountability, ethics. Believe me, I know about this stuff.'

'And Dad wasn't ambitious?' said Sam, yawning. 'What about his plans for the super casino? That was his idea, right, not Simon's. Maybe Dad brought it all on himself.'

'What?' said Tatty. 'What the hell did he bring on himself?'

'Hey, calm down, Mum,' said Ben.

'Forget it,' said Sam. 'I don't know what I was saying. What about the flowers?'

'I suppose we could turn round,' Tatty said, calming herself, 'find somewhere in the centre of town.'

'Whose idea were the flowers anyway?' Ben said.

'Mine,' said Sam. 'OK?'

'Dad didn't like flowers, did he?' Ben said.

'He used to buy them for me occasionally,' Tatty said, slowing. She could have added 'many years ago', but she didn't.

'Were you going to have a dinner or something for Dad's birthday next week?' Ben asked.

'No,' said Tatty sharply, as Goodwin House emerged ahead, beyond a vast grey modern warehouse, the Admiralty Steel place that had begun to so enrage Rich. 'Why?'

'Just asking.'

The pavement had come back, on the river side of the road, and a new dark green Jaguar, gleaming away in the sudden thick gloom, was making good use of it, parked in front of the last shuttered entranceway of the warehouse. Tatty knew whose car it was: Graham Sands', the Admiralty Steel boss. His success had taken everyone by surprise, except Rich.

'I feel even worse,' said Sam from the back. 'We so should have bought some flowers. He was going to be fifty-three, wasn't he? Oh God.'

'We're here now,' said Tatty. A short distance on from Admiralty Steel, Tatty pulled the car slowly across the road, not bothering to indicate. There was a slight thump as the car rode the kerb and then they were on the forecourt in front of Goodwin House. Two other cars were sitting there quietly – Simon's black BMW and Frank's black Range Rover.

Stupidly, Tatty hadn't anticipated this. When she spoke to Simon as they were leaving Gorleston, he hadn't said anything about being at the office. He'd said only that he wanted to come round, to see her, as soon as possible. He'd in fact said he was on his way, would be there in ten to fifteen minutes. She'd told him there'd be no one in.

She could sense Ben checking out the cars. She crept the Merc forward to the edge of Goodwin House. As always, the building's ugliness took her breath away. She wasn't surprised Simon had been trying to get Rich to agree the redevelopment of it. Rich could be fucking stubborn.

Once stopped, she leaned forward in her seat, peered round the corner. She had no idea what might still be at the back of the building, whether the authorities would have finished their investigations. There were no official vehicles that she could see, or any of those tents they put up. Nothing but a long strip of blue-and-white tape, some distance away on the edge of the quay, catching the breeze, having given up on trying to catch the sun.

With some purpose she hit the accelerator and the large engine made a whumph and the car whipped around the corner, heading straight for the steel barrier that separated the back of Goodwin House from the quay.

'Hey, steady on, Mum,' said Sam.

She stopped, centimetres short, square on. They now faced the river, and over the water Ferry Hill. Simon's daring new home, was staring straight back at them. Mockingly?

'Do you think they'll see us?' said Ben.

Tatty shook her head. 'Who? Simon, Frank?' She switched off the engine. 'I can't remember where Simon's office is, if that's where they are. At the back of the building probably, so he can admire his new home. Yeah, I'm sure they'll see us, if they look out of the window.' She opened the door, pushing it hard against the wind coming off the water. 'So?' She climbed out. She'd never liked Frank, the way he'd run around, doing anything for Rich.

'Why does this feel like we shouldn't be here?' Ben said, climbing out after her.

'Ben,' said Sam, the last to struggle out against the elements, 'it's Dad's office. It's his company, his land. We've got every right to be here.'

'Well, that's the thing,' Tatty said, looking up at the back of the shitty building, trying to work out which windows would be Simon's. The glass had a 1970s mirrored tint to it and was impenetrable from where she stood. 'It's also part his, Simon's, now.' She felt a tightening in her chest as she said it. Not pain at Rich's death. But anger, at Rich for allowing his brother into the business, and at herself. Mostly, once more, for looking the other way, zonked on temazepam. The pretty, silent wife – the role might have suited her while Rich was alive, given where she'd come from. But now he was dead. There was something else she urgently had to do at home, she decided. Rid the place of pills.

'Dad fucked up there, didn't he?' Ben shouted. 'Simon, part owner? Seriously?' He climbed over the steel barrier, and walked towards the police tape strung between the old capstans.

'I wish we'd got some flowers,' said Sam, following her brother, tentatively. 'It doesn't feel right.'

'Forget it, will you?' said Ben.

The barrier was higher than Tatty thought. Almost too high for her tight, knee-length skirt. But the soft suede had some give in it and her mac was only belted, not buttoned, and she managed to get over with some dignity – aware that people might be watching. The tarmac on the other side was puddled with greasy water and thick dark marks. Tyre marks? Rich's tyre marks? No one had said anything.

Ben was by the edge, having crossed the police line, while Sam – always the one to hold back – stood by a capstan. The wind coming off the Yare was fierce. Tatty leaned into it as she looked up and down the black rippling water. A supply vessel was some distance upriver, but she couldn't see any ships to her left, towards the river mouth, either because of the bend, or because none were moored there at the moment. It wasn't the busiest port in the world. Exactly how Rich had liked it. Too busy and every bit of land, every business, would be tightly controlled, watched, fought over. Not busy enough and any functioning concern would stick out like a sore thumb. Rich had never told her much about his businesses, but perhaps she had taken on board more than she thought.

Details had always been scarce, though there were usually plenty of pronouncements. Or bullshit.

She focused on the cluster of cheap industrial buildings, the haphazard roofs hanging to the spit of land that thinned to a point at the river's mouth. It was an acquired taste, a harsh beauty. She'd never been on a boat, a ship, as it eased out of this harbour. She fancied it now.

Sam had edged closer to her brother, Ben having stepped back. Tatty walked over to them, attempting, uselessly, to keep the hair from her face. She glanced behind her, at Goodwin House, but saw nothing but blinding light on the mirrored glass. She'd missed the moment when the sun had come back out.

'Are we meant to say a prayer or something?' Ben said.

Tatty looked at her eldest, struck by the Rich in him. She bit down on her bottom lip, knowing he was more like his dad than he'd ever admit, or be happy with. She looked beyond him, to the water. The tide was out, the river low. 'It's quite a drop, isn't it?' she said, thinking of the bruising on Rich's head. The fact that the police, the coroner, the pathologists, were continuing their investigations, even though they knew he'd drowned.

'He did do it, didn't he?' said Sam, as if picking up on Tatty's thoughts.

It was hard to think clearly, to think of anything other than the wind, and the blinding light now lifting off the water. She was finding it hard to think for herself after so long.

'I don't see how anyone could have made Dad drive over the edge,' continued Sam, her voice rushing off with the wind. 'I don't think his car could have been pushed off either. Not bumped off by another vehicle, anyway.'

'Who the fuck knows how it happened,' said Ben.

'I want to know,' said Sam.

'Yeah, well, there are lots of things we all want to know, aren't there,' said Ben.

'Why don't you care?' said Sam.

'Leave it, you two, will you?' said Tatty, remembering how they used to bicker as kids. 'I'm sure we'll find out soon enough.' She wasn't sure at all.

'What I'd like to know is who would've wanted him dead,' said Ben, stubborn like his dad. 'That's more the point, isn't it?'

Tatty could have said something then, said a few things, but Sam, thankfully, beat her to it.

'That's not our job, Ben. That's for the police.'

'You've changed your tune, all of a sudden,' he replied. 'I thought you didn't trust the police.'

'Children, children,' sighed Tatty, 'why don't we go and have a drink or something, something to eat?' Rich's shiny gold Rolex, on her thin tanned wrist, surprised her. It was nearer to lunchtime than she'd thought.

'Round here?' said Sam.

'Are we not going to go inside and see Dad's office?' said Ben. 'I want to see Dad's office. Maybe he left a note or something. Has anyone checked?'

'Yeah, I'm sure,' said Tatty. 'I would have heard. Besides, I don't have a key, a pass card, or whatever they use. I've never had one. I never go in there. Your dad didn't like it.' She wondered whether her children had any more idea than she did about what Rich had been up to all these years and where the real money and the favours came from.

'But Simon's in there now, isn't he?' said Ben. 'And Frank. They'll let us in.' He started to walk towards the building, determined.

'Still,' said Tatty, though she set off after him, sensing Sam keeping up behind her. It was a struggle once more to get over the barrier. She liked the skirt. She didn't want it torn, marked. Even Nathan had removed it carefully. Pausing for a moment to readjust her clothes, her mac, she saw a man, short and fat, come slowly round the side of the building. He lifted a camera and began snapping away at them. Another camera, with a long heavy lens, was slung over his sloped shoulder.

'Hey,' said Ben, launching into a sprint, 'what the fuck are you doing?'

The man spun round, but not in time. Ben grabbed the camera that had been hanging on his shoulder, and pulled it away from him. But the photographer seemed determined not to give up any of his equipment. Tatty closed in.

'Give it to me,' Ben demanded.

'This is assault,' the man said, his voice high-pitched, local. He was nervous, scared. 'I'm only doing my job. I'm going to ring the police.'

Tatty thought she recognised him. She knew his type at any rate.

'You're on private property,' Ben said, still holding the camera, still keeping the man reined in. 'You're trespassing.'

'Ben,' shouted Tatty, 'let him go.' It couldn't have been the best of jobs, around here.

'Is there anything you want to say, Mrs Goodwin,' the man said, having been handed back his freedom, 'about the tragic death of your husband?'

'Get out of here while you can still walk,' Tatty said, her voice rising up out of nowhere, a warmth coming to her wind-blasted cheeks.

7

'Who do we know, Frank,' said Simon, 'who can hack into a computer?'

He was over by the far wall of Rich's office, pulling files off the shelves, old grey ledgers, newer folders, thin, plastic sleeves stuffed with A4 – all smokescreens. Frank could have said, Zach. But he didn't, surprised by what Simon didn't seem to know. So Rich hadn't been completely stupid, unless Simon was lying. 'I'll get on to it,' Frank said. 'But you're going to have to give me a day or two. It is the weekend.'

'Computer hackers take weekends off, do they?' Simon said, now tipping papers straight onto the floor.

Though the office was not his patch, Frank had been around long enough to know the documents had been ordered according to the legitimate businesses, not all currently functioning – the clubs, bars and restaurants, the minicab business, the industrial equipment supply service, the boatyard. Land and property was divided between brownfield sites, the new builds and the redevelopments, commercial and residential. Then there were the arcades, the old casino. The super casino project, with Prime Poker, had its own shelf.

For years Rich had dreamed of creating a super casino on South Beach with the name Goodwin emblazoned on the front, transforming the fortunes of Yarmouth for, well, good. He felt it was his right, by birth. But it was slow going. So he'd decided to bring in Simon to help seduce the Americans, and now look what had happened.

'Hackers, Frank, where the fuck are they when you want them?'

He wasn't going to let this go. 'They're kids, mostly, Simon.' He presumed. 'Like I said, it's going to take me a day or two to get hold of someone. It wasn't my area.'

'I thought you were Rich's eyes and ears.' Simon was using his feet to sort the papers. Clearly he had no idea what he was looking for, what might be there.

Frank huffed. 'Not in this place. You know that.'

'You know people, Frank. Get on to it.' Simon straightened, pulled more folders off a shelf. 'I want someone here today, this afternoon. Fuck knows what the police are up to. Having the weekend off as well? But come Monday, first thing, they could be kicking the door down. Any excuse.' He cleared his throat loudly. 'And I don't want some glaring empty space left on the desk where Rich's computer should have been. We can't just dump it. Everything needs to look normal.'

Frank turned once more to the large computer taking up much of Rich's fat oak desk. For the last twenty minutes or so Frank had been certain it would log itself on. There'd be a ping and the screen would spring back to life and one by one the desktop icons would fill the mountainous background, each portraying the real business – money laundering, drug trafficking, people smuggling, shifting stolen goods, tax evasion, fraud, extortion, protection. There was a lot of blurring round the edges, from one activity to the next.

He'd pretended that Rich must have changed his password. Now he was waiting for Rich to play some joke on him. He'd always had a mean sense of humour. He looked over at Simon, in his neat jeans and artificially weathered leather jacket, the crap all over the floor. 'What about this mess? We can't leave the place like this.' But was it his problem now? The paper trail only went so far, if it went anywhere.

'It won't take long to put back.' Simon cleared his throat. 'I can't believe he kept all this stuff.'

'Nothing Rich did wasn't thought about, planned,' Frank said. 'He kept those papers for a purpose. Same as there'll not be anything incriminating on his computer.' Numbers and words on documents were not Frank's speciality. But he knew how careful Rich was. There'd been accusations, rumours, two police investigations, and at least a couple of HMRC enquiries, not including the current investigation, but there'd never been a charge that stuck. No one had ever landed a fatal blow, until now, it occurred to Frank. 'He always knew exactly what he was doing.' That came out quieter than he'd intended.

'So you keep saying, Frank, but Rich hadn't been himself for some time.'

Simon had a point Frank didn't want to acknowledge. For the last two days he'd been racking his soft brain while tending to his wilting shrubs. Rich's real problem was his dick. Like so many men of his age, he couldn't stop putting it in the wrong place. Frank had warned him not to go anywhere near Jess.

'Jesus Christ, there're even files from his time at the council on the Commerce Committee,' Simon said. 'Every meeting, all the minutes. Wouldn't the council have this stuff anyway?'

'He didn't trust the council – those members? He didn't trust anyone.' Frank looked straight at Simon, but Simon looked away. Slowly he realised the buzzer was going. The sound was drifting up from the lobby, two floors below, like a poisonous cloud. There was no Sian to let anyone in, or anyone else in the building. 'Simon, the buzzer's going.'

'Fuck,' said Simon, scurrying further away from the windows, and over to Rich's desk. 'Don't answer it. No one can come in with this office like this.'

Frank held his hands open, shook his head, feeling the stale air on his bald scalp. 'You didn't think this might happen?' He couldn't work with idiots, that much he knew.

'We can't answer it, Frank.'

We? 'Our cars are out the front, Simon. Have you forgotten? It's pretty obvious someone's here.' Frank went straight to the window. 'What if they've got a warrant?' He had no idea what Rich had seen in his brother. Blood surely wasn't enough. Rich was from Somerleyton, a few miles down the road, not Sicily.

The glass was smeared with salt and grime, inside and out, but there was enough of a view. The car park in front of Goodwin House still only had two cars on it, his and Simon's. Frank's breath was clouding the window as he tried to see whether he was missing anything. A deep, wide concrete ledge sheltered the entranceway so he couldn't see who was pressing the buzzer. They were still pressing it.

Had someone parked at the back? He'd been too busy watching Simon pull Rich's office apart. 'Wait here,' he said, leaving the window and Rich's office, Simon staring at him, his tanned face going pale. Frank hurried along the cheaply partitioned hallway to the empty office next to Simon's at the back of the building, and looked out at the sun smacking the wind-whipped river, the police tape strung between the iron capstans the other side of the barrier, the edge where Rich's car left dry land. Closer to the rear of Goodwin House, in the rarely used overfill parking area, was Tatty's Mercedes, glinting. He was pleased to see it.

He headed straight for the stairs. Taking two at a time, he didn't feel the exertion in his chest until he was crossing the ground-floor lobby, heading for the main entrance, making out three figures on the other side of more grimy glass. Tatty, wrapped in a well-fitting mac, flanked by Ben and Sam. Ben had Rich's height but not his weight. Sam was a touch shorter than her mother, but no less slight. He hadn't seen Ben and Sam for a long while.

He waved as he approached, sensing before he'd unlocked the door that they were far less happy to see him than he was to see them. Rich had always kept them well away from here. Zach was the only one who was brought in, used. 'Mrs Goodwin, Ben, Sam, hello.' Frank held the door open, and they came in with a wave of sharp, oily air. 'I'm so sorry,' he added, stepping back. He shook his head, feeling its weight, its bulk – Rich used to say he looked like

Brando playing Kurtz in *Apocalypse Now*. Ever since he checked the film out his head had felt so much heavier. He looked down at his scruffy deck shoes. He'd put on the wrong shoes today.

'I want you to know that Rich meant the world to me,' Frank continued, feeling himself choke up. 'I also want you to know that I worked for Rich, not Simon, no one else. That was the contract between us. I'll do everything I can for you now. I want you to know where my loyalties lie.' He knew he was speaking too fast, saying too much too soon. It was not appropriate, not now, but he wanted them to hear this before Simon appeared.

Tatty was looking beyond him. Her large hazel eyes, wide and sad and sinking ever deeper into her fine, lightly tanned face, had fixed on a point over his shoulder.

Ben spoke first, looking awkward. 'Yeah, thanks. We just want to see Dad's office.'

'Maybe he left something,' Sam said. She was looking at Ben. She seemed so young and delicate, like she should still be at school, in sixth form. Tatty had never looked her age, and he supposed Sam never would either, the lucky girl. Except, he wondered whether people took her seriously, at work. A lawyer, at a big London firm? They wouldn't round here.

'Tatty,' said Simon loudly, behind him, before clearing his throat. 'Ben, Sam.' He stepped into the group, smelling not so much of cologne – his usual Dior Eau Sauvage – but nerves.

Frank caught the look Simon threw him. It was not pleasant. Simon hesitated before putting his hands on

Tatty's shoulders and pulling her to him. She struggled free, clearly not wanting to be comforted by her brother-in-law. Slight though she was, Frank knew she was physically strong, fit, and not always shy of making her feelings known. Rich used to joke that it was Tatty he needed Frank to protect him from.

'You know, I've been trying to see you,' Simon said, clearing his throat once more. He was now holding out his hands, his arms, crouching forward slightly, not a bone of sincerity supporting the stance. 'This is the most dreadful thing to have happened, to us all. I've been walking round in a daze, trying to make sense of it, and I can't.'

Tatty nodded. 'Simon, you and I both knew Rich pretty well. I think we can both make sense of it.' She looked at Ben, at Sam, finally at Frank. For support? He didn't know how she was managing to be so calm. 'It's what we do now that matters,' she said.

'Yeah,' said Simon faintly. 'Look, can we get out of here? Go somewhere that doesn't have . . . ' he paused, looked up at the low ceiling ' . . . that doesn't have Rich all over it. I'm finding this building a bit overwhelming right now.' His arms had become wings, barriers. He was sweeping them all towards the door.

'We're here now,' said Ben. 'I want to see Dad's office.'

'Yeah,' added Sam. 'Maybe, he left something there – for us.'

Frank caught another nervy look from Simon. Though this one was directed at Tatty.

'You know what,' Tatty said, 'I'm with Simon. This building is doing my head in already – it always has. We can come back. We only wanted to see the spot.' She looked at her children, her eyes widening once more. 'It's what people do nowadays, isn't it? Leave flowers and silly messages where their loved ones died.'

'We didn't leave any flowers, Mum, did we,' said Sam.

'We had no intention of coming in,' Tatty continued, strident now. 'Ben, Sam, come on, let's get some lunch. Simon?' She made for the exit.

Frank didn't know what was going on. Respectfully, dutifully, they all followed Tatty, though Sam kept looking back, at the lift, at the stairs. Did Sam still think that Rich might have left a note – here? Was Zach the only one of Rich's kids who had any idea about what the old man had got up to at work? Not that he knew much.

Zach had no idea, Frank was sure, that the luxury yacht he was helping to relocate from the Mediterranean to Great Yarmouth contained 10 kilos of exceptionally pure cocaine. The cocaine had been cemented into the keel in a dry dock in Ibiza. Only the skipper knew about it. But the skipper didn't work for Rich. The skipper had been hired by Rare and Yare Yachts, a company with no legal connection to Goodwin Boat Services. They merely happened to occupy adjacent pockets of soft, reclaimed land. Land that Rich helped secure from the council, for peanuts, years ago. Rare and Yare Yachts was still paying Rich back. Favours in cash and kind.

Out on the forecourt, by Simon's sleek BMW, Frank thought about the £500,000 that the cocaine would be worth on the street, the cut Rich would have got. How Frank would have taken delivery of the cash. How that cash would then have been fed into the restaurants, the bars, the arcades, the casino, until it had all disappeared. It wasn't so much money these days. It wasn't worth the risk.

Except Tatty enjoyed her summers in Ibiza, Zach liked his sailing, and Rich couldn't wean himself off old money-making habits. 'Think of it as our heritage, Frank,' he used to say. 'There are some things I'll never let go.' Rich was a total cunt. There were no boundaries between his business practices and his family – he used everyone. Frank had always known where he stood. That Rich would never have let him go either. That was one of the reasons why he loved Rich. No one else had ever shown him such commitment, such trust. He could only repay it, and some.

Tatty was talking to Simon. Frank couldn't hear what they were saying. He looked down the road, towards the harbour mouth and the dead end, the industrial buildings laid low by the unexpected weight of late summer sun, and some way over to his left the top of Nelson's Monument, clear of cloud for once. He used to enjoy driving down South Denes Road and curving back round onto South Beach Parade, accelerating past the old Pleasure Beach and into a different era.

That route was blocked by the Port Authority many years ago, when work began on the outer harbour. Now there was a big chain-link fence topped with razor wire – no through traffic. Rich's idea. The more that was hidden from public view of that development the better. 'We don't want gawpers all over the fucking place,' Rich used to say, adding with a chuckle, 'watching their money float away.' Rich went to town on the security angle when addressing the council. How the port needed twenty-first-century protection from thieves, traffickers, terrorists. A terrorist being the only thing Rich wasn't.

'Frank,' said Simon, in his face, 'wait here, will you? I'm going with Tatty and the kids. I won't be long. A photographer's been sniffing around, apparently. See him trespassing again, you know what to do.'

'What about Rich's office?'

'If the police do pitch up, blame it on Tatty,' he said quietly. 'Tell them she became hysterical looking for a suicide note. Ripped the place apart before I could calm her down. Which is why I've taken her for a spritzer.'

Frank looked over at Tatty and two of her grown-up children. They were disappearing round the corner of the building, to her car. They hadn't said goodbye to him. They had barely acknowledged him. He knew that Rich had rarely discussed his business at home, but he'd always somehow thought that Rich must have talked with Tatty, the others, on occasion about his most loyal employee. Perhaps not. He would have to earn their trust. He looked at Simon, said, 'Sure.' Then walked back towards the entrance to Goodwin House, pausing on the step.

Moments later, Tatty's Merc swept round from the back of the building. Ben was up front with Tatty, though Tatty was driving, while Sam looked disconsolate in the rear. Frank watched as Tatty pulled straight out onto South Denes, going east, going fast, towards the harbour mouth, and not towards the town centre. She was a terrible driver, Rich had always complained. No consideration for anyone else on the road.

Simon's BMW took a few seconds to catch up. Frank then saw Tatty take a left onto Main Cross Road, without indicating, Simon closing the gap. They were crossing the spit, heading for South Beach Parade. They'd be going to the bar at the old casino, he reckoned. Couldn't see Tatty having a drink anywhere else in Yarmouth nowadays. Frank liked their club sandwiches, though he wished they wouldn't serve them with quite such a mound of crisps. He was getting far too lumpy. Gardening wasn't providing anything like enough exercise.

Making sure the door was locked behind him, he headed up the stairs, feeling the emptiness of the building. He kept going, past Rich's office and across the way to Simon's. He didn't know Simon's login, but that wasn't going to stop him from having a good look around – something he should have done long ago.

8

'Tatty, I wonder whether we can talk somewhere quiet?'
Simon said, leaning in.

'You want it quieter than this?' She looked around the
large plush room, the purple velvet seat covers, the heavy
drapes pulled back, but not far, the smoked glass windows
shielding them from that strange midday sun. No one
could see in or out. The bar was empty, and only two of
the tables were occupied: theirs, and one over in the far
corner. Three large men sat at that table, all wearing
sports jackets that were too tight for them, and two
decades out of style.

They looked like the jackets the casino lent to punters
who were underdressed. Tatty had never agreed with the
policy. She thought that if people weren't wearing the right
clothes, their clothes, then they shouldn't be allowed in.
God knows what the door policy would have been on the
super casino. Or how they'd have policed it with quite so
many punters.

'They're not plainclothes,' Simon said.

Tatty looked back at Simon, realising she must have been
staring. 'What?'

'They're not police, undercover.'

'I know,' she said. She smiled, at Sam, at Ben. But her children were talking to each other, and not paying attention to anyone else.

'Tatty, I do need to talk to you, in private.' Simon had leaned her way again. He wasn't quite whispering. He smelled ridiculous.

Tatty tried to sit back in her chair, but despite the plush covering it was hard, uncomfortable. Cheap. 'This seems private enough to me. We own it, after all.' Saying that felt odd.

Simon now tilted his head towards the other end of the large, low, round table, where Sam and Ben were deep in conversation. Tatty had no idea when either of them could have last been in the casino. Rich would have brought them, to show off, before he'd lost interest in it.

'I don't want your kids to hear,' Simon said.

'They're not kids,' Tatty said, annoyed, reaching for her glass of champagne. 'They're adults. Highly motivated, well-employed, young professionals.'

'I know that, Tatty. But there are certain things I don't think they know – or you know, for that matter – which need sorting out urgently. You want them to hear everything, and be compromised? Their professional standing? Your husband was a complicated man. He had a lot of interests. He was involved in many things.'

Tatty took another sip of champagne, finishing the glass. Simon, as she understood it, was involved in many things too. Disgusting things. She looked around for a waiter, a waitress, before remembering it was bar service only. Even for the owners. Things were going to change, and soon. 'I

66

don't know what gives you the right to lecture me about my husband.'

Sam and Ben were looking at her now. She felt hot, wound up. 'Ben, darling, can you pop to the bar and get me another glass of champagne, please?'

'Mum,' said Sam, 'do you think you should have another? You seem a bit upset.'

'Of course I'm upset. Who wouldn't be?'

'Sure, I'll get you a drink,' said Ben standing. 'Anyone else?'

Simon and Sam shook their heads.

'When did you start drinking champagne at lunchtime, Mum?' Sam said. She was having an orange juice, bottled, Britvic, the ice already melted.

'Sweetheart, when did you start being quite so judgemental?'

Sam stood up now, unsteadily, the colour slipping from her beautiful face. 'I'm going to the toilet,' she said, walking away across the thick patterned carpet. She did not look back.

Tatty felt terrible. She shouldn't have spoken to Sam like that. She would make it up to her. She turned to Simon. 'So what is it?'

The three men over in the corner were not looking their way. Simon concentrated on Tatty. She couldn't read his expression. 'I don't trust Frank,' he said.

Tatty felt the phone in her handbag going. It was on silent, but it was vibrating urgently. 'What are you implying? That he had something to do with Rich's death?'

'Rich committed suicide, Tatty.'

Tatty looked over her shoulder. Ben was still at the bar. 'So what's the problem with Frank? What do you want to do about it?'

'I don't want him hanging around. As soon as the funeral's out of the way, he needs to move on. He's not an employee, not of Goodwin Enterprises. Did you know that?'

'He's part of the fabric,' said Tatty. 'Rich set up a company for him: Adams and Steve Holdings, or something. It was one of Rich's more stupid jokes. I'm not sure of the exact arrangement, how money is put into it from Goodwin Enterprises. You must have a better idea. But Rich was loyal like that. He sorted Frank out, and Frank stuck by Rich. Did what he was asked, I've always presumed.'

'I don't trust him, Tatty.'

'Rich did.' Her phone started up again.

'If you ask me, Frank had been playing Rich for years. A lot of people took advantage.'

'I'm not asking you,' Tatty said. Where was her champagne? 'Besides, I like Frank.' Perhaps she'd warm to him. She had a feeling she was going to need him. 'I'm not going to tell him to get lost. Rich never suggested he was a threat, anything like a rival. Look at the guy.' She didn't think she had to say any more.

'He could make things difficult for us. He knows too much.'

'Then it's better if he sticks around, isn't it?' Her children seemed to be letting her have her quiet chat with Simon. They'd always known when to disappear. They'd spent their entire lives making themselves scarce – not that

68

she hadn't also. However, she decided she wanted them here, in on this. Too much had been kept from them, from her, for too long.

'I don't want you encouraging him, Tatty, that's all I'm saying.'

'What were you doing with him earlier, at Goodwin House?'

'I need to know what was going on in Rich's head over his last few days and weeks. People do strange things when they're under a lot of pressure. We do not want the police finding anything they shouldn't. The deal with the Prime Poker consortium could be worth over a hundred million. A hundred million, Tatty.'

'In however many years,' Tatty said dismissively. 'You think Prime Poker are still happy to invest here, without Rich?'

'Rich was beginning to hold that deal back. He was not being straight about the contaminated land, for one thing.'

Tatty could have laughed. As if Rich was ever straight about anything.

'Those Americans don't miss anything,' Simon continued.

'Rich had got the green light from the council, and the Gambling Commission.' Tatty had always been amazed at how Rich had navigated his way through officialdom. Bullied, she supposed, with the help of bribes and back-handers. 'Those bodies knew him, trusted him. He'd done the hard work. You think Prime Poker are going to proceed as if nothing's changed?' Tatty was surprising herself.

'Business goes on, Tatty. The Prime Poker consortium stretches from Las Vegas to Atlantic City. We're talking major fucking players. They know me. I'm leading the negotiations for Goodwin Enterprises. Sure, Prime Poker will proceed, as long as we keep things tight. Rich's office at home, I need to check that. His computers, we need to get into them. Before the police do.'

'Why? Why should they? Rich committed suicide. Won't they leave us alone, to deal with our grief?' She knew what had been in his desk at home. Though not what was on his computers. Zach, she suspected, might have more of an idea.

'We can't take any risks. Besides Prime Poker have investigators – did you know that, Tatty? – with a lot more muscle than the police.'

'You want to do business with these people?'

He laughed. Spat more like. 'Such opportunities don't come around often.'

Rich had set it all up, it had been his dream, but Tatty was tiring of the conversation, and Simon. 'How's Jess?' She willed herself to smile.

'Jess? What's she got to do with anything right now? Have the police told you the full results of the autopsy yet?'

'Rich committed suicide, Simon. That's what you tell me. You think that whatever an autopsy comes up with is going to explain that?' She wasn't interested in whatever the police, the pathologist, the authorities had to say on the matter. The truth was elsewhere.

'We could give Frank a small cash incentive.' Simon's voice was gumming up.

'This place is ridiculous,' she said. 'How long does it take to get served?' Ben was still at the bar, having been joined by Sam. Tatty couldn't see from where she was whether they'd actually been served any more drinks, her champagne. She couldn't see the bar person. She beckoned her children over. She didn't want another glass of champagne. Her phone had gone twice now. She was in a rush.

'If that doesn't work, we might have to resort to other means,' Simon said.

She almost laughed. 'You know what Rich used to say about you, Simon? He said you could always be relied upon to put on a good show. But you had no guts.'

'You reckon?' Simon cleared his throat, once, twice, loudly.

One of the men over on the far table caught Tatty's eye. He was not an attractive man. His face was jowly, pale, lopsided. He had small dark eyes that put a value on everything. She knew his type. She realised she knew him.

'I'm sitting here, Tatty,' Simon said, 'talking to you, while Rich is lying on a slab somewhere. Where are his guts now? Think about it.' He cleared his throat, not so loudly. 'We need to go through all Rich's things.'

'When you say *we*, Simon, what exactly do you mean?'

'I'm thinking about your interests – yours and your children's.'

'No, Simon, what you are thinking about are *your* interests. You're worried about what you might lose if certain things come out.' She looked at him, knowing how expressive her eyes could be. 'You should have thought about that when you got involved with Rich's business.'

'He asked me, begged me. He needed me, you see, Tatty. You should all be grateful.'

Sam sat first, then Ben, having handed Tatty her glass of champagne, which she no longer wanted.

'And now you need me,' Simon said, filling the brittle silence. 'You all need me.'

Ben looked at his mother. He had Rich's eyes, but not his bottle. 'Simon, as I understand it,' Tatty said, 'you are a minority shareholder, if you are talking about Goodwin Enterprises.' Ben was now staring at Simon.

'It's not as simple as that,' Simon said.

'Nothing ever is,' Sam muttered.

'Two things.' Ben casually leaned forward. 'We appreciate your concern, everything you might have done for Dad's business, but don't underestimate Mum, Sam or me. Give us a little respect, please. And some time.'

Simon cleared his throat and sighed all at once, shaking his head. 'You don't get it, do you? Time is what you don't have.'

'No,' said Ben, 'you don't get it. It's not your time. It's our time. It's our time now.'

Tatty knocked back her second glass of champagne in one, feeling the cold liquid turn almost instantly into a fiery ball deep inside her. Rich had thrived on competitiveness. 'Shall we go?' she said, proud and angry. She needed to pay so much more attention to her children. Give them the space, the credit, they deserved.

'I've ordered a couple of the club sandwiches, Mum,' Ben said. 'Apparently, they're not bad.'

Simon was out of his chair. 'This is not a joke. You can't play around with this stuff. It's not only money that's at risk. The police cannot go anywhere near Rich's offices or

72

his belongings until I've been through everything. And believe me, the Americans are a lot more fucking thorough.'

'Shouldn't you have thought about that earlier?' Sam said, coming back to life.

'I don't know what that's supposed to mean.' Simon began walking towards the exit, over a carpet that had always hosted the wrong sort of traffic. He stopped some way short of the heavy panelled door, faced them. Swept a lock of dark, well-groomed hair off a stupidly smooth tanned forehead. 'You have no idea what's really been going on.'

'We'll learn,' Tatty said to his back as he strode away, aware that the men at the table in the far corner might well have seen and heard too much.

9

The police had been waiting for them, on Marine Parade, in an unmarked car.

Tatty hadn't even unlocked the front door before they were right behind her, having scurried out and across the driveway like rats after rancid meat.

'Excuse me,' the woman said, hemming them in. It was the same two as before. 'We've been trying to ring you.' She directed this to Tatty, but was clocking Ben and Sam, closely.

Tatty stopped undoing the door. She didn't want them to have been ringing her. She had presumed it was someone else, and had been so concerned about her children noticing that she hadn't dared look at the screen. She removed the key from the lock, livid. Technically, the police were trespassing, unless they had a warrant. 'I'm not feeling well,' she said. 'We've had a rather difficult day already. What is it?'

There was no sun now, though the wind had changed direction and temperature. It was no longer coming off the sea. It must have been pushing twenty degrees. Hot and humid for Gorleston. Tatty felt trapped in her mac.

'We have some further results from the post-mortem, which we wanted to inform you of immediately,' the man, the detective said. 'In person,' he added, also observing Ben and Sam keenly. Tatty couldn't remember his name. He was too thin to have a name of substance in any case.

'Can we come in?' the woman said.

Spiros. That was her name, Tatty thought, the woman's accent helping. Rich had enjoyed good relations with the Greek Cypriot community. Better than with the Portuguese. Many still spoke Greek at home, in the dank backstreets of the Nelson ward and the brighter bungalows of Bradwell, where the more successful had managed to move on to. Rich had always made up for the fact that he had no languages by speaking English forcefully. Fuck was his favourite word.

'Is that necessary? We'd rather you didn't come in,' Ben said. 'My mum needs to lie down. These last few days have obviously been exhausting for her. There's only so much bad news she can take.'

Tatty was trying to pick up on the facial signals the man was sending to Spiros, pleased Ben was doing the talking for her. How he was rising to the task.

'We would rather come in,' Spiros said. 'You all might want to sit down.'

Clearly she didn't need to ask who Ben and Sam were. Tatty looked at her children, then back at Spiros. Why were the police always ordering you to sit down? 'Just tell me.'

The man looked uncertain, defensive. He shifted weight on his feet and his face hardened. He began speaking, fast. 'There were traces of a sleeping pill, temazepam, in your husband's urine. There was also a high alcohol level. We won't know how high until we have the toxicology results.'

Sam shivered loudly in the unusual warmth.

'The forensic pathologist does not believe that the head injury would have been fatal. We haven't yet been able to determine exactly how it was caused, though he could have hit his head on the steering wheel. Forensics believe the airbags did not deploy because the car was travelling at an insufficient velocity.'

He paused, looked up at the sky, the thickening cloud, the rising humidity. Did he sleep easily at night, Tatty wondered? What did he dream about?

'The preliminary forensic report,' he continued, 'commissioned by the police, which will be going to the coroner, suggests that your husband committed suicide by taking benzodiazepine, sleeping pills, perhaps in conjunction with a high level of alcohol, and then drowned. The investigation is not quite over, however. The toxicology report will not be known for some time. And we still need to determine how he managed to drive his car off the quay and into the river, having ingested such substances.'

'That would be obvious, wouldn't it?' said Ben. 'He was off his head.'

What if *determine* was your favourite word, Tatty was wondering, and not *fuck*?

'We always attempt to get to the bottom of any such incidents,' Spiros said.

How many such incidents were there, where a car went into the Yare, to get to the *bottom of*? Fucking police, Tatty mouthed.

'Mr Goodwin's last moments are still of interest to us,' the detective said. 'We would like to know whether you have found any notes.' He was looking straight at Tatty now, his pale sunken cheeks swamped by the warm westerly air. 'Which might explain his behaviour,' he added.

Tatty shook her head, not wanting to look at Sam. Rich was dyslexic. He'd always been afraid to put pen to paper. Predictive text messages were a godsend for him. Except the software was never quite up to some of his more colourful phrases.

'Had he been depressed?' said Spiros. 'Was he under a lot of pressure recently?'

'My husband was a very important man, a very successful man.' Tatty still couldn't look at Sam, or Ben. 'He was also a very private man. I understand that you would like more information. We all would. But there are certain things this family won't ever talk or speculate about. As for now, we would like to be left alone, to deal with our grief.'

'And to plan the funeral,' Sam added, reaching gently for Tatty's arm.

'If we find anything, we'll let you know,' Tatty said. How was she going to protect Sam?

'I have to inform you that it is unlikely the coroner will release the body until we are satisfied that we have all the information necessary,' he said. 'I can't tell you how long that will be, I'm afraid.'

'You don't have all the information you need?' said Ben.

'So what do we do?' said Sam, almost at the same time, letting go of her mother.

'We will keep you informed of any further developments,' Spiros said.

The man shook his head the tiniest of fractions, anger flashing across his sharp, hollow features. Rich had always said the face revealed everything if studied closely. Yet Rich had long given up playing poker, blackjack, knowing that the house always won. He'd long given up looking at her too closely as well. Otherwise he might have seen a few things he wouldn't have liked, certainly recently. The police weren't telling them everything.

'Your husband was well known around here,' the man in charge said – it was always men, around here. 'Obviously, we all want to be satisfied that no one has missed anything, and that we have come to the correct conclusion. Please be assured that we aim to complete the investigation as soon as possible.'

'We want to help you,' Ben said. 'We do. But we're also aware, with my father having been such a big figure, that there will be a lot of gossip. Journalists are already after us. My little brother is not even back in the country yet. We need to protect him, all the family. We would appreciate it if the police, you know, kept things as quiet as possible.'

Tatty was struck by the way Ben's voice hardened, like Rich's used to, when he was confronted by someone who thought they were in a position of authority. Ben had been surprising her all day.

'We're the victims here,' said Sam. 'I have lost my father.'

'We're all struggling to come to terms with my husband's death,' Tatty said finally, turning towards the door, feeling for the key in her hand, the sharp serrated edge, knowing another unwanted conversation had more than come to the end.

'Mrs Goodwin,' the detective said to her back, 'it's quite likely that we'll have some further questions for you, and a statement may well be necessary. We would prefer it if you kept us informed of any plans you might have to leave the area.'

'I'm not going anywhere,' Tatty said.

10

The text had hit Frank's phone as he and Simon were finishing putting the files back on the shelves in Rich's office. 'There's a problem at the club,' Frank had then lied to Simon, and Simon had raised his eyebrows dismissively because there were always problems at the club, and it was not the sort of club that Simon thought Goodwin Enterprises should have anything to do with. The thing was, it was no longer under the ownership of Goodwin Enterprises. It had been transferred to the ownership of Adams and Steve Holdings. Simon would find out eventually, Frank presumed.

Simon had then suggested Frank might want to stay clear of Goodwin House for a while. Perhaps leave town. He'd help him with some cash, if he needed it. How did £100,000 sound? Frank had told him to fuck off.

The interior of the Range Rover smelt of himself. Frank spent too much time in it, sweating. But he didn't like walking, not around here. He played with the window, though the in-rushing air only seemed to circulate the bad odour. He would have to get one of those stupid pine-tree things to hang from the rear-view mirror, advertising the fact the interior smelt, that he smelt. Rich must have been used to it, but had Tatty picked up on it? Perhaps it was the air in Yarmouth. Rotten, like everything else.

Catching a stretch of river to his left he thought of Rich's Merc, and whether the windows were open when it hit the water. Had that stopped it floating away on the tide, the water flooding in? He couldn't remember whether they were open when he saw the car being hauled out of the water. No one had given him any proper details. So far he hadn't even been questioned. He knew the police round here were easy to fool, but still.

He jabbed the button on the armrest, shutting his own windows. He wanted to give himself more of a chance, if the Range Rover were to swerve across the quay, and fly into the Yare. Cars didn't drive themselves, yet Simon was top of his list of those who'd want Rich out of the way. But there were more than a few others. Tatty, he had to concede, included.

The traffic was all one way, slow, heavy, leaving town. The centre of Great Yarmouth on a Saturday night was acrid, violent, lawless. The club was located on Regent Road, in the thick of it. Except it was the only club of its kind in town, and as such there were often scuffles outside, and in. They had to hire double the usual number of bouncers. All on the scam, and often the cause of any trouble, especially the Eastern Europeans. The graffiti on the shutters could not have been more graphic. Cocks and balls and words inciting hatred, in a number of languages. Everyone knew what sort of a club it was.

Frank was not heading for the club. They hadn't contacted him. He would visit it later anyway. He always

81

did on a Saturday night, last thing. But he was heading in the opposite direction, slowly.

Finally crossing the Haven Bridge felt like something of a relief. The sharp spit of land that was old Yarmouth had been stabbing him in the back all day. He tried cracking open the windows again, before indicating right at the Mill Road junction, waiting briefly for the lights then turning off Bridge Road, and into what Rich had always regarded as forgotten Yarmouth. Frank went straight over the mini roundabout, passing some small garages and the tabernacle, cutting onto Lady Haven Road before being forced left onto Critten's Road.

There were the backs and some fronts of small terraced houses on his left, none knowing which way they should face, and on the other side some hard metal fencing, council-planted, closing off wasteland edging the widening river. A dark blue crane sat out in the middle, lifting nothing.

Quickly the fencing became less solid, but no less pointed. Beyond it he could see the rusted corrugated roofs and breeze-block walls, some once whitewashed now yellowed with careful neglect, of the yard buildings. The gates to Goodwin Boat Services were shut and padlocked. Beyond, not taking up enough space, were a couple of old fibreglass hulls, on stilts, a forklift truck, and a dirty white transit van. Not much happened there now.

Frank drove on to Rare and Yare Yachts. The gates were open, as he'd expected. He didn't drive in immediately but continued along Critten's Road, until it ran out of tarmac. The beginning of Breydon Water was beyond the high grassy bank ahead. The boatyards lay on a strip of reclaimed land that was once a sliver of Breydon Water. A couple of decades ago there were plans to build a huge food factory here. It was where they were going to freeze peas and make potato waffles. Then they realised it would have been too costly, the land proving too unstable. They put the factory down the road in Lowestoft instead. Millions were lost to the local community, Lowestoft winning again, while Rich went on to secure a weed-clogged chunk of frontage for nothing. Rich winning too.

Frank was tempted to park up and wander over to the bank. He loved it when the sun set on Breydon Water, and the geese took flight and the reeds rustled along the banks and the mudflats, the tide low and stalled, and with the whole world shimmering purposefully. But there was no sun now and the daylight was fast fading, and with the wind having died down there was a heavy, flat stillness. It was weirdly warm, and out there in the mud were the remains of at least one man who'd made a mistake.

Frank flicked the heavy, super-charged vehicle into reverse, spun it round in the tight dead end, accelerated back along Critten's Road, passing the few homes where everyone knew better than to peep out even if they were able to, before pulling fast into Rare and Yare Yachts. He should not have received such a message.

The rare and luxury yachts, such as they were, were hauled onto the fragile land the other side of the yard buildings. Some were brought into the shed, depending on the renovation needs. Jobs like re-weighting keels were best done under cover. Mostly, the yard dealt with the sale and servicing of tired day boats and broads cruisers. The idea of shifting product out of Yarmouth on such craft by river and into the vast network of Yare and Bure broads and tributaries seemed to have evaded the imagination of the NCA's Eastern Region Special Operations Unit – those who weren't on the make. Rich, aside from paying his dues, had always been confident that Goodwin Enterprises was more than a step removed in any case.

Before Frank had climbed out, Owen had appeared, not in overalls but in a dark sweatshirt and combat trousers, a baseball cap covering his bald head.

'You shouldn't have sent that text,' Frank said, finding his footing on the sandy cracked concrete, wanting to speak first and make clear who was calling the shots. Electronic communication between them should never have been so specific. 'And not now. You do know what the fuck's been going on, don't you?'

'Yeah, well, that's the thing,' said Owen. He had some muscle on him, and height. Could frighten most people off. He had some handy tools as well. He wasn't used to being pushed around. 'The boat's pulled into La Rochelle. It's currently in the Bassin des Chalutiers.'

'What the fuck?' Frank had been there once, on an early run, when they'd had to shelter from a Force 10. He'd only been to sea twice since. 'The weather's been fine, hasn't it? I've been looking.' He had since Thursday anyway.

'For the Bay of Biscay, this time of year, the weather's been fucking ideal for a fast crossing,' said Owen. 'The lad would have been having a whale of a time.' For once Owen didn't bother sniggering.

'The boy knew about his dad,' Frank said, feeling some strength, some conviction float away. 'A message was got to him, by satellite.'

'The skipper still wouldn't have stopped,' Owen said. 'He was under orders, whatever the problem. We've used him before, plenty of times. He'd have scuttled that thing rather than put into an unscheduled port. It might be the Bassin des Chalutiers, but French Customs are not as friendly as they used to be. You don't give them any opportunity to board a vessel, whatever order the paperwork might be in.'

Owen peered out across the yard at the opened gate, as if the place was about to be invaded by a group of marines, before returning his mean, narrow eyes to Frank. Frank thought once more that this line of business had to stop, if it wasn't too fucking late. All this, for £500,000 a time? It was pathetic. Rich had only kept it going because he'd wanted Tatty to have her summers in Ibiza, his kid to have a sail. 'It's only a bit of fun, Frank,' Rich had said, not so long ago. Fun? 'For old times' sake.' Perhaps Rich had been losing it.

'The boy's dad had died,' Frank said, more forcefully.

'With the weather, it wouldn't have taken them much more than three more days.'

'So he wanted to get off, fly straight home – I can see that,' Frank said, failing to persuade himself.

'The skipper's not answering his phone. I'm not getting any communication with the boat. That's why I texted you.'

'How do you know the boat's where it is?'

85

'Sometimes, Frank, I wonder about you. There's this little thing called a global satellite tracker. I know exactly where that yacht is at all times. All my yachts.'

It seemed exactly the wrong thing for someone like Owen to know, his computer screen flashing the precise whereabouts of 10 kilos of cocaine, and the rest. The operation seemed more absurd by the minute. How times had changed. Frank couldn't believe Zach would want to rush home either. He'd had a complicated relationship with his father. Of the three kids, Zach was most like his mother.

'Do you think it's been seized?' Frank said. What the hell was he going to tell Tatty? He was certain she didn't know about this, not the real cargo.

'There are no reports – that I can find. No chatter on any channels. Maybe it's nothing more than a temporary communication problem. Which is why I want you to call the lad, find out what the fuck is going on. The only person I could contact is the skipper. He knows the risk. He's being properly paid.'

All Owen was worried about was the product, his share of the profits, which couldn't amount to more than £50,000. Frank didn't give a shit about the money, he realised, whether it was the family's or not. Zach's safety, and freedom, was his concern. The boy no longer had a father. 'Sure,' Frank said, feeling for his phone. He looked about the yard, now dimmed by the flat dusk. He tried to imagine a new use for the place. If Goodwin Boat Services officially took over Rare and Yare's land, there'd be a lot of fine river frontage. Maybe they knew better how to deal with such instability, such drainage, now. He could see a string of properties on stilts. Fine views of the reeds, the mudflats, birds taking flight. People were paying more and more for that eco-stuff. He'd talk to Tatty. He looked back at Owen, those dark narrow eyes. He was not going to call Zach from here.

'I don't like what's going on,' Owen said, looking down at his clean camouflage trousers. He had not been working on any yachts today. 'That boat shouldn't have stopped where it did. The skipper had his orders, Frank. He knew the score.'

'People are only human,' muttered Frank, not at all sure what he meant.

'Rich copping it, that doesn't make sense,' Owen said, with too much force.

'No?' said Frank, eager to get back in his car. 'Not to you?'

'Ring the lad,' Owen said, turning away.

Frank couldn't believe he used to let the guy fuck him. He shouldn't have come down here. He opened his car door, reassured by the weight of it, the black solidity. 'I'll be in touch when I hear anything,' he said. 'Don't text me again, ever.' He should throw his phone away. But he was loath to lose another number, not that this one was registered in his name, of course.

11

Heading along Southtown Road, as if the car had indeed learned to drive itself, Frank took the left fork onto Malthouse, and a further left onto the thin lane that was Riverside Road, leading down to the river. The A12 to Stansted would have to wait a sec.

It was dark now and the river was darker still. He pulled over by a row of abandoned containers before the slipway. The slipway had a thin barrier across it; next to a nearby lamp post was another post, shorter and supporting a lifebuoy, the orange picked out by the yellow-white glow of the street lamp overhead. Frank couldn't see it ever being used to save someone's life. Not round here.

He got out of the car, beeped it locked, crossed the empty road and walked back towards the steps. He was not afraid of being spotted, knowing that this stretch of Riverside Road was not visible from the top of Ferry Hill because of the steepness of the incline, or from across the river because of the redundant containers. It was where he used to drop Rich off.

He paused by the bottom of the public steps, looked both ways. The badly lit road, hugging the land, was deserted. The thick black river was deserted too, but there were pools of bright, reflected light dotting the water, growing weaker towards the harbour mouth. There was no breeze. It was far too calm. Frank was sweating before he started the climb. By the top, he wished he'd left his jacket in the car. It felt as though a storm was coming from the west, inland. The only weather he'd been looking at recently was in the Bay of Biscay. Now he didn't need to.

Having caught his breath, he headed south along Ferry Hill, towards Gorleston High Street. The road was hemmed in by residential buildings on his right and a cheap imitation of an old flint-and-chalk wall on his left. There were more working street lights up here and he was aware of being exposed, so he increased his pace until he was walking by a tall steel wall, offering even less cover. The steel had been finished with something that made it gleam. The same steel panels had been used on the ground floor of Simon and Jess's concrete box, the builder having procured some offcuts from Admiralty Steel, so Rich used to tease.

A couple of cars swept past him, their headlights glancing the smooth barricade. The double gate, set rakishly off centre, was also made of steel, with the intercom, on the far edge, glowing a ghostly blue. It looked as if you'd get a nasty electric shock if you pressed the button. Frank had never pressed it. Rich never needed to. Jess was always ready for him – always, so it had seemed. They had their codes. Timing was one of Rich's greatest strengths. Or so Rich had believed. When exactly had that talent finally deserted him?

Frank paused, caught his breath, walked on to where the property ended and another property began. This house was nothing to look at. But it had a low brick wall and there was enough space between the buildings for Frank to look straight out and across the river to Great Yarmouth, Fish Wharf and the ugly block that was Goodwin House, sticking out on the bend. He could see lights inside the building, on the third floor. Simon was still there, in his office, which, when Frank had had a snoop earlier, seemed far too neat, far too clean, even for him. Frank would need Zach's help to dig further. A hundred grand to clear off? Frank had never been so insulted.

The patch of quay where Rich's car went over was in plain view. Frank knew it would be. Some purpose. Some planning. Some audacity. Some anger? The squat capstans were starkly unreflective, darker and heavier than the night on the water. There was just a hint of the police tape strung between yet connecting nothing. The evidence was elsewhere, of that Frank was certain.

Simon had a telescope in his bedroom. Rich used to use it. Recently Rich had been visiting Jess even when Simon wasn't out of the country. Frank didn't say anything, he had long learned to keep any opinions about such matters to himself. Not that it would have made any difference. When Rich wanted something badly enough nothing could hold him back, no one could stop him. Though someone had, eventually. What sort of headspace was Jess in right now? She had some front. It wasn't all Rich.

Turning, Frank tried to discern whether any lights were on inside Simon and Jess's home. Despite being so close to the road, hugging the steep slope of Ferry Hill, the house itself, facing the other way, was well masked from the street. Its real presence could only be discerned from across the river.

Passing again the steel barricade, which had been no barrier at all for someone like Rich, or Jess, Frank was aware of a car close behind him. Crawling. He shook himself deeper into his jacket. The car slowed some more. And then it accelerated forward, its powerful engine easing into life, the wake disturbing the close night air and forcing Frank to look up. It was Tatty. Tatty's Merc anyway, heading for Southtown Road, back towards Yarmouth. He had an idea where she was going. What a family. But he was not going to follow her. He held his watch up to the light. He was short of time as it was.

12

The phone was on silent but the dull sound of the device vibrating on the glass-topped bedside table next to her head disturbed her sleeplessness. Without sitting up, Sam reached for it. In the weak dark she caught the message before it died behind the request to type in a passcode.

Need some help Sis. Call me if u r awake. Z x

It was the first she'd heard from Zach since her father had died, though she knew Ben had been in contact. She sat up, reached for the bedside light. Remembered that there wasn't a bedside light, but a light switch built into the suede-covered headboard above her head somewhere. She did not like the feel of suede. She did not like meat. She found the switch.

She'd managed to force a window open before climbing onto the monstrous bed and the air in the room now stung her bare arms as she entered her passcode and read again the message, before throwing the phone onto the other side of the bed. Where was he? It was nearly two in the morning. She thought it would be later. She was disappointed it wasn't later. There was so much more of the night to get through.

She'd been turning into an insomniac before her dad had died. Now she could see it was only going to get worse. Her mind was rushing all over the place. Nevertheless, when she was back in London she wouldn't see her doctor. She was never going to take sleeping pills. Her mother had always taken sleeping pills, and so had her dad, it seemed, at the end. A boyfriend had to be better, and not working so hard at something she wasn't sure she was cut out for. Her colleagues were all such fucking snobs. Perhaps she'd take up yoga. All her friends did yoga, or pilates. She was out of bed, looking for something to put on. Walking into the en-suite she half expected to see a couple of fat fluffy white bathrobes on the back of the door. The house had stopped being a home years ago.

She walked back into the bedroom, colder, knowing she was delaying calling Zach. He only ever got in touch when he wanted something, which was most of the time. He could have said something about their dad. Was she the only one who cared? It was so fucked up; that was why she never came back to this stupid house, this stupid town. She had always hated it here. But she wasn't sure she liked London any better.

She reached over and retrieved her phone from its goose-down cradle, and pressed the call icon, surprised that she was getting a UK ringtone. She pulled the device from her ear, looked at the screen. It didn't say it was doing anything it shouldn't have been doing. Though she thought she could also hear, faintly, another iPhone going. Ben's? Her mum's?

She stepped over to the window, parted the heavy curtains and saw nothing outside but the night and the street lamps trailing away down a lonely Marine Parade. Her room was on the side of the building, giving her an oblique view of the desolate Gorleston seafront. She put the phone back to her ear, just as it was answered.

'Sis,' said Zach. He was trying to speak quietly.

'Where are you?' she asked.

'Outside the front door, yo. I don't have my keys.'

'What? Here? You're here? Downstairs?'

'Urgh, yeah. I've been wandering round for the last ten minutes, doe. No one's left anything open.'

'You always used to climb onto Mum and Dad's balcony and get in that way. You getting old?'

'I'm not as young as I used to be, Sis.' He laughed. He was nineteen, about to go off to university, to study sports science. He'd always been fit, buff. 'Besides, I didn't want to wake Mum. Are you going to let me in then?'

She didn't bother answering, stabbing the red end call button then throwing the phone back onto her bed. She found her jumper on the padded bench thing at the end of her bed. It was like an elongated footstool. She was sure there was a name for it. Her mother would no doubt know, the amount of time she spent looking at glitzy interiors magazines. Pulling the fine jumper over her fine silk pyjamas – last year's Christmas present from her father, she remembered with a slight gulp of air, not that he'd have actually bought them – she left her room, which no longer felt like hers.

The house was dark and echoey, what faint light there was creating faint shadows. It felt too large and empty. In bare feet she tiptoed down the stairs and across the hall, not turning on any lights until she was by the front door. There was a large chrome panel to the left of the door, glinting in the dimness. There were six or so small chrome switches. She decided not to turn on any lights, knowing she was bound to switch the wrong one and hit the outside security beam.

It wasn't so hard to get out of the house, she realised, having twisted only a couple of locks. Gently she pulled open the heavy door, sure she could hear the sea. But not Zach. She stuck her head out further, swivelling round in the damp chill. Dreary light from the nearest street lamp was drifting across the forecourt with the thinnest of rains. He wasn't there. Hanging onto the door frame, she put her right foot on the mat. Leaned further forward.

'Boo!'

The bastard had hidden behind the chunky neo-classical columns, tacked around the outside of the door. They creaked when the sun hit them, which wasn't often. Sam had a good mind to slam the door in his face. 'Fucking hell, Zach. That's really mean.'

'Shush,' he said, 'or you'll wake Mum.'

'You should have thought about that, you prick.'

'That's not a very nice way to greet your little bro.'

She wanted to give him a hug, but she turned and walked further into the hall, letting him close the door. She went through to the kitchen and finally switched on some lights. It did nothing to make the place warm and comforting.

Ben had left a wine glass on the island. There was a dark pink stain in the bottom. Sam looked at the sink, the coffee machine, the fridge with its fat double doors. She didn't know what she wanted. Her feet were cold. It was still only early September. She didn't know when her mother would start to use the under-floor heating. Her father had hated being too hot. Was forever flinging open windows, telling her mum to turn the fucking heating off, it wasn't a fucking sauna.

'Are you not going to say anything?' she said, swinging round to face Zach, already knowing he was not going to make everything all right.

He was now over by the doors to the back garden, trying the handle. 'No wonder I couldn't get in,' he said. 'This would have taken some grind. The security catch has been slipped over the lock. Someone's being careful.'

'They'd have locked everything up properly before they went to Ibiza, wouldn't they?' she said, distraught. 'They'd only been back a couple of days.'

'What's the point of Nina? She's only round the corner.'

Sam hadn't seen her brother for weeks, months. He looked older, but sounded the same. 'How did you get back so quick?'

'Wings. Into Stansted. There's a direct flight from La Rochelle.'

'You just got off the yacht, and flew home?'

'Yeah. Sort of. There was a problem with the generator and the skipper pulled into this port. I would have stuck it out, doe. It wouldn't have taken much longer – that yacht was a thing of beauty. But when we moored up, I thought, you know, what the hell. Plus, the officials, the customs people, or whatever, were being heavy. The skipper was not cool about it. Who was meant to be on the yacht and so on. Seemed as though I could be doing everyone a favour if I bunked.'

Zach was still looking out into the dark, fiddling with the French doors, not facing her. 'I've always wondered about those boatyards,' she said. 'What they really do.'

'This had nothing to do with Dad. It was Rare and Yare's business – you know, the place next door.'

'They're not connected? Come on.'

'I got back, Sis. No sweat. All's fine.'

'All's fine?' She could have screamed.

Zach immediately left the doors alone and walked over to her, put his arms around her. He smelled of the sea, but she didn't know whether it was on his clothes, from the Atlantic, or whether it was in the air, having blown in from the grey swell the other side of Marine Parade. She could taste salt, too: the tears running down her cheeks. 'Aren't you sad?' she struggled to say, pulling away, embarrassed.

'Dad? It's too fucking weird. Is he really dead?'

'Yes.' She wiped her eyes. 'I saw him, in the morgue at the hospital. It was like on TV. He was on a metal tray thing, under a white sheet, and they lifted the sheet from his head and he was all pale and veiny and bloated. It was horrible, Zach. Worst thing I've ever seen. He had this big bump on his head.' She took a short breath. 'I mean, poor Dad, whatever you thought of him.'

'No way he killed himself,' said Zach.

'Ben thinks he did.'

'Ben would. It's simpler.'

'Simpler?'

'What about Mum?'

'Who knows what she thinks. No idea what goes on in her head.'

'It's fucking messed up.' He walked around the island. Picked up the dirty wine glass. Sniffed it. Shook his head. Put it back. 'I feel for Mum most. All that shit she had to put up with and now look.'

'Maybe, like over time, it'll be good for her.'

'No way you said that. You loved the old man. No question he loved you the best.'

Sam shrugged. What could she say?

'I need a drink,' Zach said, opening the fridge. 'Something to take the edge off.'

'It's like, the middle of the night. Are you not going straight to bed?'

'I've been cooped up on a stinking yacht for the last how many days. My Dad's just died. Who knows what the fuck's going on? Who knows what the fuck went on? Whoa – have you seen all the champers in here?'

'Mum likes champagne.'

'Dad didn't. Was she planning a party or something?'

'Not that she's said.' Sam couldn't believe how everything you'd loved and believed in had to have been some sort of a lie. It was so much easier being younger. Suddenly they all had to open their eyes, face facts. But she didn't know what the facts were. 'Though it was his birthday next week,' she remembered, trawling her mind for something certain.

'Dad and birthdays? Forget it. Where have you been? They didn't have people round either.'

'No, I guess not.'

'Let's crack one open.'

'A bottle of champagne, now? Are you crazy?'

'No, just thirsty.' He'd pulled a bottle from the fridge and was turning it in his hands. 'This, Sis, is vintage Moët, 2006.' He whistled.

'I'm going back to bed,' Sam said. 'My feet are cold.'

There was a pop, and Zach was reaching for the dirty wine glass as the champagne bubbled out of the bottle. He began pouring. 'Sure?'

'Oh, what the fuck? I'm not going to be able to get back to sleep anyway.'

Zach found a clean glass, filled it and handed it to her. He took a long drink from his own. 'Nicely chilled. Prefer Cristal, given the choice.'

'Where's your stuff?' She'd noticed he didn't seem to have any bags.

'I bunked, I told you. Can't say I'll miss those stinking waterproofs. Or that skipper doing his nut.'

Zach was not looking at her again. 'Those bloody boat-yards,' she said. When they were younger, their father used to take them down to his yard. They'd play on the empty hulls while he went next door for a quick business chat, as he used to say. It was never quick. What fucking business?

'I need to perch,' Zach said. 'It's still odd, being on dry land.'

'Hey, how did you get back from Stansted, at this time?'

'I got Frank to pick me up.'

'Frank?'

Zach had moved over to the table and sat down, at the head, where their father used to sit. She didn't know whether he'd done it on purpose.

'Frank?' she repeated. 'You even have his number.'

'No. But he rang me.'

'Why?'

Zach blew out a large mouthful of air. 'He wanted to know what was going on.' He took a sip, swallowed. 'He knew the yacht had pulled into port. Wanted to know if I was OK. If he could help with anything. I was just getting on the plane. Chance, hey?'

'So he rushed off to Stansted to meet you?'

'Yeah.'

'I don't get it.'

'Why not? He was trying to help – given the circumstances. I've been doing stuff for him, and Dad, for a while.'

'Like what?' She sat down now, heavily.

'Shifting stuff around . . . Heavy grind, heavy grind.' He took another sip. 'Some tech stuff as well. Those two don't know their systems from their toes.'

'What's Frank got to do with anything like that? And the boatyard? I thought he was Dad's driver, when he wanted one, taking him to the airport and so on.' She didn't think that, but she wasn't sure how else to phrase it, or even if she wanted to. She pictured Frank earlier today – yesterday, in fact – in the lobby of Goodwin House. His big bald head and sad eyes. He always looked so terribly lonely, for a thug.

'Frank does what Dad tells him – did what Dad told him. Fuck, this is going to take time to get used to.' Zach took his eyes off her, looked around the room expressively. 'Fuck's sake, Sam – all this, the villa in Ibiza, Mum's clothes, jewellery, her projects, the money we get, you, me, Ben? Where do you think it comes from? Do you have any idea how hard it is to make money, that sort of money, round here? Legitimately?'

'There's a lot of opportunity in places like Yarmouth,' Sam began, half remembering a line or two that her dad had spun in certain company. 'Land begging to be redeveloped, endless renovation projects, new port facilities, big gambling licences for the asking, councils looking for innovative ways to get the local economy back on track, plenty of grants, subsidies and tax incentives. Not much competition.'

'More bubbles?' Zach was out of his chair and walking towards the island and the opened bottle. He came back to the table with it before filling his glass and then topping Sam's up.

'I didn't say I wanted any more,' she said, taking a sip nevertheless, and seeing beyond Zach to the black back garden. They'd thrown too much money at this house, that was for sure. Its real problem was its location.

'I've never got this family,' Zach said. 'No one ever says a fucking thing about what's really going on.' He took a long sip. 'Frank's all right, by the way. He's cool.'

'Simon doesn't think so.'

'Of course he doesn't. Frank's smarter than him. He's been around the business way longer. Knows more.'

'What do you know?' Sam felt both jealous and fearful. Had her father tried to protect her more than her brothers, by keeping her further out of the loop? Because she was a girl, or because she was his favourite? Both? Sexist bastard. She reached for her glass again.

'How long have you got, Sis?' He laughed.

She looked at his thick, wild hair, getting long now he was out of school, sun-touched, the stubble on his strong chin, his clear sparkling eyes. He was suddenly a young man. But he'd always been sly, corrupt, she supposed. When he was at school he'd made a packet producing fake IDs. 'What tech stuff?' she asked, fearful.

'Playing around with the time stamps, the databases. Figures, a ton of figures. No big deal, provided you know what you're doing. And, I guess, a smidgen of expanding boundaries, searching out others' vulnerabilities.'

'What the fuck does that mean?'

'Hacking.'

He looked pleased with himself. Like his father, Zach was dyslexic, stumbled over written words. Had never done well with essays. Clearly, systems were another matter. 'Hacking into where?' she asked.

'Dad liked to keep an eye on his employees, and the competition, naturally. Look, we only had so much success, with the council mostly. Everyone's on to that one – super fucking highway.'

'What about all the figures you played around with?'

Zach laughed again, as if it were no big deal. 'Wiping documents, removing all trace, can take a bit of work. Then I might be asked to put something in their place and get the dates to stack up.'

'Why? Why did you do all this?'

'You're a lawyer, Sis. Why do you think?'

'Tax evasion, money laundering, fraud?' She didn't feel tired any more.

'Yeah,' said Zach, sounding a boastful prick. 'I guess. But, Sis, most of it I didn't understand, honestly. So many numbers. They stood over me. I did what I was asked. Ben might have had a clue.'

'Who exactly was in on it, apart from Dad and Frank?' She was never going to get to sleep, not tonight.

'Dad didn't employ many admin people, did he? The ones that he did were mostly on the level, I think. It all had to look squeaky.'

'Simon? What does he know?'

'Dad kept a lot of stuff from Simon, for sure.'

'He was his brother and business partner.'

'You know what, I'm not sure Dad realised quite who he was dealing with there. Frank hates him, says Dad should never have brought him in.'

'I don't think Mum likes him much.'

'Simon – he's got something to do with it, bet you.' Zach was pouring the last of the champagne into his glass. He'd always been hungry, thirsty, greedy. Selfish. Much like their dad.

'What?'

'Dad dying.'

'We've all got something to do with it, haven't we?' she said, amazed she did not have a headache. She wanted more champagne.

13

'Stay. Why don't you?' Nathan said, as Tatty was getting dressed.

She couldn't believe it. She must have drifted off. For years she'd struggled to sleep, and now she was dropping off just like that, in the most inappropriate places. 'No,' she said firmly. 'I have to get back.'

'He's dead,' Nathan said.

Tatty didn't like Nathan's tone of voice. 'You need to be more respectful,' she said.

'He was a bully. And a coward.' Nathan was sitting up in bed, his beautiful bare chest glowing in the gentle light. 'I don't understand you, Tatiana. Why can't we enjoy being together for once, without constantly looking over our shoulders? No one is going to leap out of the shadows and kneecap me.' He laughed. He had no idea how worried he should have been.

Tatty wondered whether it was that naivety, that innocence – or was it ignorance? – she'd gone for. It was his looks, for fuck's sake. Her body wanted to get back into bed with him, run her hands through his fine, greying hair. She didn't know what he washed it with, but his hair felt like silk, smelled like a Norwegian fjord. Rich's had been dry and sparse, while his scalp was always sticky with sweat. He'd never cared much for his appearance. She'd been so starved.

But Tatty's mind was set on leaving Nathan's loft. She adjusted her skirt, said, with her back to him, 'I have children. I have some sense of dignity, you know. I shouldn't have come. It's disrespectful. We shouldn't see each other, not until everything has quietened down.'

'Tatiana, having made your life a misery for years, decades, your husband finally kills himself, because, I don't know, he got into even more of a financial mess than anyone realised. Life's short. I don't want to stop seeing you, even for a while. We belong to each other, and now we can finally be with each other.'

'Oh, for God's sake, Nathan, get a grip.' Had she missed this in him before, this cloying mawkishness? It wasn't naivety, innocence, it was pathetic. It always was when feelings got in the way. She slipped on her shoes, grabbed the rest of her things, her cardigan, her shawl, her matt alligator Hermès Birkin handbag, and walked out of Nathan's bedroom, crossed the vast loft, heading for the old industrial steel door. They'd always felt safe enough in here, it was getting in and out of the building that was the problem – at the wrong times of day and night.

Nathan did not leap out of bed to stop her as she struggled with the bolts and mortice locks. She hurried down the worn concrete stairs, struggled with the door onto the street, finally emerging at the sea end of Salmon Road, in the filthy dark. She walked a few yards west, to her car, which she'd parked outside the next building, on the corner of Salmon Road and Fenner Road. Both buildings were former smokehouses, then semi-industrial units, a furniture factory and a PVC window manufacturer respectively. Now they were hers, nearing the end of a three-year renovation project. There were to be twenty live work studios and apartments in the Grade-II-listed shells.

It wasn't only Rich's cash that had paid for the redevelopment. Nathan, as project manager and a former English Heritage executive, had brought in some Lottery and Arts Council East grants. He had a good eye, a good business brain too, no doubt about it. Rich wasn't the only one who knew how to tap public funds. Not that Rich had ever pleaded for anything. Or that Nathan had done anything crooked, as far as she knew.

Before she got into her car, she paused on the gentle camber of the pavement-less road. She could hear the sea, smell it. She turned that way, stared into the dark. Fresh wet air was sliding across the wide stretch of beach and the large section of contaminated land that Rich had earmarked for the super casino. Out of the dirt would rise something vast and sparkling, changing the town for ever. It had always seemed such a dream, but perhaps it was closer to reality than she'd needed to consider. The base of her spine, stretched and pounded not so many hours earlier, tingled. Nathan always put the effort in, went the distance.

It was raining softly. She looked up at her own small venture, Nathan having already installed himself in the show loft. She was not pleased with herself. Call herself a Goodwin? She was so much bigger than this. She got into her car, wanting control, power, speed, and to get out of the blowy damp.

She could see that it wasn't only money. She must have always known that. 'Tatiana Goodwin,' she whispered sternly. She could also see that she was not going to get everything she wanted, just like that. She was more patient than Rich had ever been, and far more calm and considered than his brother. Stronger too.

Some distance later she found she was still wondering what Frank had been doing outside Simon's house.

14

Regent Road, a short while before dawn, was a soggy mess, the litter lying on the smudged pedestrian walkway like a flock of seagulls grounded by an oil spill. Frank had left the guys to lock up, following another dismal night. What had they said: thirty people, tops? And for this time of year? But the books would look OK, and there'd been no physical damage.

His car was parked off Nelson Road, and he turned his back on the sea and the fast-gathering chill coming in with the wet new day. Candy Kingdom, Funky Jabba, Purdy Piercing, the kebab house, were all shuttered, unlit. A hundred grand to fuck off? It would be hard to find someone around here who wouldn't have leapt at it. Frank had a different view. He couldn't get it off his mind.

The flint-and-chalk Catholic church appeared on his left, as out of place as ever. The nearest street lamps were doing little to draw attention to the medieval craftsmanship. They had been doing nothing to draw attention to the two lads, who must have been hiding behind the low wall by the entrance, either. Both were skinny, in frayed tracksuit bottoms and hoodies, filthy trainers. They scurried across the pavement towards Frank. He could smell them before they were in thumping distance.

'Yo fairy,' said one of them, 'where you going?'

Frank looked at him, then the other, said nothing, continued walking. But soon enough they loped their way in front of him. Frank didn't want to lash out yet so he slowed, said, 'You're in my way.'

'You go home?' the other kid said, the one with a tattoo on the front of his neck. A bird, tangled in barbed wire? 'You go home now? To your boyfriend?' His friend sniggered, then sneered.

They were Eastern European. Possibly Lithuanian. Probably on crack.

'Give me your wallet?' the kid who'd been sniggering said. 'Your keys.'

Frank laughed. He hadn't been mugged for years. Everyone knew who he was. He held out his arm, pushed the shoulder of the kid with the tattoo looking like it was trying to strangle him. The other kid went for his other arm, immediately had it twisted behind Frank's back in a way that he thought showed some skill, some training. It hurt. Cross now, Frank whipped his free arm round, catching the kid who had hold of him hard on the side of his head, a move that had certainly come from practice.

The kid reeled, letting go of Frank's arm. At the same time Frank brought up his foot, in the direction of the other kid. He got him on the thigh, but the kid was too far away for the kick to have meant much. The kid had also pulled a gun, something Frank was not expecting. Yarmouth street scum did not usually carry guns. He was now advancing on Frank, knowing Frank wasn't going to try to kick him again, with the gun out in front of him and pointing straight at his chest. Anyone who pointed a gun at your chest, from such a distance, knew what they were doing. The smaller target of the head, Frank might have thought differently and done something about it.

'Where's you car?' he said, dead serious now.

'Round the corner,' Frank said. 'Bermondsey Place.'

'We go,' he said, the tone urgent.

The kid with the tattoo rearranged his hoodie and took the lead. The other lad, the talkative one, walked at Frank's side, making no effort to shield the weapon from any CCTV cameras that might have been working.

Nelson Road was deserted. Rounding the Prince Regent, in complete darkness, then passing the shuttered off-licence and the fish and chip shop, neither showing any signs of life, they came to a slow halt by the narrow beginning of Bermondsey Place. There was a chance, Frank thought, that the guys from the club might catch him up after battening down the hatches, because they too parked their cars on Bermondsey Place. But it was a slim chance, and even if they did, he couldn't see Scott and Terry being much use. They weren't employed for their muscle.

The gun was waved at Frank. 'It's down there,' Frank said, pointing into the darkness. He could make out a row of industrial-sized wheelie bins and the scruffy backs of some buildings, and flat garage doors that he knew no one had bothered to smother with graffiti. Further on, though not in view, were more large wheelie bins and some vehicles, his included. There were no street lamps and certainly no CCTV. It was where the street scum went to shoot up when they couldn't make it back to their overcrowded bedsits in time.

'Move,' the kid said, doing his nationality no favours and prodding Frank in the side with the gun.

'Where did you get your piece?' Frank said, taking a step or two.

There was a snort. 'Shut up, fairy.'

Frank kept looking ahead, looking for his car, feeling the gun in his side. Two big wheelie bins were now on their right, and Frank would have liked to shove the runts inside, slam the big lids shut, let them rot with the rest of the garbage from Regent Road, but he had a feeling they might pull the trigger. Eventually they reached his Range Rover, tucked into the last pocket of the night on the narrowing lane, and that was where one of them made a mistake. Another mistake.

'Keys,' the kid with the gun demanded, holding the weapon with one hand, the ghost of his other hand, perhaps shaking, held out for the fob. He was off balance, weakened by years of substance abuse, petty criminality and shocking welfare.

As Frank reached inside his pocket, he dropped to his knees, swinging his left arm round hard into the back of the kid's legs. He went down immediately, cracking his head on the uneven tarmac. Frank swiftly elbowed him in the throat for his trouble. The gun was lying free on the pavement, by his side, the stubby matt black barrel and sharply pitted handle darker than any lingering night air. Frank was nearer to it, and faster than the other kid; he had it in his hand and was standing, pointing it at him, in a fraction of a second. It was a small, heavy, well-manufactured weapon.

'We not hurt you,' the kid standing said, the one with the tattoo. He kept looking back the way they'd come, clearly weighing up his options for bolting. 'Only frighten.'

His mate was wriggling by Frank's feet, and Frank kicked him, with purpose this time, in the kidneys. He stopped wriggling so much. The gun was a Glock 19, newish. Worth two grand on the street. This was certainly not standard Yarmouth drug-dealer issue. 'Where did you get the gun?' Frank asked again, keeping it trained on him. It felt good in his hands.

'To frighten you,' his tattooed friend repeated.

'You wanted my money, my car?' Something wasn't stacking up. Looks deceived around here, always had.

The one still standing hunched his weak, bony shoulders. 'Frighten.'

'You picked the wrong man,' Frank said.

'You Frank? Frank Adams?'

'Who put you up to this?' Frank said, moving straight towards him, stepping on the kid on the ground as he crossed the short distance.

But he didn't wait for Frank to catch him. He turned and ran, an awkward, panicked, stumble of a run, his filthy trainers picked out by the faint dawn. What had given the lad the lead was the direction he'd gone: not back the way they'd come down the alley, but the other way, towards Wellesley Road. Frank could have let off a couple of shots, but he didn't shoot messengers, not in the back. Besides, he didn't want the police crawling all over here.

He got into his Range Rover, reached over, put the gun in the glove compartment, started the motor and gently negotiated the vehicle's exit from its tight parking spot, making sure he didn't run over anything squirming around in the dirt. Pulling away, he sniffed. There was that stench again: the wrong side of Yarmouth. Frank longed for his garden, early autumn there was always a lot of clearing, but he knew better than to head straight home.

15

Ben couldn't believe how well he'd slept. It was nearly 10 a.m. He'd missed two texts and a call from Avani. He thought about ringing her back, but not for too long. Climbing out of bed, he realised what had finally woken him. The doorbell was going. Where the hell were the others? Was no one up? He shook his head as he searched the room for his clothes. Pulling on his jeans and a sweater, he walked barefoot out of his bedroom.

Grey light was gushing in from the tall landing window by the stairs. Glancing outside he was not surprised to see that it was raining. He hurried the rest of the way down the stairs, slowing once he reached the ground floor, remembering that his father was dead. It was something he felt compelled to project. But for how long? The stupid bell went again as he was grappling with the locks. Pulling open the door he found Simon looking the other way, out to sea.

'Take your time, don't you,' Simon said, turning back towards the house, and pushing straight inside.

'It's Sunday morning,' Ben said, retreating. 'Is Mum expecting you?'

'Where is she, Ben?' he said.

They'd reached the kitchen. 'Still in bed, I guess.' Ben had no idea.

'Have you lot been having a party?'

Ben could see three empty bottles of champagne, one on the counter, two over on the kitchen table. Corks and their accompanying detritus of foil and wire were blocking one of the sinks. The kitchen reeked of cigarette smoke, Ben realised, though he couldn't see any butts. Sam didn't smoke, nor his mother. At least, neither of them used to. 'Do you want a coffee or something?' he asked.

'I want your mother,' Simon said, though not unkindly.

'Sure,' said Ben, 'but I'm not waking her up.'

Simon was in his slim-fit distressed leather jacket again, and his neat jeans. He didn't look like he'd slept at all. His tanned face was both taut and creased. He had tight grey bags under his eyes. He walked over to the far wall of glass, observed the tidy wet garden. 'Are you going to miss him?' he said, his back turned, running his fingers through his hair, perhaps catching a reflection.

'Dad? Yeah, of course,' Ben said.

'Do you think your mum will?'

'Did you want a coffee or not, Simon?' Ben felt under-dressed.

'I've been drinking coffee all morning, mate. I'm fine, thanks. Look, I'm pushed for time. Do you mind if I take a look at your dad's study?' He was facing Ben, walking back into the centre of the kitchen.

Ben was now certain his mother had forced the locks on the desk. Wondered whether she'd found what she was looking for. 'There's nothing in there. We've been through it.'

'Who do you work for?' Simon asked.

'What do you mean?'

'In London, your fucking job, Ben?'

'I work for a company in the City.' As soon as the words were out, Ben thought of other things he could have said. He wasn't enjoying being on his own with Simon.

'What's it called again?'

'Winslow Investments.' Ben was certain Simon knew that. His father had made enough fuss about it when he'd got the job – when the job had been got for him.

'What's it do?'

'Currency trading mostly, on the Forex.'

'The Forex? Shifting vast sums of money from one currency to another for tiny margins, but large profits?'

'That sort of thing.'

'Is there a lot of risk involved?'

'Not if you know what you're doing.' He felt on slightly firmer ground. It was a technical business. But he understood it.

'They let you have some control?'

'Yeah.' They didn't, yet; Ben was still climbing the ladder.

'How much do you personally get to play with?'

'Anything up to ten billion dollars.' The company dealt in those sums. Ben's exposure was far, far less, and always under the supervision of one of the senior managers. He'd only been there for eighteen months. He needed a coffee. He certainly didn't need Simon to be here. Decided he'd have another go with the machine.

'Why did your father not want you to go into the business? Our business?'

'He did, I think. I didn't want to go into it, not so soon, anyway. He always said I needed to work elsewhere, out of Yarmouth, after uni. Get some experience of the real world.' Simon was making him spill the ground coffee, making him say things that weren't quite true.

'He was no fool, your father, was he?'

'I don't know what you mean.' His dad had always said he needed to prove himself before he could come crawling home, begging for a proper salary.

Simon cleared his throat. 'You, working in the City, playing with all that money, and your sister now a lawyer – think about it. Young Zach – I'm not quite sure how your dad thought he'd fit in, but I'm sure he had something in mind.' Simon cleared his throat again, a couple of times, let his right hand slap the marble top of the island, then drummed a short beat. 'Your dad had you all exactly where he wanted you.'

Ben looked at the spilled coffee, aware of a dull pain at the back of his head. But he wasn't the one who'd been up all night, drinking champagne.

'But did he?' Simon continued, an edge to his voice now. 'Are you going to see if your mother's up, or do you want me to?' He slapped the top again, hard.

The coffee machine started to make promising noises. 'I'm not waking her up,' Ben said, anxious and cross now. He was in his house, his kitchen. 'She doesn't sleep well. If she's asleep, then she can stay asleep.'

'Fine,' said Simon, walking out of the room. 'I'll be in your dad's study.'

118

Ben left it perhaps a second or two too long before, breathing heavily, he went after Simon. There was now no hope of physically barring Simon from the room, even if he'd had the guts.

'We've been through it,' he said. 'What do you expect to find?'

'Who forced the locks?' Simon was standing at the desk, opening and closing the top right-hand drawer. Split wood was visible.

'We were looking for a note,' said Ben quickly.

'If your dad had left a suicide note he wouldn't have locked it in a drawer, would he? You sure the police haven't been here? Anyone else I should know about?'

'It's not the police that you're worried about, is it?' Ben's mother was at the door. She was in her dressing gown, which stretched no further than some clear tanned skin well above her knees. The material was thin and silky, and it was practically translucent. Her nightie underneath was no more substantial.

Ben was embarrassed for her. But pleased too that his mother could still look so good first thing in the morning. As a kid, a teenager, all his friends used to fancy her. Her hair was something of a mess though, and for the briefest of moments Ben wondered whether she had been in bed alone.

'Morning, Tatiana,' said Simon, glancing at her briefly, then back at the desk. He pulled open another drawer, rifled some papers.

'What you want is not in there,' she said, her voice clipped. 'Get out.'

Ben looked again at his mother, felt that dull pain in the back of his head once more. His feet were cold. He thought his mother must have been freezing. Boiling with rage, yet freezing cold.

'It's come to this, has it?' Simon said, still not leaving the desk alone.

'You think I didn't know where Rich hid his secrets?' Tatty said.

'I don't remember hearing about you ever confronting him,' Simon said.

'You and I, Simon, yeah, we're partly to blame for his behaviour, aren't we?'

'What are you getting at?'

'You think he cared what I found? You wouldn't have believed some of the things – not just the receipts. Pathetic, intimate things.' She laughed faintly. 'Once a thief, always a thief, that's what they say, isn't it?'

She was looking straight at Simon, and Simon seemed more uncertain. Ben realised how gloomy the room was. No one had switched on the lights. Flat grey light was making little effort to penetrate the study through the one triple-glazed window, which was meant to look out onto a sunny forecourt, a glimmering sea in the distance. He didn't want to be here.

'What is it you're really after, Simon?' Tatty said. 'Something to hurt us with?' She laughed again, louder this time. 'Proof that Rich was seeing Jess? But you must already have that, surely?' Simon cleared his throat, but Tatty continued before he had a chance to speak. 'Or are you worried that the police will find out, then come to the conclusion that you had all the motive you needed to kill him?'

'He committed suicide, Tatty.'

'When did you find out?' Tatty asked, still remaining by the door. 'I'm genuinely interested. Did you confront him the other day? Wednesday night?'

Simon was facing them, his back to the grey view, but steadying himself on the edge of the desk. Ben almost felt sorry for him. He wasn't sure he'd ever heard his mother sound quite so calculating, steely.

'I think you might have imagined this one, Tatty. Are you still taking those pills? Rich was concerned about all the pills you took, you know.'

'Where's Jess now?' Tatty asked.

'Jess went away for a few days, to stay with her sister. She thought I was going to be in the States. I was meant to be in the States, as everyone knows, putting the finishing touches to this deal that Rich kept cocking up.'

'That's convenient. She couldn't come back to support you, your young wife? Poor love's probably distraught. Assuming she's not dead too.'

Simon looked at Tatty, saying nothing. The silence was as heavy and dull as the weather. The triple glazing was not doing a very good job keeping it out. Ben wished he were in the Mediterranean, well away from here. He hadn't gone to the villa this year. He'd spent all summer trying to impress his boss and shag Avani. He wasn't sure either were worth it.

'Some of us focus on the real world, Tatty,' Simon eventually said. 'Keep taking your happy pills. I'm responsible for the business now.'

Ben knew he should say something. But he felt sharply out of his depth today.

'All the decisions are mine,' Simon continued. 'First priority is making sure everything is in order, given the circumstances. If that means working all hours of the day and night, so be it. At least someone round here behaves like a professional.'

He pushed himself off the desk, pushed past Tatty in her wispy nightclothes, and marched out of the room. 'You think you're going to get anything out of this?' He stopped by the front door. 'You might want to think again. You've no idea who you're dealing with.' He opened the front door without fumbling, not bothering to shut it as he left.

Ben glanced at his mother, who'd remained by his father's desk. He was sure she was smiling.

'He's always been a bit hot-headed,' she said. 'Don't worry about him. He doesn't know who he's dealing with.' She smiled.

'Is it true about Dad and Jess?' Ben asked.

'You know what, Ben darling, I think we all need to sit down and have a proper chat. You, me, Sam and Zach.'

'When the fuck are we going to do that? When's Zach getting back anyway?'

'Didn't you know? He's back. He got in late last night.'

16

Frank's second cup of tea tasted no better than the first. The milk was not past its sell-by date, because it was UHT, but it was foul. He threw the steaming liquid into the tiny sink, then the mug after it. It was too hot and he didn't have time to finish it anyway. He looked about the galley kitchen. Walked into the bedroom. Caught the film of salt on the cramped plastic windows.

No matter how clear it was outside, it always appeared foggy from in here – the deep stretch of North Beach slowly slipping into the North Sea, the wind turbines, more every year, lazily pinning the Great Yarmouth shore back. The view was not what it once was. Holidays in Yarmouth were not what they once were, despite all the recent Enterprise Zone grants, the public and private investment in the tourism sector. Rich had always disputed the fact that Yarmouth was the third most popular seaside resort in the country, supposedly worth five hundred million a year. 'Where's all that fucking money going?' he'd say, with a smile on his face.

Frank picked his jacket off the hook on the back of the door, feeling the weight of the gun. He wasn't going to take any chances. Which was why he'd decided to sleep in the company caravan, as Rich liked to think of it. Frank guessed it was all his now. Few people knew about it. Rolly Andrews, Sian's dad, kept an eye on it for them, but he'd been given more than enough favours to stop him blabbing. Enough favours that Rolly Andrews, traveller, had stopped travelling.

This dull morning Frank couldn't quite see why Rich had thought this stretch of Yarmouth, the holiday park, was so desirable. It seemed the holidaymakers had all packed up and pissed off the moment the August bank holiday was over. There was no sign of anyone about outside, and it was not early. The blasted caravan shook with every step Frank took to get a better angle, and the view got smaller and more dismal. But then Rich had always seen things others hadn't. Hadn't he?

Frank put his jacket on before removing the gun. Looking about, he picked up the small towel on the corner of the bed. It was damp, yet crusty at the same time, and even at arm's length it stank of rotten cotton. He tried to wipe the gun carefully with it, making sure none of his prints got on the beautifully hard Glock polymer. He then folded the stiff towel around the gun, took a few heavy steps to the galley kitchen. Put the gun on the draining board, reached above the sink, tapped the panel on his left at eye level, felt it loosen, got his finger around a bottom corner and pulled it off.

Inside was a slim compartment that held a thick plastic bag containing five thousand euros and a passport. Frank had forgotten what name the passport was under, but he knew the photograph was of Rich, taken quite some time ago now. Frank guessed the passport had to be approaching its expiry date. Frank had sorted it out for Rich back when it looked as though the fraud squad was closing in. There was also the small issue of the minicab franchise with the Portuguese. Both problems went away, albeit in a somewhat muddy fashion.

Frank pushed the plastic bag further behind the adjoining panel, reached for the towel-wrapped gun and managed to balance that on the ledge and get the panel back into place, securing it with a thump. He checked his watch, looked around the caravan, then let himself out and into a thud of low pressure. Heavy rain was not far away. His car was further off, on Freemantle Road, and he swore at himself for having left it there. Last night, taking no chances, he'd cut across the racecourse, by the stands. This morning, almost lunchtime now, he decided it would be quicker to walk straight to the pier than get his car. Sod the weather.

By the time he got to the boating lake a heavy drizzle had begun. However, there were quite a few people about now, either wrapped up and clutching umbrellas, or so out of it they weren't noticing or didn't care. It wasn't freezing. His phone was going, and he swept across and into the tour bus shelter opposite the old theatre. No one was waiting for a tour of the Golden Mile. The electric vehicle, comprising one too many open-sided compartments, and supposed to resemble a steam train, was slumped along the kerb, gathering water and grime.

It was Owen's number. Fucking Owen, who'd just been told never to call him again, whatever the fucking issue. Frank stared at his phone, letting it ring out, not believing it. A short while later a beep notified him that Owen had left a voicemail message. A voicemail! Frank tried to imagine the words, the phrase, that would have been coursing through Rich's brain.

'The boat's left La Rochelle, without your boy on board. Thought you might want to know that,' Owen's message said.

Frank immediately deleted it. Put his phone back into his pocket. Thought. At least Owen was a couple of steps behind. Still, he could be a mean bastard. He was greedy too. Now Rich wasn't around, who knew what he might do. Frank walked out of the hopeless shelter.

A week ago the Golden Mile was almost thick with people braving the August bank holiday washout. A week ago Frank was at home in Bradwell, in front of the box, hoping the weather would let up so he could get on with refashioning the outside of his property – he was creating a shingle garden in what had been the carport, using coastal plants. Rich and Tatty were returning from Ibiza. Zach was sailing through the Straits of Gibraltar. Ben and Sam would have been in London, keeping some distance.

The soft, wet bowling green was now on his left, the beach beyond. He was moving fast, full of purpose. He was late. Then he was finally at the entrance to Britannia Pier, the strip of hoardings advertising attractions few wanted to see sitting below the thin neon sign, *Britannia Pier*, which no one had bothered to switch on, despite the dullness of the day. Further on were the lurid green plastic mounds of Joyland. Everything was so familiar yet so different.

He stopped. Looked back across Marine Parade, at the beginning of Regent Road, at the grand Victorian façades on that side of the road, hiding the decrepit B&Bs, the bedsits, the creeping deprivation. He wasn't sure whether one super casino would change all this. He wasn't sure whether that was Rich's real aim anyway. But he was going to do his best, for Tatty and the kids. Who knew what they could achieve. Because what else was there to do? Carry on as normal, when there was no normal? He couldn't leave this place, as much he hated it. Rich had made him feel he belonged.

The vast plastic ice-cream cone, complete with Flake, guarding the entrance to the pier, had been upended. A fallen sentry stretched between the Pier Tavern and the hot doughnuts and waffles kiosk. No one was skirting it, because no one was bothering to venture onto the sodden walkway. Frank bent down, grabbed the sticky cone by the Flake, and tried to haul it upright. It was slippery, greasy, and he tightened his hold. It wasn't so heavy, however. At least the weight was all at the bottom of the cone, the bit that Frank used to love best as a kid. His summers were short and brutal. There were few treats. Few memories he wanted to hang on to.

No one appeared to have appreciated his efforts rescuing the cone, and he dipped through the entrance, emerging onto the tired pier, which stretched over the smooth flat sand, falling short of all but the highest of tides. Frank was glad that only sand was below, and not too far below the sodden planking at that. They'd been wrangling about renovating the structure for years. Rich had been happy to watch it rot. The new Goodwin Casino was to have not one but two piers, joined at the end by a sparkling glass ball-room.

He walked past the dripping kids' rides – a horse on bucking wheels, a bright yellow-and-orange clown car – none attracting any interest, with the amusements hall on his left emitting the usual shrieks, shrills and clatters. The pier widened by the large theatre and Frank skirted the entrance to the show bar and walked along the side of the large structure, the yellow-and-red bumpy slide looming over the remaining rides ahead.

Britt Hayes was already waiting for him beyond the bottom of the slide, at the far corner of the pier. She was facing out to sea. The spot was well sheltered from any working CCTV cameras, if not the weather. The walk had warmed Frank and he was glad of the wet breeze.

'Autumn already,' said Hayes, turning, before Frank's footsteps could have alerted her to his presence.

'Then winter,' said Frank, 'and the end of another fucking year. Do you ever have the feeling you're getting too old for this carry-on?' Mortality was stalking him badly today.

'Too young, too old, what difference does it make? We shouldn't be in it anyway. But we're stuck, aren't we? Once you're in, you're always in. There's no going back. You have to keep going forward. Get better at it. Be smarter, more careful. I'm sorry about Rich. We didn't always see eye to eye, but still.' She shrugged her slim shoulders.

She was leaning against the railing, backdropped by the sea and a cluster of wind turbines, turning slowly but steadily. She was in a tight, light waterproof, the hood up, black leggings and trainers. She could have been going for a jog.

Frank was staring at her. She knew what he wanted to know.

'We haven't been called in yet, Frank. The local guy, Leonard, is still in charge. I can do my best to keep it that way.'

'You know what Rich was like. You think he'd want the police anywhere near this?'

'What about his wife, the family?'

'We can handle it.' Frank forced a smile.

'What do you think happened?' she asked.

Frank looked beyond Hayes again, and towards the shallow North Sea. The tide was out. He thought he could see waves breaking on Scroby Sands. There'd be seals frolicking in the gentle surf. Rich had wanted to build the casino there, out on the sandbank, until he looked into the costs and felt the first sniping of the environmentalists. It was one thing building an outer harbour, quite another a pleasure dome. Frank shook his head.

'He was in the shit,' Hayes said, 'and not only from HMRC. That's easy to deal with on a personal level, but the fraud boys, when they get a sniff of anything organised? We have a new boss. He's revamping the whole set-up. Cuts might be going on elsewhere, but we're getting more resources. Part-funded by a few recent successes.' She laughed. 'We get to keep some of the cash, Frank. Did you know that? The criminals are funding the police. Funny, isn't it? The better they are at it, the better we're equipped.'

'You wouldn't find much cash, however hard you looked at Goodwin Enterprises, so tell them not to bother. You knew what Rich was like. He wasn't stupid.'

Hayes looked over his right shoulder, Frank following her gaze, towards the funfair, the ancient big dipper dominating the Golden Mile. And beyond, perhaps, to the rough, deserted land where the casino complex was meant to go. Three blocks, each ten storeys high, two piers, and the giant crystal ballroom. Forget the marine energy supply vessels, Rich had hoped that one day the outer harbour would be used for cruise ships carrying gamblers across the North Sea. The Dutch, the Belgians, the Danes, especially the Swedes, loved their gambling, even more than the Brits. 'You have to think far enough ahead,' he used to say. But he can't have, Frank thought now. Not that far.

'Thanks to the whole terrorism thing, we have powers that we never used to have, Frank,' Hayes was saying. 'Organised crime – fraud and extortion especially – we're in a much better place to tackle it. As for the drugs, and the people-smuggling, that's bread and butter. Most of you lot are way behind. It's only a matter of time.'

'Like I said,' said Frank, 'you knew Rich, you knew how careful he was. He ran a tight ship. The operations are solid. Nothing could look more legit.'

'Not his brother, Simon, I don't know him.'

'You wouldn't like him.'

Hayes looked at Frank. She was an attractive woman – fit, full of guts. Loyal too. To those she loved anyway. 'Rich didn't trust him? His own family?'

Frank shook his head. 'At first, maybe. He thought he needed him to persuade the Americans.'

'Then what happened?'

'I'm not sure,' said Frank. 'Different visions? Money, power, it goes to some people's heads.'

Hayes laughed. 'I can get this escalated pretty quick. We can pull Simon in, see where it goes from there. If we look hard enough, we'll find what we want.'

'I don't want it all to collapse,' said Frank. 'Rich wouldn't have wanted that. There's too much at stake for those he left behind. He spent twenty, thirty years, building up the business. This casino deal comes off, we're in a whole different league.'

'Maybe that's the problem,' said Hayes. 'There are plenty of hungry eyes around here.'

'Let the family work it out.'

'And you, Frank? Where do you fit in now?'

She looked at him through tiny dark pupils, and Frank was reminded that you could only ever know someone that much, even those you loved. He said nothing. Listened to the soft waves. Hayes was not going to answer for him.

'Someone took him out,' Frank finally said, the breeze getting in his eyes now, some grit too. 'But it might just be best if everyone thinks it was suicide.' He knew more conversations with Tatty and the kids were needed, and soon. Then there was Simon to deal with.

'Why did you want to see me?' she said.

'Who might be supplying Glocks around here? You don't come by them often on the street – in the wrong hands.' He looked at her now, distrustfully. 'Do you?'

She looked over her shoulder again, as if someone might be running up the beach, armed. 'You want a Glock? There're plenty of cheaper alternatives.'

'I don't want a Glock waved in my face by a couple of crack addicts.'

'That doesn't sound right.'

'I know. They knew my name as well. Lithuanians.'

'Fuel to the fire.'

'Thought they could frighten me.' He laughed.

'They picked the wrong guy.'

Frank smiled some more. He'd met Hayes through her on-off boyfriend, Howie Jones. Howie was the best bouncer he'd ever come across. He'd trained for far more dangerous things. Been paid higher rates to keep the peace as well. He was not handling retirement well. He handled his relationship with Hayes better. Both had unusual and demanding tastes. 'One ran off,' Frank said. 'I left the other in the gutter.'

'That was nice of you.'

'I can be nice when I want to be.'

'I don't envy them now.'

'No.'

'I'll ask around,' said Hayes.

'Thanks. You want an ice cream?'

Hayes pulled her phone out of the side pocket of her waterproof. 'Not quite the weather for it, is it?' She checked the screen. 'Anything else you want to tell me?'

There was always a trade. 'Rare and Yare Yachts?' he said. 'I think it's time that yard's closed down.'

'I need more than that, Frank.'

'A yacht will be coming in, middle of next week.'

Hayes was already shaking her head. 'The old ones are always the best.'

'Fancy thing, all the way from the Balearics. Up for a refit. You might want to check out the keel, once they've got it on dry land.'

'You think there is any dry land around here?' she said, pushing herself off the railings.

17

They'd missed lunch. Tatty looked at her watch again, Rich's glinting gold Rolex. At this rate, they'd miss tea. She'd forgotten how difficult it was to get all her children out of the house at once. Ben was too particular, Sam shy, Zach forgetful. School was so long ago. But she'd often had help. A succession of German and Scandinavian au pairs, pawed relentlessly by Rich. Two left in the middle of the night, leaving notes, blaming the kids, their unruly behaviour. It was Nina who inadvertently told Tatty about the amount of cash one of the girls had squirrelled away in her room.

'Children,' Tatty shouted by the front door, 'can we please get out of here.' She could hear one of them, Ben, in the cloakroom, but there was no sign of Sam or Zach.

Ben emerged, in another strange jacket. 'They're outside, Mum, waiting.'

'Oh.' Tatty opened the front door, realising that perhaps it was she who had been keeping everyone waiting. She for one didn't know what to wear any more. What was suitable for a widow? A mother, a mistress, a mobster? Suddenly none of her clothes seemed suitable, but she was smiling, broadly, as she held the front door for Ben. *A mobster!* Her time, her terms.

'Oh God, Zach, do you have to? And Sam. When did you start again?' They were both smoking, standing by the car in the drizzle. The smoke was hanging heavy in the wet air. 'Put them out, come on, guys.' She would like to have stepped over and swiped the cigarettes from their mouths. They weren't even e-cigarettes. But her children were adults now. They'd been controlled enough – all of them had. She beeped the car unlocked, thought for a moment, then beeped it locked. 'You know what, let's walk, it's not far. Do our bit for the planet.'

Ben laughed. 'Yeah, right, Mum.'

'It's pissing down,' said Zach.

'It's not pissing down, darling,' said Tatty. 'A bit of drizzle, that's all.'

'It's not that near,' said Sam.

'You've just spent a fucking week on a boat in the middle of the Atlantic, Zach,' said Ben, almost at the same time, 'and you're fussing about the rain?'

'I don't like the seafront here,' said Sam, perhaps answering for Zach, 'it's always given me the creeps.'

'I know what you mean,' said Zach. 'Too fucking dead.'

'It's changing,' said Tatty quietly.

'Are you telling me no one parks up to stare out to sea all day?' said Sam. 'I can see them.'

'Pervs,' muttered Zach.

'We'll all be there one day,' said Ben.

'Mum's gotta move,' said Zach. 'But would she dare?'

'No way,' said Sam.

'And do something on her own?' said Ben.

'I do have a voice,' said Tatty, louder, leading them out of the drive and across the empty road, swamped by not just the drizzle but that low Sunday afternoon feel, and no doubt too many cloudy eyes. She tightened the belt on her mac. Sam, Zach, they were right. Marine Parade, the Gorleston seafront, had depressed her for years, for decades. She wasn't sure it had changed that much. There was more money around, she supposed. Some of the big houses on the front had been added to, revamped, like theirs. Some younger people had moved in. But it smelled the same. The weather hadn't changed one bit.

However, she wasn't going to do the easy thing and run away – yet. She'd decided over the last day or so. She'd spent years running away, one way or another – keeping quiet. Gorleston had once been a haven. Compared to where she'd spent most of her teens! From one smoggy squat to another, always the wrong end of the city. Earning cash in the only way she knew how. Abandoned by her parents. Or was it the other way around?

Fuck the weather, her business was here. Rich had always seen opportunity, the bright side. If he could make it work, so could she – though better, more comprehensively, more successfully. She had a lot to prove, and was surprised at how happy she felt about the challenge.

They were now on a near-deserted upper esplanade, no car parks this end, walking towards Gorleston's Yare Hotel, with Yarmouth's cranes striking the grey sky further ahead. She was running through what she was going to say to her kids. Four days with no temazepam or any of the other pills she took now and then, and her mind was clearing beautifully. Rich had never taken any such medication in his life, not that she knew about, not voluntarily.

She glanced over her shoulder. Her three children were walking together, talking quietly among themselves. How much had Rich looked out for them, protected them? More perhaps than she'd ever realised. It was her job now.

They'd reached the kink at the end of Marine Parade where the upper esplanade joined Cliff Hill, with the hotel hugging the top a short distance away.

'You think they even do tea and cakes?' said Sam.

'I don't know,' said Tatty, 'I haven't been there in years.' Rich had had a feud with the owner. He had wanted to buy the property and the owner had not wanted to sell it, at least not for what Rich was offering. What pissed off Rich most of all was that even when the fire so mysteriously broke out in the kitchen forced the place to close for six months, the owner still refused to sell. 'If they want to lose that much money, they're in a different game,' he'd said. Tatty saw what he meant now. Saw too that he must have backed away.

They entered by the main door, sinking into a small world of soft, thick beige. There was no one at the front desk, because there wasn't a front desk, just a cramped lobby full of fake antique furniture. It wasn't clear how you checked in, or out. Perhaps you didn't, perhaps it was all front. Music was being piped from somewhere – tinny pop that had even less place here than they did.

'Fucking weird, man,' Zach said loudly.

'Didn't Dad want to buy this once?' said Sam.

'Yeah, I was just thinking about that,' said Tatty.

'Another mad venture?' said Ben. 'What the hell would he want this place for?'

'Because he wanted everything,' said Tatty.

'And then he got bored, once he had it,' said Sam.

They all looked at Sam. There was nowhere to hide from that sort of comment, not here. Tatty briefly looked up at the low ceiling, dotted with halogens on dim. There were no cracks. 'I don't know where we're meant to have our tea,' she said. 'There doesn't seem to be anyone around to ask.'

'I've always thought the service industry in this neck of the woods needed a good kick up the arse,' said Ben.

'Now's your chance to do something about it,' said Tatty, leading them through one of the doors without giving her eldest enough time to ask her what she meant.

They emerged into a long, thin lounge area with more plush beige and a tiny bar over in one corner. There were hunting prints on the walls and a view of Gorleston Pier, or the South Pier as it was properly known, directly down and out of the string of plastic-framed windows. Large, once white gulls were flapping about nearby, the weather having brightened for the afternoon. There were even people out on the pier and strolling across the thick corner of Gorleston beach, directly in front of the model yacht pond. There were no toy boats on the yacht pond, and no proper ships going in or out of the harbour. However, sitting on the blue-grey horizon, Tatty could make out a couple of large vessels. Perhaps they were waiting for Monday, when a few more people did a few more things around here.

'It's not without potential,' Zach said, walking towards the far corner. 'Yeah, I can see why Dad might've wanted this place.'

Tatty thought about it. The hotel's view stretched across the mouth of the River Yare to the pointed end of the Yarmouth spit. Over the low-lying industrial roofs, the high-rise casino would have dominated the skyline. A boat service could have whisked gamblers from one joint to the other in a matter of minutes. Could still. Rich had had vision, that was for sure. Tatty hummed.

A few old but smartly attired folk had melted into some of the deeper chairs in the room. A group of not bad-looking twenty-somethings were at the other end of the lounge, grouped around the fireplace, which sat naked and unlit. They looked like they'd been in town for a wedding the day before and were still hanging on to the occasion, dressed in their skimpy party clothes, reluctant to return to their normal lives.

The Ocean Rooms, down at the beginning of Gorleston Pier, had long been used for such occasions. Rich had thought about many other uses for it as well. How, under different economic conditions, in a different climate altogether, it would be the perfect location for a cluster of upmarket bars and restaurants, with decking spilling out onto the new golden sands of Gorleston beach. Except Gorleston would always be 'a shady place for shady people'. She had a feeling that Rich's words were going to haunt her forever.

The Ocean Rooms – God, that was where she'd first met him, Tatty remembered with a shiver. She shouldn't have been there that evening. She'd practically been kidnapped.

She looked away, back towards her children – their children – knowing that at least two of them hadn't made such mistakes at such a young age. There would always be sunshine with them around. She would never regret Rich's contribution there. There were mistakes, and mistakes. Besides, the future was not Rich's but theirs now.

'Right,' she said, clapping her hands. 'Let's make our presence known.'

'I'll go and find someone,' said Zach. 'What do we want – tea and fucking scones?'

Rich would have said the same. 'Yeah, I think so,' said Tatty, as Ben and Sam settled themselves in chairs that were trying too hard to be chairs from a different era, for a different sort of clientele. 'Tea and fucking scones. Ben, Sam?'

'The dog's bollocks,' said Ben.

Tatty sat in the biggest chair, which had been left empty for her, and which was placed strategically in the corner, with the windows on her right, and the lounge unfolding in front of her. No one could creep up on her. She even felt in charge. 'Don't forget to ask for the clotted fucking cream,' she said, too loudly, after Zach. He was by the door now, near the underdressed young adults. He turned his head, as if waiting for more instructions. There'd always been more with Rich.

'And the fucking jam,' Sam added, for them all, perhaps.

'I think I'm going to miss Dad's language the most,' said Ben, as Zach disappeared. 'Boy, did he put some effort in there.'

'That's because what he was really saying was such bullshit,' said Tatty, her mood slipping. She smiled, a fake

140

smile, at Ben and Sam. They were both staring at her. Now who was the fraud? She had been completely disrespectful. 'I'm sorry, I shouldn't have said that.' She was nervous.

'It's OK, Mum,' said Sam. 'We do know.'

'Some things,' said Ben. 'But not everything, not by a mile.' He glanced over his shoulder, straight out of the nearest window.

'That's why we're here, seeing as we're all together for once,' Tatty said. She looked up and saw Zach walking back into the lounge towards them. The opportunities he, they all, had ahead of them. Could she still provide for them? The way Rich had? 'I'll tell you everything I know,' she said.

'Shouldn't we be having this conversation somewhere more private?' Ben said, as Zach reached them and sat heavily in his own over-stuffed chair.

'I don't know what the fuck we're going to get,' Zach said. 'They seemed a bit fucking clueless when I asked for clotted cream.' He looked at his siblings, his mother. Opened his mouth to say more. Closed it again.

'It's not always great, scurrying around in the shadows,' Tatty continued, trying to get the tone right. 'Your dad didn't believe in making too much of a statement. Unlike Simon, he didn't like to go flashing his weight and wealth around. However, there are some people around here who need to know how things are going to be from now on.' Where had that come from?

'Who's the boss, is that what you mean, Mum?' Zach said, sitting forward in his chair.

'If you want to put it like that, sweetheart, yes.' Perhaps this was going to be easier than she'd thought. 'Look, your father exerted his influence in many ways. We have some tough decisions to make, like how do we keep the business going, what do we want from the business, what bits of it can go, what needs to stay . . . '

'Who goes and who stays, as well,' said Ben. 'Let's not forget that.'

'True,' Tatty said. 'And who comes in to help with all this.' She looked at each of her children, knowing that what was going to be said over the next hour or so could change everything between them. 'Your father,' she began, 'was more than happy for you all to go and earn a living elsewhere, wasn't he? I mean, he still supported you, Ben, Sam, but he wanted you to get away from here, get some experience of life, some knowledge. He was pleased too, Zach, that you were off to Loughborough to study sports science. But you all know this.'

'Yes, Mum,' said Sam, nodding.

'But then what?' said Ben. 'He wanted us to come back and work for him, on one of his dodgy fucking operations?'

Tatty wasn't sure of the look on Ben's face. As with Rich, you could never be sure when he was joking.

'He believed in giving you opportunities,' said Tatty.

'Telling us what to do, more like,' said Ben.

'Mum,' said Zach, 'I worked for Dad for years. Computer stuff.' He sat back, looking pleased with himself.

'You needed some pocket money. I got that,' said Tatty. She hadn't got it at the time. She had tried to ignore it.

Zach was now shaking his head, puffing his cheeks. 'It was off the scale.'

'Ah, tea,' said Ben, sweating.

A waitress was walking towards them with a large tray loaded with perhaps scones and cake, and tea things – Tatty couldn't quite see. Such a tiny, skinny waitress shouldn't have been carrying such a tray on her own. Nevertheless, she managed to put the tray down carefully on the low coffee table, her slim black trousers and stained white blouse barely having anything to hang on to. 'Thanks,' said Tatty.

There were scones and neon pink jam, and some cream in a small silver bowl. But it was far too white and fluffy. She was going to leave a tip nevertheless.

Tatty had been so focused on the girl she hadn't noticed who had walked into the lounge behind her. And Graham Sands was a very large man. The owner of Admiralty Steel seemed to be trying his best not to look their way. He was with his wife – Tatty had forgotten her name, but not how thin she was also. She was as thin and pale as her husband was fat and red. She reminded Tatty of the young waitress.

Finally he made eye contact and began walking over. 'Excuse me,' Tatty said to her children, getting up, not wanting their tea sullied. 'Someone I know has just walked in.'

'The geezer over there?' said Zach loudly behind her. 'Dad's best mate?'

'Tatiana,' Graham Sands said as she approached, with Zach's laughter still ringing in her ears. 'I was so sorry to hear about Rich. My deepest condolences, to you and your family.' He looked round her, to the others.

'Thanks,' said Tatty coldly.

'The whole of Yarmouth is shocked. He did so much for the business community, for everyone. We're going to sorely miss him.' He was trying to smile, sadly.

'Graham, we both know what Rich thought of you. There's no need to trouble yourself, or me, with false sentiment.'

'As I said,' Sands stated, no smile on his face now, 'my deepest condolences, to you and your family.' He glanced over his shoulder. His wife was still by the door, talking to the thin waitress – it could have been her daughter, Tatty thought. 'I've already expressed as much to Simon,' Sands continued. 'He'll have a lot on his plate from now on, I expect. But he seems a capable chap. Enjoy your tea.' He surveyed the lounge proudly. 'We know there's room for improvement. But give us time. We've got big plans for this room, for the hotel.'

'You own the hotel?' Tatty said.

'Oh yes. I bought it a couple of months ago. Cheap as chips, it was. I thought it was time to get into the hospitality business. The steel industry is heading for the scrapheap, the way the Chinese have been manipulating the market, and no help whatsoever coming from the EU – thank God we're leaving. As Rich always knew, you don't want all your eggs in one basket, not round here.'

Sands retreated with a surprising burst of speed for such a colossal man. Tatty returned to her family, though she waited for him to leave the room with his stick insect of a wife before opening her mouth. 'Where was I?' Her children looked at her.

'Zach was telling us about working for Dad,' Sam said, raising her eyebrows, looking at her younger brother.

Tatty wasn't sure what her children might have been discussing while she was talking to Sands, but she knew one thing. She shifted her gaze to the nearest window, watched for a moment the rippling river, the deeper troughs between the north and south piers where the Yare met the sea. The dirty gulls dancing on the waves. 'The tide runs very quickly here. I'm not sure how well your father had been keeping up.'

18

'We're still waiting, Mum,' Ben said.

Tatty checked the room once more. Leaned forward. Was about to speak.

Sam beat her to it. 'You didn't actually want Dad dead, did you?'

Tatty sighed. 'Darling, I've wanted him dead many times, believe me. But no, I didn't want him dead enough to actually do anything about it.' She shook her head. 'I didn't kill him, if that's what you're asking.'

Sam sucked in the warm, stale air, stuck the wrong side of a bank of cheap double-glazed windows.

'He wasn't on sleeping pills, was he?' Ben said.

'No. Not that I knew. I don't understand that bit.'

'Could he have taken some of yours? Sneaked them from your packets?' Sam said.

'I guess so. I have been wondering that. I probably wouldn't have noticed – I'm sorry.'

'Was he really having an affair with Jess?' Ben asked.

'Where were you last night?' Zach chipped in. 'Until whatever it was o'clock in the fucking morning.'

'Are you seeing someone, Mum?' Sam said.

Her children were asking the questions, Tatty realised, blinking. The same way they used to badger her. She should have been leading this discussion. It was meant to be her moment. She had some serious questions to ask them. 'One at a time, one at a time, darlings.'

'How involved are you in all his businesses?' Ben asked, holding his hands up and making quote marks with his fingers.

'I'll get there,' she said, taking a breath. 'Was your father having an affair with Jess? Yes, I'm pretty certain. It had been going on for some months, possibly longer. I found things. Did Simon know? That's troubling me. How did he find out? When did he find out? Half of me thinks your dad told him.'

'Why would he do that?' said Sam.

'To humiliate him? I don't know. A power thing, maybe, related to the Prime Poker deal – who knows?'

Sam sighed. Ben too. Zach chuckled, said, 'Grown-ups, man.'

'Isn't business more important?' said Ben.

'In your life, Ben,' Sam said.

'So who have you been shagging, Mum?' Zach said.

'Nicely put, bro,' said Ben, reaching forward only to find that the tea had all been consumed.

'Have I been having an affair, Zach, is that what you are asking?' Her gaze shifted past her youngest, to the window and beyond. She blew out some air. 'As a family, we really should do something about our language, how we talk to each other.'

'It's too late,' Ben said, shifting awkwardly in his tight chair.

Tatty was worried for Ben. He was never comfortable talking about his relationships, his girlfriends. He didn't do intimacy.

'I did ask you too,' Sam said.

'Yes, I have been having an affair,' she said. 'But it's no big deal – if you can believe that. The guy means nothing to me – not now, anyway. Also, it's only the second affair I've had in all the time I've been married to your father. I'm not sure you need me to talk you through his indiscretions, the ones I know about at least.'

'Spare us, please,' said Ben.

'Two?' said Zach. 'Go you.'

'Did Dad know?' Sam asked.

'If he did, he never mentioned it,' Tatty said. 'I honestly don't think he thought I'd dare.'

'So you do think he was losing it a bit?' Ben said. 'You know, with the business and everything?'

'Frank doesn't,' said Zach. 'No way.'

'Frank was very loyal to your father,' Tatty said.

'Unlike you,' muttered Sam, wounded.

'I understand how it might appear to you, Sam, to all of you,' Tatty said. 'Relationships, marriages, are complicated. And they don't get any easier over time. I wasn't always perfect. But I tried.' Tatty wondered then whether that was the case. She'd certainly tried to block plenty of stuff out.

'Come on, Sam,' Zach said. 'Dad wasn't exactly squeaky. Women aside, he was the biggest fucking crook in Great Yarmouth.'

'I'm not so sure about that,' said Tatty, wondering, wishing. 'But he was up there.'

Ben, as if following her train of thought literally, looked at the ceiling. 'Which leaves us where?' he said.

'We have our futures to think about,' said Tatty, staring at the table, the finished tea things – Graham Sands had a long way to go with this place. She wondered whether he'd have the time. 'I'm not going to ask any of you to do anything you don't want to do. Please understand that. I'm not sure I'm going to do anything I don't want to do myself – not any more.' She tried to laugh, but only a small, tired sound came out. 'But I'm buggered if I'm going to let the business go, all that your father set up, the opportunities that can still come our way. All that is ours, our future.'

She caught Ben's eye, cynical, dark, distant, looked to the others. 'Simon is not going to push us out,' she added. 'Neither is anyone else, for that matter. If your father has left us anything, then we're having it.'

'I need a smoke, man,' said Zach, feeling his pockets.

'Do we really want everything that's left, everything he was involved with?' said Ben.

'I don't know everything he was involved with, yet,' said Tatty. 'I honestly don't. But I'm going to find out, and then I'm going to make some decisions. Actually, we're all going to make some decisions, if you'd like. I know you have your own lives elsewhere, and I'm not asking any of you to change anything, not right now.' She paused, desperate for a cigarette for the first time in years. 'I'd completely understand if you wanted to turn your backs on Goodwin Enterprises. I wouldn't love you any less.'

'Sam, you coming?' said Zach.

'Children, you want to kill yourselves that way, fine.' She would have loved to join them. 'Give me a minute more. I'll never turn my back on you, Zach, Sam, Ben. I know I haven't been the most together mother.' She was tearing up. How could she have been so fucking casual, neglectful? A bullied, pathetic little thing, concerned only with her suede skirts and Hermès handbags and endless spa treatments, while her husband brazenly fucked his way around a fucked town. He found money where no one bothered to look. Not all his means were so admirable, but it was not a very admirable part of the world. 'From shit to shit,' he used to say. 'Take it or leave it.'

'Are you OK, Mum?' Sam said.

She had so much time to make up. Determined, she dabbed at her eyes with the knuckles of her clenched fists, said, 'I promise you all this: from now on I'll always be completely straight with you. I'll tell you everything I know. I won't hold anything back. I think we've all been under something of a cloud.'

'Mum,' said Zach, standing, 'thanks for saying all that, and everything. Yeah, it means a lot. Sam, are you coming?'

Sam got up, followed her younger brother out of the soft beige lounge. Ben smiled at her, strongly.

'Didn't know you had it in you, Mum,' he said.

'Let's keep surprising ourselves, shall we?' She wasn't quite sure what bit he was referring to. 'A drink, darling? A glass of champagne? It has to be that sort of time.'

'Do you care what sort of time it is?'

She smiled, shook her head. 'Where's that skinny waitress?'

19

Call me asap. Frank, the text said.

Zach looked at his phone again, felt pressured. Things were becoming real now. He got on his knees, his stomach, crawled a bit under the bed, so he could reach further, to the area in the middle up against the skirting, below the headboard. Finally he got hold of the old Adidas box and pulled it out. It still felt heavy, but not as heavy as it had at the beginning of the summer. Putting it on the bed, he had to sit down next to it. He was dizzy. It had been a mad twenty-four hours.

When he did lift the lid, he saw the rolls of cash and his beautiful brass-studded, bone-handled Laguiole knife with its corkscrew. Frank told him he'd once seen a man have his eye removed with just such a corkscrew. He took a roll of cash, knowing there'd be exactly £1,000. Knowing too that no one else had been anywhere near his money. Nina the cleaner was safe as houses. That's what his mum used to say. 'She should be, we pay her enough.' How that line used to reverberate around the house – as if money bought every-thing, which it did. Zach still didn't think that Nina knew he'd slept with her daughter Clara – was still sleeping with Clara, he reckoned. Didn't think his mother knew either.

Clara was cool. Worked as a waitress at the Star Hotel. Wanted to go into fashion. She had a good eye. Good hands too. His father had once said to him that there were two types of women: ones who gave and ones who took. 'Make your choices wisely,' he'd said. 'Or you'll end up taking shit and paying for it.'

Stuffing the roll of notes into his pocket and standing, Zach realised that everything was going to be so much quieter now. No barked orders to obey. Maybe he wouldn't go to Loughborough. Maybe he didn't need to get away after all. But the fucking weather here was going to drive him insane.

He looked around for his jacket. Decided on his dark blue All Saints mac, which was hanging on the back of his bedroom door. Putting it on, he glanced over to his large bed, where he'd fucked Clara the last time he'd seen her, shortly before he flew out to Ibiza. He thought she gave more than she took, but he wasn't sure. He wasn't sure he'd totally understood what his father had meant.

He walked over, replaced the lid on the box, then took it off again and removed the knife, which he put in the right-hand pocket of the lightweight mac. He bent down, feeling the knife swinging against his leg, and shoved the box under the bed, before walking out of the room.

The others were either asleep or in their rooms being quiet. It had gone ten, and stepping outside Zach was pleased to find that the rain had stopped and the air was dry and crisp. Light from the nearest street lamps was drifting over the forecourt in clean sweeps. His mum had left her Merc at a stupid angle as usual. For a moment Zach considered taking her car, if he could find the keys. However, he reckoned there was enough space to get his Mini out of the garage and around it. He preferred his Mini anyway. It was faster, tidier, hotter, with more than enough room to get a decent blow job in the front – the only blow jobs he'd ever had. Perhaps he'd text Clara once he'd spoken to Frank and bought a wrap of C. How he needed a bump. He couldn't remember whether she worked on a Sunday night or not. He couldn't imagine she'd be too busy if she did. She liked her blow as much as he did. She was all blow.

'Frank,' he said, serious now, into the hands-free, driving along Marine Parade, heading for Yallop Avenue, 'what's up?' He was going to take the Lowestoft Road, the dual carriageway, to Yarmouth, feeling the Mini needed some exercise having been cooped up in the garage for the last month or so.

'How are things at home?' Frank asked.

'Not sure how I'm meant to answer that, man.'

'No more awkward visitors?'

'Not since this morning, I don't think.'

'Good,' said Frank. 'Look, I don't want you going anywhere near Rare and Yare. Don't contact Owen either.'

'He owes me money.' Zach accelerated to 62 mph by the James Paget, a 40 mph zone, suddenly remembering that that was where his father's body was, wedged into a big fridge. Moments later, he was braking for the first roundabout.

'You think he'd still want to pay you, seeing as you abandoned ship? You'll be lucky if he hasn't got some other idea for you.'

'Special circumstances, Frank. My dad had just fucking died. Besides, that skipper, man, I told you how antsy he was getting. I wasn't going to stick around. Haven't we gone through all this?'

'I know what you're like. Also, the boat's on its way back. Seems the French found everything in order.'

'Even more reason for me to get paid.'

'That's not how Owen would see it. Your father's not around any more, Zach. He can't protect you now.'

'If he ever did,' Zach muttered, though he knew he had. He approached the next roundabout, too fast. It wasn't as if he was going to be paid much anyway, but there were principles. 'Never undersell yourself, lad,' his father used to say. 'I'm always suspicious of people who do things on the cheap.' Not that he'd ever paid anyone over the odds.

'Besides,' Frank said, his voice coming over thin and straggly for such a formidable man, as Zach negotiated another couple of empty roundabouts at speed, 'Owen won't be the only person meeting it here.'

'Right,' Zach said, before thinking about it. 'You should have said, Frank.'

'Use your brain.'

'Fuck you.' But Zach knew he hadn't been using his brain lately. Sometimes there was just too much to compute.

'Calm down, Zach. There are certain things it's better you don't know about. I don't want to have to spell everything out, especially not on the fucking phone.'

The low Haven Bridge was looming. 'Fine. Whatever you say.' Zach finished the call confused. His mum was telling him she was going to be dead straight with them all.

154

Would hold nothing back. While Frank was saying there were still things he was better off not knowing. 'Information is key, son,' his dad had said, more than once, without telling him a fucking thing.

Zach hated it when his father used terms like son or lad, trying to be chummy. His father was never chummy, nor casual. He'd preferred it when his father had called him a little cunt, and then laughed.

A police car, the Beamer estate, Yarmouth cop shop's top rig, was idling in the parking bay in front of Barclays Bank, facing south, towards the harbour mouth. Zach had been intending to pass the Star Hotel, where Clara might or might not have been, before cutting up to Trafalgar Road and hitting Connaught Terrace that way.

Even though he wasn't laced, he decided to go left, the long way round the one-way system, to avoid attracting any unnecessary attention. Most of the local traffic cops knew who he was, knew the markings on his Mini. It was a small town, despite the fact that his father was no longer around barking orders, commanding respect. 'You fat cunt,' Zach found himself saying, as he sped along North Quay, angling towards yet another roundabout.

There was more traffic going towards the front, and people were hanging around the twenty-four-hour Eastern European corner shops, and the kebab places on Nicholas and Nelson Roads. The chip shops were shut, however, and the pubs were fast emptying. End of the weekend rubbish was spilling out of the gutters and drifting idly across the pavements and pedestrianised Regent Road. Then Zach was taking a left without indicating, onto

Connaught Terrace, past the cramped rows of social housing, past the two brothels masked by nothing more than net curtains and chronic indifference – one of his mum's phrases – and the crack house with its fortified windows and front door, and on towards the dead end, and the bump store, another Eastern European twenty-four-hour operation.

There were no CCTV cameras aimed anywhere near here, of course, and no one who cared for their lives was prepared to notice anything or anyone anyway. Most of the street lamps had been vandalised, and what flickering light there was leaked round shabby curtains.

Zach had always felt invincible. Hey, he was fucking Marvel man. But as he parked up tonight – squeezing his Mini between a knackered Vauxhall Vectra and a stupidly new Nissan Qashqai, and climbed out, letting his light mac settle – he was glad he'd pocketed the knife, feeling it knock his leg once more.

The house, in total darkness, was the end of the terrace but one. The front door was wide open, which was odd. Zach paused on the pavement before stepping across the small front yard, through a chill of fresh air, and straight into the dark, narrow hallway, which reeked of old sweat and something acrid and metallic that Zach couldn't place. 'Yo,' he said softly, not wanting to surprise any of them. They were usually friendly enough but understandably they could be a bit jumpy. They dealt from the room at the back, when they weren't playing on the Xbox.

There was no noise coming from that area. No noise at all, though faint light showed. Zach found he was gripping the knife tightly in his right hand while pushing himself on. The air in the hall seemed to be getting thicker, as if it were somehow coating him. Zach broke forward, wanting to shake himself free of the air and the smell he couldn't place, thinking he'd been stuck on the high seas for long enough and it was time he scored some bump for a bump, then he was going to locate Clara for a hump. He always got what he wanted sooner rather than later because he was a Goodwin. But he wasn't smiling.

The door to the back room was open and Zach didn't have to move any further before he realised what he was seeing. 'Oh fuck,' he said, immediately glancing up at the coiled bare bulb hanging from the middle of the ceiling, feeling his chest pound. But he couldn't keep his eyes from looking straight back down. He felt vomit rising.

Lukas was on the floor, on his side, blood having pooled around his head. Dominy was face down on the table. An oil spill of blood was sliding off the surface, running slowly and thickly down the table legs onto the worn, filthy carpet. There was so much blood on the floor Zach couldn't determine whose blood was whose. Both boys were still, dead, the silence now even more present and lethal.

Zach began to back away, his eyes still fixed on the bodies. He'd had no idea blood could smell so strong, like metal, like iron, an iron smelter, whatever that was. He couldn't see how they had been killed. Stabbed, he presumed. Maybe tortured first, because Lukas' face was a mess of lumps and bruises. But his tattoo, the sharp tattoo that curled around his neck, was hidden behind the blood . . . and, the closer Zach looked, behind flesh. Small flaps of torn flesh.

A taste of sour doughy flour and fluffy cream from the scones, and jam like children's medicine, hit the back of his throat. He swallowed harder than he'd ever swallowed before, desperate to keep the vomit down as he ran out of the dim hallway and onto the street, leaving the front door exactly how he'd found it. He daren't touch a thing, nothing, nothing at all. He mustn't be seen. He was thinking now, his mind rapidly calculating, computing shit.

The street was still and quiet and empty, and at last he could breathe the fresh North Sea air. He fumbled his key fob out of his pocket, his hands slippery, as if they were covered in blood, though it could only have been sweat, nervous sweat. He'd thought he was so much tougher than this. Used to such violence, such scenes. But he wasn't. He wasn't prepared at all. Just who the hell was he? His father's son?

As he began negotiating the small, powerful vehicle out of its wretched spot, he worried whether he might have left any prints in the house. Footprints on the floor. Whether his trainers might have picked up fibres, blood. He would throw them away, as soon as he got home. That was the obvious thing to do. He couldn't drive through Yarmouth in bare feet, not when the lone traffic cop would be waiting by the bridge to pull him over, just for fun. Spoilt young bastard needs to be shown who's in charge now, Zach could hear the cop thinking, sitting in his well-equipped rig, his shiny, rainproof officer's cap pulled low over his corruptible eyes.

But the police were not in charge. They had never been in charge, not here. His father had been. The fat cunt.

Without thinking, Zach pulled out of Connaught Terrace and turned onto Trafalgar Road, then headed left on the Golden Mile, swiftly passing Joyland and the kink by the theatre. Before he knew it, he was on North Drive, looking out for Jellicoe Road, which he knew he couldn't miss because there was the sign to the racecourse. He would take the long way back. Go over the new bridge at the start of the A12. Clara would have to wait, though he didn't think Frank could. He needed to talk to Frank. But he didn't think Frank would be too impressed with what he had to say, his fondness for bump. It was one thing smuggling the stuff – yeah, he got that now – quite another taking it for fun.

You couldn't mix business with pleasure, wasn't that what everyone always said? There was no playing at this business.

Zach pressed the screen, not bothering to anchor his phone into the socket. Put his phone to his ear, heard it ring.

20

She didn't feel like Rich; she felt too light, too thin, too well dressed. The leather on his desk chair felt sticky. Grubby. God, he didn't use to shag his women here, did he? Was he that much of a cliché?

Tatty sprang to her feet, walked round his oversized desk to the centre of his office. She looked the other way, at the walls lined with deep shelves. They were a mess. There were files and folders at odd angles, some in heaps. Bits of paper were poking out here and there. Someone must have been looking for something, in a hurry, and then made no effort to put everything back carefully. Simon, she presumed.

She would get to the files, in good time – not that she was sure she'd be able to interpret the information, yet. Ben and Sam were heading back to London for a few days, while Zach planned to stay at home. She'd been unable to wake him earlier this morning – had no idea what time he got in last night. The young! Stepping back to the desk, and the large computer screen planted in the middle, she was reminded of how much she was going to need them all – she needed Zach now if she was to get into Rich's digital files. But that wasn't quite what she had in mind for first thing this morning.

She sat, listening. Goodwin House was quiet, empty, tingling against the bright, warm weather. It wasn't only the tide that seemed to be on the turn. Frank had said he'd come inside with her and wait, having let her into the office block. She'd said, no, she wanted to be here on her own. He'd respected that, acknowledging her position now, but he'd made her promise to ring him if she needed anything. He looked at her in such a way that she knew exactly what he'd meant. 'I won't be far away,' he'd said.

She opened and shut the desk drawers again, shocked by the cheap normality of Rich's office ephemera. The mints, the gum, the cracked Biros, the twisted paperclips, the balls of fluff. A few pills not in their casing, though some shapes she recognised – the bloody thief. A packet of Durex, purple. He bothered to use condoms?

She sat forward on the chair. Moved the heavy glass paperweight of Caesars Palace across the desk. She'd never been to Las Vegas, or Atlantic City, where they also regularly went. It had always been Rich – Rich and Simon, Rich and Simon and Amit Sharma, the accountant, or Will Keene, the company lawyer, and who knew who else. Oh yes, that strangely attractive scientist from the local university, an environmentalist. She'd gone more than once, hadn't she? And who did they meet when they got there? Just what had they got up to? Businessmen and those in their sleazy pockets – it was pathetic.

'What the fuck are you doing here?'

Simon was by the door. Tatty had left it open, wanting to hear anyone coming that way, Simon particularly. But she hadn't heard him approach. He'd snuck up on her. Was he always this quiet, practised? Wanting to catch Rich out? For a second she wished Frank was here with her, in the building anyway. 'Morning, Simon,' she said, trying to sound calm. 'At least the sun's out for once.'

He'd come a step or two into the office, though he remained closer to the door than the desk. 'You're in Rich's office. You're sitting at Rich's desk.'

He looked like he'd had another great night of sleep. The only thing kempt about him was his hair. 'Has Jess come home yet?' she said. She glanced down at Rich's fat gold watch on her thin brown wrist. It was not yet eight.

'How did you get in?'

Tatty looked up at her brother-in-law. Wondered if he was really as stupid and shallow as he looked. 'What time do you normally start work? I thought you'd been working all hours. Keeping the business going in such a crisis.'

He shook his head. 'I don't know what you're playing at, Tatty. But you're making a big mistake.'

'No, Simon, that would be you.' She stood up, walked over to the bank of windows, prised wider a couple of the blinds, blinked. 'It had been bothering me that you got to have the best office, the best view. But you missed what was really going on. Or did you?'

'I think you should leave, Tatty. You're obviously still in shock. Go on, get out, will you? I've got work to do.'

'The thing is, the future is in the other direction, Simon. I'm looking at it now. Rich's office was always facing the right way. All this land that will be redeveloped. I can see the towers of Goodwin Casino rising straight ahead.' She was still holding the blinds apart. Still looking through the dirty glass. Still feeling Simon's eyes boring into her back, hating her.

It was hard to imagine how long it might take for the shabby roofline of low industrial buildings to change. Looking more intently, she could see Nelson's Memorial rising up into the faint blue. Though she didn't think she could see the traditional roof of her smokehouse, so Rich wouldn't have been able to discern any of that building from here. There was too much shit in the way.

A thought came to her. 'What's the deal on this place, on Goodwin House?'

'Why?'

Tatty turned, walked back towards the desk, went round it, slowly, conscious of her well-fitting orange dress, the colour of a bright dawn, or a fiery dusk, and her figure, which was still perhaps defying her age. What would she do for exercise if her activities with Nathan were to come to an end? She ran her fingers over the dark oak veneer and sat lightly in Rich's foul chair.

'I'm trying to work out exactly what goes on in this building, and how necessary it is to the operations,' she said.

'Tatty, Rich found this place, years ago. He was more than happy with it – believe me.' He cleared his throat. 'This is the headquarters of Goodwin Enterprises. Always has been. It's where we run everything.'

'Everything? The legal stuff and the illegal stuff?'

'I don't know what you mean by the illegal stuff.' He didn't clear his throat this time, but sighed. 'You might want to talk more quietly in any case.'

Tatty was beginning to understand Simon's tics more and more. He'd have made a crap poker player. He was leaning against the door frame, not casually, but anxiously, aggressively. He didn't look like he wanted her to get the fuck out of there. He was blocking her exit.

She laughed. 'What are you afraid of? You think this place is bugged?'

'As far as I know, the police are still looking into Rich's death. They could turn up at any moment, with a warrant – who knows?'

'Frank, he thinks this too?'

'Yes.'

Tatty knew that wasn't the case – she was testing Simon. Frank had been pretty certain, earlier this morning, that the police would be backing off, for the moment anyway. But Frank had also thought it might not be such a bad idea if Simon still thought the police were about to swoop. 'Any advantage we can get over him, Tatty, the better,' Frank had said. 'He's a fucking snake with no balls.' She didn't think snakes had balls in any case, but she'd let it go.

'The others will be in shortly,' Simon said, filling the shrill silence. 'Mark, Sian, Celine. A couple of temps were meant to be starting this week on the casino project team, and the industrial equipment supply services arm. Which reminds me, Rich was due in Athens this week.' Simon closed his eyes briefly.

How had Rich put up with him? 'So if the police were to bash down the door, everything they might find here is legit, in order, is it?' she asked calmly.

'That's what Frank and I were trying to work out over the weekend. There are a lot of files, papers everywhere. And we haven't started on his computer, his personal electronic files. We can't get into the system. You wouldn't happen to know what his passwords might be? Frank's meant to be bringing in some kid to help. He say anything to you about that?'

Tatty shook her head, knowing that Simon must have realised that Frank helped her get into the building. No bad thing, she thought. But it didn't seem that Simon knew about Zach and his computer wizardry. Surely Frank wasn't intending on bringing Zach in? She made a mental note to talk to Frank urgently about this, and then sat back in the chair, trying not to think about the state of the leather. 'Which parts of the business are you directly involved with, Simon? Just how big is the legit end? Not many people are employed here, are they?'

'Everything I do is completely legitimate, Tatty. What Rich got up to without my knowing, fuck knows. But my side of things, I can tell you, is all dead on the level. Why do you think Rich brought me in? I'm the person people can trust. My reputation is spotless.' He paused, sucked in his cheeks, let go of the door frame, a spring to his small actions.

She hadn't heard anything negative about his business reputation, it had to be said. Not in a business that relied on ruthlessness. But Rich had once suggested that Simon had a personal weakness, one that, if he wasn't careful, could get him into serious trouble. Rich never said anything more than that. It always amazed Tatty how Rich managed to keep his mouth shut when he wanted to.

'Did Rich have that reputation, honestly?' Simon was saying. 'Night and day, that was us, Tatty, think about it.'

'Oh, don't be such an arsehole, Simon.' She leaned forward. The chair would have to go, but she liked the view from behind such a desk. 'It's all linked. Don't tell me it isn't. Sure, Rich might have spread the risk while keeping the opportunities flowing. But there's no way you didn't benefit from the whole package.'

She stood, knowing how much her lifestyle, and the kids', would have cost, and how much more Rich could have spent on them. 'So let's cut the bullshit and devise a plan of how we're going to work together.' She wasn't about to tell him it was only a temporary measure, for the sake of immediate continuity and the Prime Poker deal, assuming he really was that essential. She'd soon see.

'Work together?' he said.

'There are certain lines that I'm sure will have to go. Drugs, for instance. I—' She shut her mouth. There was no need to go into detail about why she didn't want anything to do with drug smuggling, prostitution, or people trafficking. She didn't care about fucking over corrupt corporations and inept councils, she realised, or any shoddy business. She smiled, added, 'I expect there'll be other areas that we will need to explore and exploit. The world's a very different place to when Rich started out. And I'm not sure you've moved with the times either.'

'What the fuck do you know about any of this?' Simon was laughing as he walked towards the desk. 'You with your designer clothes and your silly handbags, and your endless holidays and spa treatments, and kids you could

166

barely be bothered to bring up. Your stupid pet projects that Rich financed to keep you out of the way. What the fuck do you know about the real world? You've spent God knows how long zonked out of your head.'

He was closing in on her now, and she could feel his hot stale breath on her face. There were traces of his cologne as well. It was not a smell she was appreciating.

'The difference is, now I'm in charge,' she said, still backing away, but she was already behind the desk, and there was a solid wall behind her. Where was Frank?

Simon was rounding the big desk, coming behind it too, into the narrow gap between the desk and the solid wall, suddenly thrusting his right arm forward. He grabbed the front of her lovely orange dress and moved his hand up, clasping the light but strong material so his fist was nestling into the space between her chin and her neck, pressing on her windpipe. The material wouldn't give, nor would his fist.

She was finding it hard to breathe, while Simon was breathing all over her face. She tried to look round him, beyond him, caught something glinting on the desk, down to her left. She looked up at him now, looked into his eyes, looked longingly, pursed her lips, as if she were about to kiss him. She tensed, then lurched forward, so her body was pressing against his.

Simon was not expecting this – Tatty throwing herself at him. He recoiled, and in that instant she grabbed the heavy glass model of Caesars Palace from the corner of Rich's desk with her left hand and swung her arm up and thwacked him on the side of his head with it. Simon instantly let go of her and staggered to the far side of the desk, clutching at his ear.

'You fucking bitch,' he squealed.

'Call me that again and I'll really make you feel it,' she said, catching her breath and moving out from behind the other side of the desk. She'd hit Rich harder, though not for some time.

Simon appeared unsure what to do next, while Tatty recognised that things weren't going quite according to plan this morning, her first day at the office. She would listen to Frank more closely in the future.

'Oh,' came a small voice from a small person entering the office.

The young woman ventured further before stopping still and letting her tiny mouth, which was encased in thick dark lipstick, fall open wide. 'Who are you?' Tatty said.

'Sian. I'm Sian. I work on reception, on the floor below.' She had a soft, local accent. 'I was also Mr Goodwin's PA, and I do a lot of the general administrative and secretarial work,' she added brightly. 'I've been here for nearly a year. I come from Yarmouth. My father is' – she coughed – 'was, a good friend of Mr Goodwin's. He owns the North Beach Holiday Park. Rolly Andrews?'

'Whoa, slow up a minute,' Tatty said.

Simon, still clutching his ear, strode out from his side of the desk, past Sian, his head turned the other way, and left the room like a sulky schoolboy. Sian looked over her shoulder as he went, then back at Tatty, but closing her mouth this time and sucking in her painted lips, leaving a thin tight line where her mouth should have been, a hint of dark gloss.

'He had an accident with this,' Tatty said, holding up the heavy glass paperweight.

'Oh,' Sian said again, though not sounding quite so surprised. 'You're Mrs Goodwin, aren't you? I haven't seen you here before.'

'I'm Tatiana Goodwin,' Tatty said. 'You can call me Tatty.'

'I thought I heard people talking up here,' Sian said. 'I work on the floor below. I didn't know who it would be, not in Mr Goodwin's office.' She paused, looked down at her tiny feet. 'I'm sorry about Mr Goodwin.'

'What time do you start work?' Tatty asked.

'I thought I'd come in early today, make myself useful. Mr Goodwin, that's Simon, will have a lot on his plate, what with Mr Goodwin, your husband, having passed on. Oh God, that doesn't sound right, does it?'

'Don't worry about it,' Tatty said. 'We all have a lot to get used to.' She looked back to the shelves in Rich's office, the disorder. 'Look, why don't you give me a hand to sort this lot out properly, and while we're at it, perhaps you can tell me more about what goes on here.'

'I'm not sure I'd be able to do that,' Sian said. 'You see, your husband and Simon, well, they've always been very strict about what we can and can't say about the business to people who don't actually work here, friends and family included. I'm not allowed to tell my dad anything. There are a lot of big deals going on, worth a lot of money, and it's important that things aren't said to the wrong people, even by mistake. It's sort of the mantra here. Yarmouth's not such a big place and you know how people talk. A lot of livelihoods depend on Goodwin Enterprises.' She smacked her lips.

Tatty felt sorry for her. Someone must have once told Sian that her mouth was her best asset. Tatty wasn't so sure.

'We're reshaping the local economy,' Sian continued proudly. 'Who wouldn't want to be involved? There's not a lot of money in this part of the world to go around.'

Tatty laughed. 'I like your attitude.' Though she wasn't at all sure Sian would be able to remain at Goodwin Enterprises. 'Did you go to school here?'

'Yeah, sort of. You know, when I went. My dad didn't see a lot of point in that sort of education. But I always tried to work hard – when I was there.'

'Right, well let's get to work now,' said Tatty, walking briskly to the wall of shelves. Like Sian, she hadn't had much of a formal education, had barely gone when she was meant to. She picked up the nearest file: *Arcades*, a hand-written label on the spine said, *2013–14*. Some of the pages inside were loose, falling free. She had a quick flick, saw numbers, names of venues, locations, some she recognised.

Sian shook her head. 'I don't think you should be looking at that, Mrs Goodwin.'

Tatty put it back, walked a couple of steps further along, picked up another folder. *Equipment, Shipping, General, EU, 2015–16*, it said. She didn't bother to pick this one up. On the shelf above there were a number of box files, all the same shade of mottled grey, all labelled *Enterprise Zone*, with dates, years. They were in the wrong order.

'That's mostly the old council stuff,' Sian said. 'He doesn't – didn't – do so much work for the council any more. Most of his time recently was spent on the casino project, and the equipment supply business. What comes over from Greece, and the like.'

Perhaps Sian would be able to stay for a bit. 'The arcades, who looks after them, those accounts?' Tatty asked.

'Well, we all do, one way or another,' Sian said. 'Frank keeps an eye on them in person. He goes around, checking everything is in order. When's the funeral, Mrs Goodwin?'

Tatty's phone started ringing. It was in her bag, which was at the foot of Rich's desk. 'Excuse me,' she said, moving towards it. 'I need to get this.'

She grabbed her bag, put it on the table next to the paper-weight of Caesars Palace, and retrieved her phone. Saw that it was Nathan, and took a deep breath. Sian hadn't moved, stayed staring at her. Tatty tapped the phone, the red decline call icon. Put the device to her head neverthe-less, said, 'Hello?' while waving at Sian to leave her office. Tatty sat, as if to emphasise her need for privacy, and that this might be a long call. Business had to be so much about acting, putting on a front, she decided, this sort of business anyway, saying, 'Yes, OK,' into the phone, the cancelled incoming call.

21

Frank drove south on Nelson Road, the town coming slowly back to life. The sun's brightness was disturbing the inevitable autumnal gloom. Decelerating, he glanced either way as he crossed Regent Road, catching shutters going up, street boards coming out, the odd pedestrian starting an empty day early, a loose dog or two.

There was more traffic, then traffic backing up, as he got closer to Connaught Terrace. He knew why. He didn't need to get any closer. The concrete spill of St George's Park was on his right, so he took a left when he could heading for the front and the Golden Mile. He'd drive as far as the proposed super-casino site before cutting across to Goodwin House. He was anxious about Tatty, and Zach. This world took some getting used to.

He hadn't got as far as Amazonia World of Reptiles when his phone starting shrieking. Glancing over at the screen he saw it was *Unknown*, but he knew exactly who *Unknown* would be. He was constructing his way out of the mess, thinking up excuses, before he said hello.

'I seriously fucking hope you had nothing to do with this, Frank,' Hayes said.

He sighed. 'You know me better than that, Britt.'

'Two guys, both Lithuanians – ring any bells?'

'Should you be calling me?'

'I'm investigating a double murder now, Frank, I can call who the hell I want, when I want.'

'Nice talking to you again so soon,' Frank said, his large dark Range Rover – tinted windows, personalised plate – crawling by the Merrivale Model Village. He thought about ending the call. Thought better of it. The model village had stopped being a draw years ago. There were better escapes from the raw reality of Yarmouth nowadays. He began wondering whether he should get rid of the vehicle. Perhaps buy one of those electric things, a Prius or something. No one would expect that.

'Is this some sort of turf war?' Hayes said.

'What makes you think these guys were the same two scum who held me up?'

'Did one of them have a nice tattoo of a piece of barbed wire roped around his neck?'

'I told you.'

'The barbed wire's all but gone, Frank. Seems someone else didn't appreciate the artistry.'

'Knifed?'

'They both were. Ruthlessly. No signs of much of a struggle, in situ, but one of them had been badly beaten somewhere. No firearms were recovered. But we found a fine medley of class-As. Plenty of cash too.'

'Cash? So it was personal, not property?'

'Depends how you look at it. The perpetrators could have been disturbed. The money at least was well hidden. We'll be trawling every CCTV camera in town. Asking around, for what that's worth. Every resource is being redirected, Frank. And I mean every resource. ANPR, the lot. The digital bods here have rarely been so excited.'

'I can believe it,' said Frank, thinking of Zach.

'I only hope we don't spot anything we shouldn't.'

'Britt, you know me, you knew Rich, how we've always done business. This is not our style, besides—'

'I don't remember you being quite so passive over that minicab franchise.'

'I've no idea what you're talking about.' He was now cruising along South Beach Parade, the big dipper between him and the sea. It wouldn't have taken much for the hundred-year-old structure to be reduced to driftwood. Rich had thought about arson. 'It's become a fucking eyesore,' he'd said. 'I can't have it ruining the view for my new guests.' Frank had told him that a storm would get it soon enough. It was proving remarkably resilient. Not the only thing in Yarmouth that was.

'Look, Frank, something has shifted in this town over the last few days. You think it's all coincidence?'

'Are you tracking that yacht?'

'The Border Agency's been alerted – not that they've got a lot of time on their hands. We'll be watching it from the moment it gets anywhere near Yarmouth, I can assure you of that.'

'These murders – when are you going public?'

'That's already out of our hands, the amount of vehicles we've got down here. Everyone hoping they can sell a report for a few quid to Sky News. It's a bloody mess, Frank, and I'm not joking.'

'Tape the street off, for Christ's sake. The whole area. Publicity like this is not going to help the casino deal,' Frank said, as much to himself as Hayes. 'Prime fucking mess, more like.' The air inside the plush elevated cabin of the Range Rover was suddenly stifling. He jabbed the window button with his index finger.

'I can't think who would have wanted to invest here anyway,' said Hayes. 'Not even a bunch of American gangsters.'

'Come on,' said Frank, feeling fresh air flow against his cheek. 'We need all the help we can get, improving this place. Are you telling me that the public sector doesn't believe in providing opportunities for growth? The right environment?'

'Not the sort of growth you have in mind, Frank. You know what the public round here are like – those that have any say.'

'Rich did his best to change all that.'

'Rich is dead, Frank.'

'Yeah,' sighed Frank, finding that he was pulling across the empty South Beach Parade and turning into Salmon Road. He stopped at the corner.

'There's always trouble when there's a vacuum,' Hayes said. 'You sure you can handle it?'

'There is no vacuum. As far as I'm concerned, Tatiana Goodwin is in charge, for now.' He switched off the engine. 'Let's give her some time.'

'You think there's still time, Frank? There's only so much I can do for you, or Goodwin Enterprises.'

'You said all your resources are focused on these two murders, didn't you? I suggest you get your officers to stick to that.'

She blew air straight into her phone, a short hard blast. Where was she? He presumed not at police headquarters in Wymondham. She wasn't stupid.

'If anything points your way, Frank, it's going to be bloody difficult not to follow it.'

'I've told you everything I know,' Frank said. 'Two guys tried to frighten me. They got nowhere. That's it. I came to you with that, remember?'

'You wanted to know who'd kitted them out, given them orders.'

'Yeah, I did. Thought you might be interested as well. The fact they are now dead has nothing to do with me, or the business. I didn't kill them. I'm doing everything I can right now to help a bereaved family.'

'Spare us the tears. What is it with that family, anyway?' said Hayes. 'Now Rich is dead?'

'Where did you grow up, Britt?'

'You don't want to know.'

'Let's keep the personal stuff out of this then. Help each other with the here and now.'

'Like I said, let's hope that doesn't become too uncomfortable for you, or your blessed family.'

'If I hear anything, anything at all, Britt, you know you can count on me.'

'I hope so, Frank. I've got a job to do as well.'

'How's Howie?' Frank had a feeling that some extra muscle might come in handy. It was one thing keeping an eye on one person, but four?

'He's away,' she replied, too quickly.

Hayes could be very protective of Howie when she wanted to be. Frank said his goodbyes, pressed the end call button. He supposed they could all be protective of those they loved, if they loved them enough. Howie never went away. He wasn't the easiest person to get hold of either.

Frank peered up at the Smokehouse. Tatty had done a good job, albeit enabled by Rich's cash and clout. He was still looking up at the building, the acres of bright red brickwork, the small stone windows, the long rows of stumpy, slated chimney stacks, when he heard the roar of a car. A dark green Jaguar shot out of Fenner Road, mounting the low kerb as it swung, far too tightly, onto Salmon Road, all but glancing Frank's Range Rover before accelerating away.

Frank got out of his car, amazed that the offside wing mirror was still calmly sitting there, reflecting clear sky, until his shiny bald head got in the way. He had dark bags under his eyes. His forehead was a maze. He pulled his head away, straightened, looked back down Salmon Road towards South Denes Road and the river. The car was long gone and the road was empty again, the worn tarmac beginning to sparkle under a swiftly strengthening sun. Bad drivers were not uncommon in Great Yarmouth, but he knew whose car it was.

Enjoying the warmth, he reached inside his vehicle, retrieved his phone. Called Zach from the kerb.

Zach answered on the second ring. 'Frank?' he said, urgent but wary.

'Where are you?' Frank asked.

'At home. I'm still in bed.' He yawned, unnecessarily.

'You can't hide under the covers all day, Zach.'

'I'm getting up, I'm getting up.'

'Have you done what I said?' It wasn't only his trainers the kid needed to get rid of.

'Sure, I'm on it.'

'In bed? Fuck's sake, Zach. A full valet job, inside and out. Ask them to wash away those stupid stripes as well.' Not that it would make any difference in these days of ANPR.

'Frank, give me a break, man.'

'What do you want to buy that crap for anyway?'

'You ever feel the need to get blunted?'

'Not any more, mate,' said Frank.

'Shit,' said Zach.

'What? What is it?'

'Someone's at the door. What the fuck do I do?'

'See who it is?'

'What if it's the police?' He was whispering into his phone.

Frank could almost hear Zach's heart thump. For about the first time in his life he had some idea of what parenting might be like. The responsibility, coupled with the emotion. Frank contemplated heading over there. The boy needed calming down. 'Zach, just remember who you are.'

'They're going away,' Zach said. 'No, they're not. Fuck.'

'Ring me if there's any trouble,' Frank said, ending the call as he spotted Nathan Taylor emerging from the far end of the Smokehouse, where there was a large slab of a steel door. Taylor looked around suspiciously, appeared to think all was clear, then checked himself as he noticed Frank. He was dressed, head to toe, in fine grey cloth, clearly chosen to complement his hair. He didn't know which way to turn. Rich had always joked about the man's sexuality, wondered whether Frank might be interested in fucking a piece of fine English heritage. Frank knew Taylor wasn't gay. Told Rich as much, though he didn't tell him everything. Rich never listened, except when it suited him.

Taylor started walking towards him. It would have been rude not to.

'Hello, Frank,' he said, holding out his hand.

'Mr Taylor,' Frank said, shaking his hand. He hadn't come across Taylor much over the last couple of years. Rich wanted Tatty to think she was in charge of the project. She was, more than Rich ever realised. Taylor seemed changed since the last time Frank had encountered him.

'Are you meeting someone, here?' Taylor said, flicking his hair off his forehead. He reminded Frank of Simon, though he was older, and perhaps more comfortable, more suited, to the finer things in an easy life. 'Lovely day,' Taylor added, before Frank had time to reply. Yarmouth would never be the place for him.

Frank glanced up and down the street, finally latching on to the acres of empty space at the end of Salmon Road, across South Beach Parade, where the super casino was to be. 'No,' he said. 'I'm not meeting anyone. Simply enjoying the weather.'

'How's Tatiana?' Nathan said. 'Terrible thing for her to have to deal with.' His voice didn't suggest there was anything terrible for her to have to deal with at all.

'She's got the rest of her family supporting her,' Frank said. 'She's a tough lady. She's doing what she has to do.' He smiled. Taylor didn't.

Frank's phone was going again. He glanced at the screen, shielding it from Taylor. It was not who he expected it to be.

'I'll leave you to it,' Taylor said, turning and hurrying back across Fenner Road to a white Audi TT, which he beeped unlocked.

Frank knew exactly what Rich had thought about such cars, those who drove them. He returned his attention to the phone, pressed the answer button, put it to his head, said, 'Jess?' Jess! But he'd missed her. She'd either hung up or voicemail had kicked in. He waited for the signal to inform him that he had a message. It didn't come.

22

'Nina!' said Zach, opening the door.

'I'm sorry, Zach love, I've had a problem with me keys,' she said in a rush. 'I don't want to worry Mrs Goodwin with anything else at the moment. I wanted to explain in person, you see. I'm not sure what I'm meant to do about it.'

She was still on the doorstep, and Zach stepped to one side to let her in. 'No worries,' he said, able to breathe at last. 'I was here. Mum's in Yarmouth, I think. Sam and Ben are back in London.'

She edged inside, and before Zach shut the front door for her he noticed how bright it was outside. He smiled. He'd rushed on his ripped Diesel jeans and an old Jack Wills T-shirt, which he'd had forever and hated. All he needed was to find his flip-flops, and then he'd be set. 'I'd forgotten you come on Monday mornings,' he said vaguely.

'I don't, normally,' she replied. 'Tuesdays and Thursdays are my days. The thing is, I wanted to explain to Mrs Goodwin, in person, what's happened to the keys. I know what your father used to be like about security. Besides, you can never be too safe nowadays, with all these people moving to these parts. Can't trust everyone.'

Zach was still breathing so much more easily, but he paused in the stark hallway. The kitchen door was ahead, leading the way to coffee and cereal. 'Can I get you anything? A coffee?' he asked, wanting to get on with his breakfast.

'I'm all right, love. As I said, it's not one of my normal days. I shouldn't be here.'

This was not something Zach had ever paid much attention to, Nina's normal days. When he had brought Clara home, she'd always known where her mother was, that she wasn't about to walk in on them.

'But if there's anything you, or Mrs Goodwin, want me to do, now I'm here,' Nina said, 'I'd be happy to stick around, given the circumstances.'

Zach turned, faced her properly. She hadn't followed him far into the house. He was confused. She hadn't said anything about his dad's death, directly. Was he meant to? 'Yeah – Mum's not here.'

'The keys,' Nina said, 'I've come to tell you about the keys.'

'Sorry, Nina,' he said, 'I'm losing the thread.' He shook his head, relieved more pressure. 'You've lost your keys? To this house?'

'That's the thing,' she said. 'I haven't lost them. I never lose keys. I never lose anything.'

Zach tried to see where Clara got her looks from, her fit, young body. He was struggling. But he doubted he'd know Clara when she was Nina's age. It wasn't as if he was going to marry her. His mother might have got married young – in a rush, by all accounts – but he had his whole life. Things were different today. It wasn't the fucking nineteenth century.

Nina continued, 'They've been taken.'

'What do you mean, they've been taken?'

'All my keys – gone.'

'What, stolen? From your home?' Zach wondered whether she might be about to cry. 'Hey, it's no big deal.'

'But it is,' she said stridently. She was looking down at her feet.

Zach was sure she was wearing a pair of Clara's trainers. 'When were they taken, then?'

'Sometime over the weekend,' she said quietly. 'I can't be sure exactly when. You see, I keep them in the cupboard in the hall. All my keys, for the houses I clean. I only work for eight families, but there are quite a lot of keys. Everyone has so many locks nowadays, you wouldn't believe it.' She looked up at him – Clara's eyes. Yes. 'But no one has ever stolen anything from my home before.'

The word *protection* formed in Zach's mind. Something else Frank had said late last night, about personal security, that they would need to watch their backs. He'd do what he could for them. Zach exhaled loudly. 'Who was around, over the weekend? Anyone notice anything?' He looked down at the loose, worn T-shirt with the naff logo. It was a stupid thing public school kids wore. He didn't like to think he'd ever fitted into that world. 'You got any idea who might have taken them?' he added. He wasn't going to spell it out. Not Clara, surely.

'Clara's been out a lot, working mostly.' Nina put her hands to her face. 'But no – no, no. My Clara would not have taken them. Not for anything. She's a good girl.'

'That's not what I meant,' Zach said. But he knew Clara wasn't exactly a fucking angel. He coughed. He was not good at smoking. 'Were you in all weekend?'

'No, not all weekend. I can't say that I was.' Her hands had dropped to her sides and she was looking at the floor again, colour rising to her cheeks.

'They'll turn up – bet you,' Zach said brightly. 'Look, I need caffeine. You sure I can't get you anything?' He headed for the kitchen, then, sensing Nina was not following, he stopped in the doorway and glanced over his shoulder. She hadn't moved. Her head was still bowed. She was shaking. 'Are you OK, Nina?'

She wiped at her eyes. Wiped them again. Began shaking uncontrollably. She couldn't leave her eyes alone. 'I'm sorry,' she attempted to say through the tears. 'I'm sorry. Everything's happened at once.'

'Nina, hey there, it's OK,' Zach said, moving back towards her. He couldn't quite bring himself to give her a hug. 'They're only keys. Easy enough to replace.'

She was trying to smile. 'I'm sorry,' she said once more, the shaking subsiding. 'I remember when your mum and dad moved in, when my mum used to clean here. This place has changed, hasn't it?' She looked up, caught his eye, turned to face the uncluttered hallway. 'You kids have all grown up so fast. Seems like only yesterday this hallway was full of pushchairs and toys.'

Zach somehow doubted it ever was. His father hated clutter. He nodded.

'Your folks have been very kind to me, and Clara. Your dad, he was a good man. Whatever you might hear, please don't forget that, Zach.'

Zach thought she might be welling up again. 'Cheers,' he said. 'You sure you don't want a coffee?'

'No, I'm all right, love. It goes straight through me.'

'Do you know when the rubbish gets collected?' he asked, realising he had no idea of this either, heading for the kitchen, but not at all sure where Nina was headed next.

'Thursdays,' she said. 'First thing.'

'Cool.' He'd spent too much time in bed or on the computer, when he wasn't at school. Or skiving off in town someplace, smoking weed.

'Your father never liked rubbish hanging around, though. If you've got anything you want getting rid of, I can take it with me in my car. No problem, love. It'll be got rid of properly, I promise you. I use different bins every week.'

Zach was looking at Nina hard. He still hadn't made it to the kitchen. How much did she know? He'd been careful with Clara, he reckoned. Never told her about the hacking, not for his dad anyway.

'Your dad, he bought me my car,' Nina was telling him now.

'Yeah?' said Zach, though not as surprised as he thought he should have been. Your home, did he buy you your home too, he wanted to ask, picturing Nina and Clara's neat bungalow, with its crazy chimney crawling up one end, on the Mariner's Compass estate. It wouldn't have been that cheap, even years ago.

He could feel the muscles in the back of his neck tensing as he realised he had no idea where Nina's mother used to live in Gorleston, where Nina was brought up. She was practically family. He should never have fucked Nina's daughter. 'Actually, you know what, Nina? I might have some crap in my room. You got a minute?' He'd not even made it to the kitchen, and he was now heading back up the stairs , almost as nervously as he'd headed down them.

'That's no problem at all,' Nina said behind him. 'Anything, anything at all.' Her voice, rising in volume and purpose, followed Zach onto the landing, where a sharp wedge of sun lay on the thick carpet. 'It's a lovely bright morning – bit blowy. Doesn't seem quite right.'

23

The files had got her nowhere. She'd only just resisted calling Ben. Why had they gone back to London so soon? She felt exhausted already – her first day at work, and it wasn't as if she'd even had to commute very far. Come on, Tatty, she told herself, get a grip.

Her lips were dry. The weather being all over the place. No wonder Sian wore so much lipstick. Tatty wondered if she lived on the front, in one of the static caravans on the North Beach Holiday Park. Some people did, year round.

She remembered now an occasion when Rich came back from a meeting with Rolly Andrews. 'He's a stubborn little fucker, but it's prime fucking land, Tatty,' he'd said. He couldn't seem to get the word *prime* off his mind then. The meeting had gone on all night, supposedly. Rich smelt of sex as he undressed before walking into the shower. She'd said nothing, once again, as she climbed out of bed, knowing it wasn't Rolly he'd have been screwing.

Tatty sat back, reached for her phone, hurriedly tapped the screen, then held it to her ear. It went straight to voicemail. Now, when she wanted to, she couldn't reach him. Fuck him. Frankly, Nathan had always been long past his prime.

She stared at her phone until the screen went dark. Clear thoughts were taking their time to surface this morning, and it felt as if a void was opening up inside her. She caught a faint reflection of herself, sitting at Rich's desk, in Rich's office. She had a swift, terrible craving for temazepam. She thought of the small pills in the top right-hand drawer of Rich's desk, and the other shit in there from his sleazy life. When had he started to steal her pills? Had he really stored them up, to use in one go? She couldn't see it. Never.

She got to her feet, went over to the window, peered down at South Denes Road, the few trucks trundling past, no pedestrians. No paparazzi. The story of Rich's death was blowing over already. Yarmouth was still Yarmouth. Even if the weather wasn't normal.

Trying not to get too close to the grubby blinds – did this place have cleaners? Nina needed to get in here – but leaning as far forward as she could, she caught the edge of the building next door. Admiralty Steel, Graham Sands' business. There was a Jaguar, a long, low, slimy green thing with thick black alloys, parked up on the corner. It was stretched across the pavement, as if he now owned that too, the selfish sod.

Was there anywhere to get coffee round here? Where had Sian gone? She left the window, headed out of the office, only to bump into Frank by the door. He was such a big man. For a second she wanted him to put his arms around her, hold her tight against the emptiness swirling deep inside her. Instead she leapt back, feigned shock. 'Frank!' she said. 'Christ, you made me jump. Why does everyone creep around this place?'

'I hurried straight up. Couldn't hear anything. For a moment—'

'I've been working,' she said, 'at my desk. But still.' She looked down at his feet, which were strikingly small and encased in delicate black shoes. Office shoes.

Having followed her gaze, he tapped the floor. 'These carpet tiles, they muffle a lot of noise, I guess. You'll get used to it,' he said.

'Not sure I want to.' She thought of the Smokehouse, the acres of reclaimed wooden floors. It was meant to be live work. What if it was work work? She had to kick Nathan out anyway. The thought had been forming for a while, she realised.

'Where's Simon?' Frank asked. 'He's not in his office. Is he not in yet?'

'He was in all right,' she said, looking back at Rich's desk. 'Did Sian not tell you?'

Frank shook his head. 'I came straight up, like I said. You stop to talk to that girl, you never get away.'

'He had a confrontation with a paperweight.'

'Mrs Goodwin, you were meant to ring me if there was a problem. I wasn't far away, I never am, remember that. A paperweight?'

She watched him scan the room, his eyes settling on the desk, the mini Caesars Palace as heavy as bullion.

'That?' he asked.

'You think I can't handle him?' she said, looking at him hard. He had surprisingly fine eyebrows, for a man of his age. They appeared plucked.

'Be careful.'

'I lived with Rich long enough.'

'I don't think Simon's as predictable.'

She looked at him hard again, raised her eyes. 'Like I said.' It was his phrase.

'Jess rang me,' Frank said.

'What the fuck did she want?'

'I didn't answer the phone in time. She didn't leave a message and now her phone is going straight to voicemail. She might know something.'

'What the hell was Rich's problem? His own brother's wife – whatever we might think of Simon.'

Frank shrugged, shook his head. 'Rich gave her my number, told her to ring me if she was ever in trouble. She's never rung me before.'

'Frank, I'm really not interested in Jess right now. You understand? Is there anywhere to get a coffee round here?'

'Sure, there're places. There's the River Cafe a couple of blocks up the road, but they don't exactly grind their own beans. You want me to take you into town? Rich always used to go to the old casino, or the Star, about this time. I could show you around while we're at it.'

'I do know my way around Yarmouth, thanks.'

'What I was thinking was, I could show you some of Rich's other businesses, what he owned, and who owed him. How we look after our interests and theirs. Rich helped out a lot of people. So you get some sense of the scale.'

Tatty glanced over at the shelves, the files she'd made no headway with.

'I'm not good with numbers, paperwork,' Frank said. 'The street's my place. Though there might be a few streets we want to avoid today.'

'This office is in a fucking mess.'

'Simon's been having a look. But you won't find anything useful there. Let me show you, on the ground – at least what's yours now,' he said.

'And Simon's,' she added.

'A lot of this has never been written down. What goes on outside of this building was always Rich's, far as I'm concerned.'

'And in here?' Tatty asked.

'Like I said, paperwork is not my thing. I'm sure Will Keene can put you straight. Rich used to pay him enough.'

'The lawyer?'

'Yeah, Rich's lawyer. They had an understanding.'

'What about the computers?' Tatty asked. 'What's on those – or should I be asking Zach?'

'Rich always fed the numbers. If you want to know the truth, all Zach did was provide some access, some systems know-how. It was kids' stuff for him.'

'No risk at all?'

'I've got my eye on him, Tatty, believe me.'

She went back to the desk for her bag, grabbed her mac too, which was on the back of one of the hard black leather armchairs for visitors. They wouldn't be coming to the Smokehouse with her, none of the chairs. The desk would, though, to remind her – if she needed reminding – who used to be charge. She joined Frank by the door and they headed down the hallway.

'Why are you doing this?' she said, as they approached the lift.

'Let's take the stairs,' he said. 'I've never trusted the lifts in this place.'

'Why are you helping me, Frank?' she repeated, as they headed down the stairs. She could feel the steps shaking as they went. Frank was a very big man. She was finding it comforting.

They got to the bottom, were about to push into the empty ground-floor lobby. Through various windows in various doors, Tatty thought she could see people outside, on the forecourt. There were two or three figures. Frank suddenly put his arm across her, stopping her going forward. 'Rich always helped me,' he said. 'Why wouldn't I help you?'

'You could just walk away,' she said.

'That's what Simon's hoping,' he said. 'Thinks I can be paid to fuck off. You know what, Mrs Goodwin, let's go out the back.'

'Who's there?'

'I'm not sure.'

'The police?'

'No, it's not the police. I'm not expecting them here today. They've got more urgent things to be getting on with at the moment.'

Frank led Tatty round the stairwell to a blank white door at the back marked *Fire Escape*. She hadn't noticed it before. He pushed on the bar and the door opened out onto the overflow car park at the back of the building, and a blinding sheet of sun, and some way beyond the quay edge a glistening river. Beyond that, on top of a sharp hill, with the sun hitting it square on, the metallic box that was Simon's house. Towering flashes of orange and white were on the periphery of her vision – bits of ships moored up- and downriver. The air, coming cool and swift off the sea, swirled around her, getting under her mac. She was wearing tights, but the wrong denier. The sun was no contest for the wind around here. Even in September.

Frank was beeping unlocked his Range Rover, saying, 'I normally park out the back. Rich always preferred it that way.'

Tatty climbed in, not sure of the smell, though the acres of cream leather appeared clean and new enough. Frank spun the giant car round tightly in the empty car park, Tatty trying as he did so to work out how Rich's car might have got on the other side of the barrier. 'Do you think Simon did it?' she said, remembering that it would have been Rich's birthday in a couple of days. He'd have been fifty-three. She didn't want to think about how old she'd be next birthday.

'Kill Rich?'

Tatty nodded, but Frank didn't seem to be looking her way. 'Yeah.'

'He knows something.'

The heavy, powerful vehicle eased along the side of the building, up onto the forecourt. Her Merc was there, but Simon's car was gone. Not so the small group of people standing on the wide doorstep. Slowly they turned to face Frank's car. There were three men in dark blue overalls. One seemed to have some sort of equipment on his back, another a sledgehammer, the last what looked like a large pair of bolt cutters. Frank accelerated straight out onto the road, crossing over to the empty lane heading towards the harbour mouth.

'Who the hell are they?' Tatty asked.

'Pest control,' Frank said, laughing, but not sounding too happy about it.

'Rentokil?' she said. 'I didn't see any vehicle.'

'They work for another organisation.'

'Someone sent them?' The low-rise industrial buildings stretched either side of the road. They were in shade now, though the buildings didn't seem high enough. Tatty leaned forward, peered up through the Range Rover's large wind-screen. Cloud.

'Yeah,' said Frank. 'Looks like it.'

She got it now. 'Who were they after? Simon?'

'Me. You.' He whistled. 'They'd have known Simon wasn't there. I guess they were waiting until we stepped outside. They hadn't come far.'

'What about Sian, the others?'

'They're not interested in them.'

'They were going to attack us, in broad daylight?'

'No, not today. They were just going to remind us who they worked for, and what some of that heavy-duty equipment could be used for, I expect.'

'Who do they work for?'

'Like I said, they hadn't come far.'

'Sands?'

'He's not the most subtle of men.'

'You can say that again.' Tatty looked out of the window, saw that they were passing the River Cafe, firmly without an accent on the e. It was in an old Portakabin, very old. There were two Portakabins, in fact, and a couple of large signs advertising all-day and all-night breakfast, open twenty-four hours. The place offered baguettes and filled rolls too. You could eat in or take away. Tatty was not hungry. 'Who goes there at night?' she asked, pointing across Frank.

'Guys off the ships, mostly. Some of the industrial units operate all night. Admiralty Steel used to. And the power plant, across the way – that never shuts. You see the odd hooker as well. Not so many now. Most work out of the brothels and parlours around Queen's Road. It's safer for them there.'

'Yeah, right.'

'I keep a close eye,' Frank said, 'on all Rich's properties. There's never any trouble. They're pretty clean, well run. We can start there.'

'You know what, let's leave the brothels for now.' Tatty hadn't been in one for a very long while. She wasn't ready, even if it was to check the cleanliness, the safety measures, how best to move that bit of business on.

Frank took a left on Hartman Road, and an awkward silence seeped into the car. Some empty land was fenced off on their right, with a forgotten warehouse slumped windowless in the middle. On their left was the large, grey, gas-fired power station. For something that still relied on fossil fuels, it looked almost clean and modern, sitting effortlessly upright behind an endless chain-link fence topped by razor wire.

'What's the point of all those fucking windmills,' Rich used to say, looking out to sea in despair, 'when Yarmouth's got this?' Though he'd have preferred it to have been a nuclear power station. He loved nuclear power.

'There's something you need to know,' Tatty said, as the Range Rover came gracefully to a halt at the junction with South Beach Parade – fenced-off scrub appearing straight ahead, across the empty main road, with some low dunes and the sea beyond that. The sky was sinking into the grey sea somewhere out towards the Netherlands. It was not the sharpest of horizons.

'Yeah?' Frank said, pulling out, heading north.

Scrub stretched on and on. Soon it would merge with the land intended for the super casino. She didn't know exactly where the plot began and ended. She would. Plans forming thick and fast.

The old mock-Tudor pub on the corner of Monument Road and South Beach Parade was for sale, Tatty noticed. They'd need to acquire it sooner rather than later. But she doubted there'd be much competition for the freehold.

'Were you going to tell me something?' Frank said.

Salmon Road was fast approaching. 'I've been seeing Nathan, Nathan Taylor,' she said.

'I saw him earlier this morning,' Frank said, deadpan, looking straight ahead. 'He was wearing all grey. Does he always wear grey? And then he gets into a white car.'

'He's image conscious,' Tatty said. 'That's the designer in him – far too vain. I've been a fool, Frank.' She paused.

'We all make mistakes, in a time of need.'

'Did Rich know?'

'If he did, he never told me.'

'And you kept quiet?' Had Frank known?

'No need for people to get hurt unnecessarily. To be honest, Rich thought Nathan swung the other way. At least, he used to rib me about it. But Nathan Taylor's not my type, don't worry.'

'I wouldn't. He's history anyway.' There, she'd said it. She was going to be a woman of her word from now on, wasn't she?

Frank was still not looking at her, still staring at the road ahead. The big dipper was looming. 'Are you going to keep him involved in the Smokehouse?'

'That's nearly finished,' Tatty said. 'He did a good job, I'll give him that. It might not be easy, getting him out though. You should see what he's done with that penthouse.'

'You want me to deal with it?'

'I'll let you know if I do, thanks.' The log flume was now across the central lane of parked cars. Except there were no cars parked there this morning. The flume was not working either. It had been the kids' favourite ride. She remembered when it arrived, not long after she and Rich had got together. 'Are you really doing all this because Rich helped you?'

'He was very accepting, and generous.'

'He could be that.' It hadn't taken Rich long to find out how she actually made a living, when they first got together. 'But I still don't get it.'

Frank snorted, clearing his airways. It was not a pleasant sound. 'I don't have any family of my own,' he said. 'I was in care from the year nought. I don't have a boyfriend. I'm not good in relationships anyway. You lot are all that I've got, the only family I've known. Besides, there's too much money floating around just for me. I wouldn't know what to do with it all.' He laughed.

It was a good laugh. Hearty, honest.

24

'That's Rich's – yours,' Frank said, pointing to a building next to the old Windmill Theatre that was now Laser Quasar. Tatty's eyes were focused on Harry Ramsden's World of Famous Fish and Chips. She was feeling twinges of hunger. They'd had a coffee in the casino, but it was weak, watery, no better than what they might have got at the River Cafe, she reckoned. The place had not long opened, that was the excuse they were given, the machine not properly warmed up. Tatty thought the casino was meant to be twenty-four hours. That's what Rich used to say, after another whole night out. 'Yarmouth, the town that never sleeps' – he'd actually said it.

Then Frank took a call and announced he needed to be somewhere else because someone he'd been looking for had been spotted down the road. Though he'd promised he wouldn't be long, Tatty had refused to sit there, in that empty casino, waiting for him to come back for her. Some tour. 'You're the boss,' he'd said.

'What did he want that for?' she said now, looking at the run-down building.

'He didn't. He wanted the Windmill Theatre. Couldn't get it at the time. Thought he'd put a squeeze on.'

She considered the small but elaborate building, with its light-bulb-studded wooden windmill blades stuck halfway up the outside. The shutters on the ground floor were down, spotted with graffiti. There was a good view from the plush safety of Frank's vehicle. Perhaps she'd get one. Mercedes coupés didn't offer anything like enough protection. 'It's got something,' she said.

'He thought it was the only windmill round here that made any sense. Thought he could turn it into the Moulin Rouge. At least get a troupe of girls to dance around topless. There isn't a strip club along this part of the front.'

'He never told me.'

Frank looked at her, smiled. The car eased forward a block, pulled into the next largely empty parking bay. 'That arcade' – he was pointing across Tatty now, while still keeping an eye on what was going on around them – 'that's yours. The one next to it as well. In season, we used to be able to wash fifty grand a week in these places, and could put through triple that in the casino. Times aren't what they used to be. Not enough punters, too many accountants. You wonder why Rich was so keen on a super casino? He thought it would be able to take care of all his operations, any conceivable expansion, without anyone batting an eyelid, as long as the crowds came – and even if they didn't.' He laughed. 'And that's not to mention the corporate tax advantages of such a development in a regeneration area.'

'There'd be the small matter of partners, the Prime Poker people, wouldn't there?' Tatty said. 'Who'd be accountable to them? Wouldn't they want some of the benefits?'

'That relationship was a work in progress.'

'With Simon in charge?' She was conscious of the engine softly idling, conscious too that Frank seemed to have more than a head for numbers. He knew the whole operation inside out. He'd been under-selling himself.

'His job, as I always understood it, was to get them on board. The project needs a huge amount of investment to begin with. We're a couple of years away from such a complex finally opening. You saw that land back there. How long does it take to build a palace, fit for ten thousand people, in the shape of a G, complete with a couple of piers, a glass ballroom – all the permissions aside?'

'Did I see you outside Simon's house, Saturday night, on the street?' she asked.

'Yes,' he said, not hesitating.

Tatty was glad he hadn't lied. 'What were you doing?'

'Where were you going?'

'I think you know that now.'

'I was reminding myself of the view across the river.'

'You said you think Simon knows something about Rich's death. What?'

'I'm working on it, Mrs Goodwin, believe me.'

'For God's sake, call me Tatty.'

'Tatty.'

'Sands? Is he behind it? Working with Simon?'

'No, I don't think so. Sands has never been able to command much loyalty. He might be old but he's new to this game. However, a vacuum has opened up,' Frank said. 'There isn't so much to go around.'

Hadn't Sian said something similar?

'Simon would be pretty easy to exploit,' Frank said.

'But he's not in charge,' Tatty said. 'I am.'

'Not everyone knows that. Not Sands, not his people. I doubt it would ever occur to them.'

Tatty thought of her conversation with Graham Sands in his new hotel. 'Sexist bastards.'

'You want to know what I've had to cope with?'

'I can imagine.'

'Yet these things can be used to our advantage,' Frank said. He was peering ahead, through the wide windscreen.

'How?'

He sat back, flicked the supercharged motor into gear, stamped the floor, swung out, accelerated beyond the Flamingo arcade, leaving a flash of lurid pink and lilac imprinted on Tatty's brain. This was soon replaced by a deeper shade of lilac decorating the outside of the Circus arcade, and then the red and gold adorning the façade of the Golden Nugget. A block further on and the car swerved into another largely empty parking bay, coming to a stop behind a large black Mercedes G Class, personalised plates. A man was sitting behind the wheel, on the phone.

'If people don't know who you are, just what you represent, they're less likely to be on their guard,' Frank said. 'They might say things they shouldn't, prejudice aside.' He flung open his door. 'I won't be long. Stay here.'

'So now I'm supposed to wait in your car?' she shouted after him. But he had slammed shut the driver's door and was jogging down the middle of the road, passing the Silver Slipper. He was going at some speed, with some agility for such a large man in city shoes. He passed a rusty brown

Ford saloon then strode up onto the pavement and disappeared down the side road at the end of the block.

Tatty leaned over, removed the key from the console. It was a nice big car, on a rough road. She gathered her bag from the footwell, opened the door, climbed down. Beeped the car locked. Was aware of a lot of other beeping going on around her. The doors to the Silver Slipper were wide open. A cacophony of cheap electronic sound was pouring out. She stood on the wide pavement a moment, hearing also the gentle sound of the sea, and the wind, and gulls squawking.

She was not cold, nor hot, but she tightened the belt around her mac, took a firmer grip of her handbag, began walking fast in the direction Frank had gone, trying not to look at the man in the jeep. She went left at the end of the block, down a narrow shady street. The first buildings on either side were painted black. One seemed to be a club, The Finest in the East. There were some large terrace houses further down the road, brick and cream. She could see some green ahead as well, grass and trees, as the road opened out. A park? She wasn't sure she'd been down this road, not for decades anyway. But she didn't get to the end.

Halfway along she realised that a number of the houses were painted the same shade of cream. There was a sign, vertical on a near wall, which could perhaps light up in the dark. In the strong daylight it was a smudge of faint orange letters spelling out *Sunrise Lodge*. Closer, the cream paint job didn't look so neat or new. The windows were not in good repair, nor the brickwork. The entranceway was in a porch with a bay window above.

Frank was standing by the porch, with another man. The other man was wearing a cheap, mismatching track-suit, the top a shiny dark blue, the bottoms a matt grey. He had on filthy black trainers, soft and misshapen. He was bent over, not struggling. His thin, shaved head was being held in the crook of Frank's thick arm. Frank looked up as Tatty approached. He shook his head. He was not too happy to see her.

She shrugged.

'I said stay in the car,' Frank said.

Tatty nodded. 'I'm trying to catch up, Frank, fast.'

'OK, your call. This,' Frank said, 'is Mr Shawcross. Say hello, Kenny.'

The man mumbled something that sounded like 'cunt'. Frank stepped on one of the man's soft trainers. Frank's fine black shoes must have had proper heels, shaped from well-cured leather. The man mumbled something that sounded like 'fucking cunt'.

'I've been looking for Mr Shawcross for weeks,' Frank said to Tatty. 'He owes us a lot of money.'

'Don't have any, do I,' the man said clearly. 'What are you talking to her for anyway? She your copper friend?'

Frank stamped on his other foot, then back-heeled the man's flimsy shin, encased in even flimsier material. 'She is someone you do not want to get on the wrong side of.' Frank then back-heeled the man's other shin.

There was a long-drawn-out yelp, but no swearing. Tatty thought the man had given up. He looked like he'd given up weeks, years ago.

'Where's the money?' Frank said.

'It wasn't a good summer,' the man managed to say. 'I had to close my stall.'

'It's never a good summer here, is it?' Frank applied more pressure on the man's neck.

'What's this prove?' the man said.

Tatty was wondering too. The poor sod. By all accounts, the weather had been even worse than normal.

'I'll get it to you. I'm working on it,' he said.

'You know the score,' Frank said, squeezing harder.

There was another yelp, more of a squeal.

'They never learn,' Frank said to Tatty.

Tatty looked away, then up and down the street. She didn't see anyone else around, no one peering out from any window, no parted net curtains. Someone had to be watching. It was broad daylight. But perhaps that was the point. It was another way of getting the message across. 'How much does he owe?' she asked.

'Forty grand,' Frank said.

Kenny Shawcross shook his head, as if to say no way.

It was much more than Tatty had been expecting. She felt like stepping forward and kicking the man herself. 'Bloody hell, what did he do with all that money?' He didn't look like he'd been spending it on clothes.

Frank looked up at her. 'It accumulates. They take out short-term loans, blow it on crack, and then forget to pay us back.'

'You know me,' Kenny wheezed, 'I don't do that stuff. I'm telling you.'

'Crack, booze, the bookies, they always deny it,' said Frank. 'And we're here to help you lot – the only people left, in a high street full of sharks, who'll lend you a hand. But I'm afraid this time, my friend,' he changed his hold on the man, and began squeezing him an awful lot harder, 'you pushed your luck too far.'

The man's legs were shaking as he was being lifted off the ground, and Tatty wondered whether Frank might actually break his neck.

'Wait,' Shawcross managed to wheeze, 'your boss, I heard something.'

Frank stamped on the man's foot again, before easing the pressure. 'What?'

'I heard something,' Shawcross repeated, sucking in air, his pale ravaged face a jigsaw of purple patches.

Frank straightened him up, grabbed the front of his tracksuit, pushed him against the entrance of the Sunrise Lodge so the door banged. 'What the fuck are you trying now?'

'An American, small black guy, has been asking a lot of questions. You understand?'

Frank leaned forward, tensed. 'No, I don't understand.'

'Says he'll pay for answers.'

'They always say that.' Frank then head-butted Shawcross, sharp and hard, so there was a loud crack, followed by a loud clatter as Kenny's body crumpled against the door.

25

'Forget it,' said Frank. It was the first thing he'd said since they'd got back into the vehicle.

The Mint, Atlantis, Caesars Fun Palace, all shot by in a blur of unlit neon, but Frank stopped at the first set of pedestrian lights. Tatty was surprised he bothered, and she took her eyes off his glistening forehead – she couldn't believe there was no bruise, no mark. Focused instead on Yesterday's World, A Glorious Emporium of the Past. She shut her eyes, trying to imagine what was behind the dark red shutters. Nothing came to mind, so she looked back at the road ahead, wondering why the car hadn't budged. The lights were green, then she noticed an old couple. They were taking a century to cross the road, but at least they were making the effort to walk unaided.

'Forget what?' she said.

'What you saw.'

'Why did you let him go?'

'He'll have a sore head for a few days.'

'But he still owes you forty grand.'

'He owes you forty grand.'

'I think I want it back.' The car was moving now. They were passing a row of fish and chip shops clumped around

Magic City. 'What did he mean about an American, asking questions?'

'Buying time, probably. Kenny's not the sort of guy who normally knows a fucking thing. But I'll check it out. I've not finished with him.'

'Why did he think I was your copper friend?'

'Like I said, I've not finished with him.' Frank turned to her, slowing. 'Look, I'll never lie to you. But there are some things you are better off not knowing, if you want to make a go of this business. Someone in your position, at the top, it pays to let others keep your hands as clean as possible. Trust me. Some pretty nasty stuff is going down at the moment.'

Tatty blew out air. 'Did Rich go debt-collecting with you?'

'No,' he laughed, 'no way. He left that to me. It's old school stuff. When I say stay in the car, stay in the car.'

She'd think about it. 'The cash that washes through the arcades, the casino, the bars and clubs, where does most of it come from?' They were at the top of Regent Road, where a fat chunk of the pedestrianised walkway spilled onto the Golden Mile. Leaning forward she thought she could see a couple of police vehicles halfway down.

'There are a lot of different operations.'

'So everyone keeps telling me. Just what can I know, if I am the fucking boss?'

'We can talk in the car,' Frank said. 'But it's best not to make a habit of talking about this at Goodwin House. Or at home. Did Rich ever discuss what he was up to at home?'

She looked at Frank, his great big head hard as granite, and sighed. He caught her meaning all right.

'You don't know who else might be listening,' he said.

'My kids? The cleaner?' She laughed.

'The National Crime Agency has more power than ever.'

Rich had mentioned the NCA, though not as much as he banged on about HMRC. 'So?'

'They have some pretty impressive surveillance equipment,' Frank said. 'Underhand bastards. The thing is, you don't want to find yourself an accessory to this or that. Rich kept office hours, if you know what I mean.'

'Like fuck he did.'

'It's tough work making the legit businesses stack up.'

'Frank, do me a favour, seeing as we're in the fucking car – the cash, I'm only talking about the cash for now, OK, the stuff that needs to be washed. And don't you dare tell me I'm better off not knowing about it.' The grand old theatre was on their right as they entered the one-way system. It was currently a cinema, Hollywood something. It seemed to change hands and purpose every time Tatty passed.

'To be honest, we were trying to move out of cash,' Frank said. 'I kept telling Rich, "For God's sake, it's the twenty-first century." Our key partners now, especially those on the continent, like to exchange goods, services, expertise. It's an electronic world, Tatty. Bitcoins and the like. Cash has had its day, the further from the street you go.'

'Let's stick with the street then,' Tatty said, annoyed. 'The cash that you loan out to people like Kenny. It doesn't come from a hole in the wall, does it?'

'Mostly drugs, the parlours, and some of the transport businesses – depends on what's being ferried around,' Frank said, his eyes firmly on the road. 'And yeah, there's the short-term loan business, that's predominantly cash. What comes back, though, sometimes includes assets. And we make some from protection. Not enough, if you ask me.'

'Protecting what, around here?'

'People like to feel safe, in a town like this,' Frank said. 'And they like their materials not to disappear, their property not to be vandalised. They can rely on us.'

'Yeah?'

'We're trying to reverse a fifty-year decline, Tatty. We provide a better service than the council ever has, believe you me. And the amount of money we're putting into the local economy? I'm telling you.'

It could have been Rich talking. 'But the drugs, the brothels, what was Rich thinking?' An old anger was rising. 'Frank?'

'It's not where the real money is any more. More of a habit, the drugs particularly. All these synthetic manufacturers – the Dutch, the Chinese – have altered the landscape forever. The old rules of supply and demand have all but gone.'

They had slipped over the mini-roundabout at the back of the old theatre. She remembered Rich taking her to see Les Dawson there, shortly after they got together. The evening's entertainment didn't begin until they walked out ten minutes before the interval. They were now on North Drive, with the lush bowling greens on their right, the cold grey sea beyond. 'Well, those habits stink.'

'If we weren't still involved, others would be, Tatty. Do we want that?'

'The trafficking? What did you just call it, the transport business?'

'Smuggling, not trafficking, there's a big difference, whether we're talking drugs or people.'

'Is there?'

'You know, getting people into the country, even through a port like Yarmouth, is not easy. We don't charge as much as we could.'

'Who are we talking about – those poor, desperate kids from Syria? Afghans fleeing more terror? The persecuted? The starving? Those North African women who've been sliced?' Tatty had never thought of herself as political. She supposed she'd never thought much about anything, for decades.

'Why do you think Rich went to Greece so often? To make sure we were dealing with the right people. Refugees, migrants from Syria mainly nowadays, sure, but these people are being given opportunities, new beginnings, that this government certainly isn't offering.'

'What are they paying for it? How?'

'They need our help, believe me.'

'Fucking hell,' said Tatty. 'What do you do, get them over here and stuff them in the brothels? Are you telling me these things are not linked, by you, by us?' She kept her eyes firmly ahead as they passed the big Edwardian hotels, most now leased by social services, lining the road on their left, and the car parks, largely empty, spread towards the beach on the other side.

'I understand what you're saying, but it's not like that, believe me.'

What had Rich told Frank about her past? 'Where are we going?'

'I thought we could swing by the North Beach Holiday Park. Then the racecourse – you know Rich had plans for that too? – before dropping in on the boatyard. This is the future, Tatty. We get the super casino under way, and then the other pieces will fall into place. We've just got to get everything lined up, which includes keeping the competition at bay, keeping the town clean and safe.'

Who was meant to be running this business, Tatty couldn't help thinking. The first clumps of dunes were emerging, mounds of soft natural world. Her phone was ringing. She was going to ignore it. 'That's as maybe, but first things first. We've still got to do something about the past, the old habits, haven't we.' It wasn't a question either.

Frank blew out some air, a long steady blast from his two massive lungs. They must have been like oak trees deep within his huge chest. 'There are certain positions we don't want to drop, we can't drop, not just like that. We have the wrong people wandering around, scruffing the place up, and bang goes the whole project. The best way to keep scum off the street is to prevent them getting any purchase. There's no point relying on the authorities, as Rich knew all too well – they gave up on Yarmouth years ago.'

'You think Rich did a good job, honestly?' The holiday park was now on their left – large white static caravans and chalets tethered behind a low hedge, topped up with some tired chain-link fencing. Many of the dwellings had fancy balconies and balustrades, more suited to some suburban mansion, but in miniature.

'He tried. We're all trying.'

'I've got kids, Frank. I don't want them mixed up in the drugs, the prostitution' – the word felt sharp and painful in her mouth – 'and not the trafficking. Not that, for God's sake.'

'Smuggling, not trafficking.'

'Like I said.' It was catching.

'You might want to contemplate the figures first,' Frank said.

They had come to the entrance of the holiday park, and the end of North Drive, the end of the road. Ahead were vast stretches of undulating marram grass and sand. The area was officially recognised as an Area of Outstanding Natural Beauty. It was an acquired taste. Frank swung the Range Rover round, braked, so it was facing back towards town, the only direction you could go by road from here. There was the old Coastwatch tower on their left, a red-and-white corrugated-iron box hanging off the side of the narrow esplanade. The naked and mutilated body of a drug-ravaged prostitute was found a short way out in the dunes from here, not so long ago, Tatty remembered. No one had yet been charged for it.

Frank's phone was going now.

'I guess some of this could depend on the conditions,' Tatty said, more to herself. 'What we can do for them.'

'I've got to get this.' Frank pulled his phone from his jacket pocket and climbed out of the car in a blast of squally air, leaving the motor running.

No one was quite who they seemed to be, herself included, Tatty decided, watching Frank talking into his phone, hunched against the wind. Tatty retrieved her own phone from her bag. Brought the screen to life. Finally, among the other missed calls, she saw that Megan had tried to reach her. Friends for you when you needed them most. But Megan wasn't much of a friend. Tatty didn't have friends. Rich had seen to that.

26

'Sis?' said Zach. But it had gone straight to voicemail. He didn't bother leaving her a message. He texted her instead. *Ring me when you can. I need to speak to you. Zx.* Ben didn't answer either, so Zach left him a message too.

He got off the edge of his bed, walked over to the window, looked out at the patchy sky. He'd driven to the car wash in his flip-flops, but it was not flip-flop weather. He liked those trainers. Decided he needed some more, urgently, but buying them online would take a day at least. Perhaps he'd drive to Norwich. He'd never get the right pair around here. Even in Norwich it wouldn't be easy.

Scanning further down Marine Parade, he caught sight of a large black Mercedes G Class parked up on the road, a short way from the small public car park on the front. It was not quietly lined up, facing out to sea, like the other sad vehicles. It was aggressively facing Zach's way. He couldn't tell if anyone was inside. The windscreen was slick with glare, while the side windows must have been tinted. The alloys were chrome and sparkling. He couldn't quite read the number plate from here, though it looked short, personalised. Zach thought he'd seen the vehicle before, in Yarmouth. It stuck out a fucking mile.

Zach was not going to drive to Norwich today. He was not going to drive anywhere. He stepped back from the window, crouched, looked under the bed. The house was giving him the creeps. He should have been used to the space, the quiet. He'd grown up here. Spent much of his life in these well-padded rooms. He retrieved the old Adidas box, took out the knife once again, and a roll of cash, because you never knew. Kicked the box back under the bed.

His laptop was open on his desk, but blank, the screen having shut itself down. He'd been Googling the local news, seeing what was being said about the double murder. The details were scarce. Then he'd wiped all trace of his search activity. He was certain not even the most diligent of forensic computer scientists would be able to get anywhere with his equipment, his history. He knew how to clean the metadata, and not just what was under the hood.

Nevertheless, he didn't hang on to his laptops for long. More than a few were at the bottom of the Yare. His old phones would have to follow suit, he realised, wondering where they all were. He'd never bothered to sell on his old equipment – his pocket money, on top of his wages, meant that he didn't have to. He was spoilt, he guessed. Careless as well.

His current phone leapt into action, startling him. He took a deep breath, answered. 'Sis.'

'What's up?'

'I'm lonely, man. When are you coming back?'

'To Gorleston? I haven't been back in London long. I'm at work, catching up. In a couple of days or so. Depends.'

He heard a car bump onto the forecourt. 'Have you thought about what Mum said yesterday?' He walked over to the window once more, saw that his mother had arrived home. Felt surprisingly relieved. Saw also that the big Mercedes jeep was still there.

'About what?'

'The business.'

'The business?'

'Yeah, the stuff Dad set up. Us all playing our part.'

'We haven't even had Dad's funeral. How can I think about any of this now?'

'What did Mum say about Dad not keeping up with the times, or some bullshit? What she meant was, we need to get on with it – business like this. Things move fast here.'

'Could have fooled me,' she said.

'Mum's getting to grips,' he said.

'She's not being herself, Zach.'

'What do you really know about Yarmouth? It can be pretty fucking ugly.'

'Great,' she sighed.

He wanted to tell her, but didn't, so he said nothing.

'I'm at work, Zach. I can't talk about this now.'

Zach heard his mother come into the house. Heard her shout, 'Zach?'

He walked over to his bedroom door, opened it, shouted down, 'I'm in my room, Mum. I'm on the phone.'

'OK, darling,' she said, coming straight up the stairs. 'I'm going to have a lie-down. I'm exhausted. I'm not here if anyone comes to the door, all right?'

She'd left her car sprawled across the forecourt, blocking the garage, making it pretty obvious that she was in. And that he wouldn't be going out in his car, even if he'd wanted to. 'Sure,' he said, catching a glimpse of her on the landing. She was still in her mac. It was not the moment to tell her about the missing keys. He retreated into his room, gently shutting the door. He wasn't certain he'd be able to protect her, with only his knife. Perhaps he'd ask Frank about getting him a gun. Surely his father had one, stuffed somewhere. Or had his dad always relied on Frank for firepower?

He pressed his phone back against his ear. 'Sam?'

'What are you doing?'

'Talking to Mum, sorry.'

'I've got to go,' she said.

'It's better when you're here,' he found himself saying. 'You and Ben.'

She was gone, and he stared at his phone. Then he put it in his jeans pocket, the knife in the other front pocket, with the cash – you never knew. He left his bedroom, headed downstairs quietly. He went straight into his father's study, shutting that door quietly too. It was a small, dim room with some bookshelves, a desk, a leather office chair, a big TV, and a tiny window. It was the sort of room that made you feel trapped. This was where his father would let rip at them, out of sight of their mother.

Zach immediately saw that the desk had been broken into, without any consideration for the workmanship. In haste? In desperation? By his mum, according to Ben. Had there really been nothing to find in there? No note? No evidence? Nothing incriminating? The whole house needed to be pulled apart.

Zach started with the right-hand drawer, tipping the contents on the floor. Among the various papers and receipts he found nothing more than an old calculator, some paperclips and a lot of dust and fluff. The next drawer had more of the same. The next as well.

He was working swiftly now, the floor of his dad's study piling up with bits of paper and card, and small presentation boxes. Old presents. Presents Zach recognised; birthday and Christmas gifts they'd given him. In one such box was a memory stick in the shape of the Eiffel Tower – that had been from Sam, he recalled. Pull off the tip and there was the USB plug. It was a stupid present for a man who was barely computer literate. In another box was a Mont Blanc pen; from his mother. It had not been used either. Another drawer, more unused presents, including some cufflinks in the form of silver dice. Solid silver. A present from him, via his mum's purse. His dad had worn shirts that required cufflinks, though not these cufflinks.

The drawers at the bottom of the desk were deeper, heavier. There was a green Rolex box. This was empty. Zach threw it across the floor. Below it were what appeared to be some old hand-drawn, hand-painted birthday and Christmas cards, amid even grainer dust. He pulled them out, opened them up. Fucking hell. There was at least one from him, when he must have been six or something. It was a sort of boat, with a lot of crinkly dark blue sea. There were others that could have been his work, or his siblings'. Stick figures, square houses, brown blobby trees. There were quite a few. He couldn't believe the sentimental old cunt had kept them.

All the drawers and contents were on the floor now, and Zach was on his knees, looking at the empty shell of a desk. Banging the sides, the underneath of the top, looking for false panels, proper hiding places. Where a gun might have been kept, perhaps. Anything that was dark and wrong.

He stood, pulled the desk out from the wall, far enough that he could turn the thing onto its side. It was heavier than he'd thought, and the edge of the top hit the wall as it clattered over, digging into the plaster.

Pleased, Zach turned, took in the few shelves and even fewer books on them. Stuff he knew his father had never read. James Patterson's *Now You See Her*. Another one by him: *Private*. He swept them onto the floor, wondering if there might be a secret panel lurking behind them. But there wasn't. He shoved the rest of the contents of the shelves onto the floor – including some framed photographs of his dad and his mum at an evening do, a group shot of them all by the pool at the villa in Ibiza. Playing happy fucking families. Yet none of the glass broke. He lifted his foot, ready to stamp.

'Zach? What the fuck are you doing?'

It was his mum. Fully dressed, but dishevelled. He froze, feeling nine years old.

'You woke me up. I couldn't understand what the noise was. It sounded like someone had broken in.' She stepped further into the study. 'I thought you were in your room.'

'What's that in your hand?'

Tatty looked down, pulled her hand, the hand carrying the small matt black pistol, behind her back. She flushed.

'What I think it was?'

'What the hell have you done to your father's study, Zach?'

Zach felt his eyes watering up. A nine-year-old boy. He looked away, at the mess on the floor. 'He kept our old birthday cards and stuff, the ones we made.' He poked the mound with his foot, trying to unearth one of his. 'There were a load of presents in his desk too – you know, things we gave him. Things he never used.'

'He was impossible to buy things for,' his mother said, still holding her hand behind her back.

'But he kept them,' Zach said.

She smiled at him. 'He did love you.'

'Yeah, right,' said Zach. 'Where did you get the gun?'

'You don't need to know.' She was still trying to conceal it.

'You said you wouldn't lie to us.'

'I'm not.'

'Well, you're withholding information then.' He knew the lingo. 'How can we trust you, if you don't tell us a fucking thing?'

She sighed. 'It was your father's. He kept it locked in his desk – in that old Rolex box, if you must know.' Her foot pointed the way. 'I didn't want anyone else finding it after he died, so I got it out the other day.'

'You broke into the desk?'

'Don't ask me what he'd done with the keys. Still can't find them.'

Zach remembered about Nina and the keys to the house. But that didn't seem important now. Besides, something Nina had said about Clara, or the way she'd said it, was not sitting right. He knew Clara – better than her mum knew her, probably, at least some of her ways. 'You thought you might need it, the gun?' he said, refocusing on something that was fucking crucial.

She was shaking her head. But Zach couldn't tell whether she meant yes, or no, or was simply embarrassed.

'What were you looking for, Zach?' Her foot was now prodding the jumble of stuff on the floor.

'A gun?' He shrugged. 'I don't know. Something.'

'Don't be so angry, darling.'

'I'm not fucking angry.' He was scared but he wasn't going to tell his mother that. 'None of this stuff helps.' He was looking down at the mess he'd made, thinking of the mess and blood in that horrible room in a terrace house in a Yarmouth backstreet. Two guys with their throats slit. Just because they were dealing bump? 'It doesn't make sense.'

'People only see what they want to see, don't they?'

'I don't know what the fuck you mean.'

'Forget it, it doesn't matter.'

Zach watched his mother bend down and retrieve a large old envelope. The seal had long lost purchase and she pulled out a fat wodge of even older-looking bits of newspaper, yellow and crinkly. 'Bloody hell,' she said. 'I missed this.' She began flicking through the cuttings.

'What is it?'

'Old news reports, about your grandfather.'

222

'I didn't think I had a grandfather.'

'Your dad's father, who died before you were born.'

'Oh, him. Didn't he go to prison?'

'Not for long. He was set up.'

'Dad told you that?'

'Common knowledge. These cuttings seem to be about the case.' She was still shuffling the yellowed papers, still trying to shield the gun from him as well. 'Not something your father wanted to forget, I guess.'

'Let me see.'

'Haven't we got other issues to deal with first? Like getting this place tidied up.' She smiled.

Yeah, as if he were still a kid, being told what to do by his mum. 'All yours,' he said, storming out of the room.

27

Frank looked up at the building. He'd had to walk some way down Riverside Road, having parked up in the usual place, to get a view. Still, it was quicker and easier than trudging up the hill. The back of Simon and Jess's house was in shadow. Ferry Hill was in shadow and the late afternoon, late summer gloom was creeping down the slope fast. Frank stepped back as if it were about to wash over his feet.

She wasn't here. She said she'd be here, by the slipway, the lifebuoy, twenty minutes ago.

He walked on as far as the small park, with its few benches clinging on to that precarious patch of land. He was about to take the path through the park and on up the hill when something made him look over his shoulder. Walking towards him along Riverside Road at some pace, in shadow, was a tall, thin woman in jeans and a tight-fitting jacket. She had quite a pair of heels on her feet, which, despite their height, seemed to be doing nothing to slow her down. Practice, persistence, determination. They were making some racket too, drowning out the gulls.

'Frank,' she shouted, 'wait.'

As if he hadn't already stopped in his tracks.

'Frank,' she said again, unnecessarily. Her shoulder-length blonde hair was billowing in the breeze like a cheap spinnaker.

'Hey,' said Frank as Jess reached him, immediately clinging on to his arm. She gave off a perfume he couldn't name, though it wasn't dissimilar to Simon's cologne. Her hair smelt clean and fresh too, while a waft of salt and diesel blew in from the port around them. 'What kept you?' He wanted her to let go of his arm. He didn't like her, thought of Tatty. She would not have been amused.

'Simon. We had things to discuss.'

'I bet. He's still in the house?'

'No. He just left for a meeting, in London. He won't be back until tomorrow. He likes his nights in London.'

'He didn't want to stick around? There's a lot going on.'

'He was not in a good mood.'

'No surprise there. Did he have a bump on the side of his head?'

'Simon?'

'Who did you think I meant?'

She shook her hair out, trying to look perplexed. She let go of his arm, and stumbled backwards. It was a very uneven strip of road. 'How come you're still talking?' he asked.

'It's complicated,' she sighed, long and hard, gazing out at the dim, narrow road. 'That's life for you. Look, Frank, I've just come back from my sister's to all this.' She held out her thin, bony hands, a few precious gems barely hanging on. 'There are some things I don't want to talk about, not now. All right? God, everything's so messed up.'

'Does Simon normally let you fuck whoever you want?' He'd never have said such a thing to her, of course, if Rich had still been alive.

'We'll work something out, we always have.'

'You're fucking joking.'

'No, I'm not fucking joking. What's it to you, anyway?'

'There are things I still need to know, Jess.'

'Things you need to know? Look, I've been pretty fucking accommodating as far as Simon's concerned, I can tell you.' She was shouting now, out in the road. 'Do you want to know what Simon gets up to, with others, half my fucking age? What he likes me to do to him – in bed? I could ruin him.'

Frank was going to need some time to think about this. There'd been rumours, always brushed off by Rich, who was never one to criticise people's sex lives. 'But fucking his brother?' Frank couldn't help himself now. 'I don't know what world you're living in, Jess.' He glanced round her to the river, saw a huge, dirty, blue-and-red-hulled ship negotiating the corner by the base of Gorleston Pier, ready for its slow, gentle chug the short way upriver to its mooring.

'Same as you,' she said.

Well he didn't know what world Simon was living in. 'When did Simon find out you were fucking Rich? Last Wednesday?'

She shrugged, held out her skeletal hands again. 'It's complicated, OK?'

'He always knew? What are you saying, Jess?'

'No, he didn't always know. But I don't know when he found out for definite. That's the thing. Before last week? It doesn't matter.'

'And he did nothing about it?' Frank shook his head, glad he was single. Something he realised he'd been pleased about for quite some time.

Another shrug. 'You don't know Simon. How his mind works. Or his body.'

'Why did you ring me?' Frank said, looking into her light blue eyes surrounded by thick black mascara. They were bright and glistening, too bright. She'd eventually rung him back. Said she'd been driving. Was in and out of signal, then her satnav packed up, had to keep looking at the route on her phone. Didn't have a charger in the car. 'Why did you want to see me, Jess?'

'Rich – I can't believe it.' She sniffed, but didn't look too sad. 'You knew him. You drove him around. I couldn't talk to Tatty, could I? Why did he do it, Frank?'

'When did you see Rich last? Wednesday evening? Don't fucking lie to me.'

'Frank, can we get out of the road?'

He looked over his shoulder, saw the ship was closing in. It was flying an Estonian flag, riding low in the water. 'Yeah.' He set off towards his car.

'Why don't we go this way,' she said, not following him, gesturing towards the harbour mouth. 'Walk?'

'I thought you wanted to get out of the road?'

'Let's walk up to the pier. Get a cup of tea.'

'You don't like my car?' Did she think he was going to drive her off somewhere, put a bullet in her head? That was Simon's job.

'It's a nice evening. I need some air. I've been in cars all day.' She set off, heels clattering once more.

He guessed he could stretch his legs too, it'd be good for him. 'Sure,' he said, turning his back on his Range Rover. He caught her up and they kept as close to the water's edge as possible, the ship taking some time to pass them coming the other way. Its engines were spluttering hard, producing a dirty trail of diesel, which was slowly masking the acres of industrial buildings and depots across the river. All could have suggested a hard-working port, but Frank knew otherwise.

'How is Tatty?' Jess eventually said.

A large block of apartments was being built on the Gorleston side of the Yare, where some old warehouses and scruffy business units had once been. Boards gave an artist's impression. Gentrification. Frank didn't know who the developer was. 'What's Simon know about this?' He slowed as they neared.

Jess shrugged – she was doing that a lot. Kept walking. Frank should have known who the developer was paying protection money to. It was a big site. Materials for residential blocks usually commanded a higher tariff than industrial sites. Rich was particular about what they got involved with on this side of the river, being even closer to home – but still. It seemed like a lost opportunity to Frank.

'How's Tatty?' Jess repeated.

'How do you think?' Frank said, looking out across the water, soft evening light skimming the surface, gulls swooping. Squawks battling it out with the diesel chug and splutter. All the way from Estonia!

'They'd been married a long time,' Jess said. 'It didn't seem like they still had much of a marriage. Their kids are grown up.'

'Doesn't seem like you have much of a marriage, Jess.' He glanced at her in her tight designer clothes. She left little to the imagination. She was so skinny though, except for the tits. Brittle. Like she might snap if you pressed too hard.

'What are you, my moral guardian? I thought you respected Rich. Would do anything for him, so he told me. Well, I made him happy, Frank, those moments we were together.'

Frank shook his head. He thought there might have been some truth to that. But he didn't like the idea of Rich having spoken to Jess about him.

'He was a passionate man,' she added.

Greedy too, Frank could have added. 'What's Simon want now?' he asked.

'What do you mean?'

They were approaching the lifeboat station. 'Richest fucking charity in the country,' Rich always used to complain. 'How many people do they actually save a year? Fuck all, for the money.'

Had Frank missed some subtext here? He looked across the water once again. Rich went into the drink, the other side of the river. There was no one to rescue him.

'What does Simon want with the business?'

'He never talks to me about that.'

'Yeah? Did Rich?'

'What do you think?' She looked down, her chest restricting the view.

'Last Wednesday evening, did you see Rich?'

'Haven't you already asked me that?'

'Did you see him?'

'No. No.' She shook her head, the highlights doing their thing. 'I was at home, packing. Simon was on his way to Las Vegas first thing the next morning. I was off to my sister's. She's not been well. Thought I'd help her out with her kiddies.'

Frank's mind was racing. Simon might have been flying to Vegas from Schiphol first thing the next morning. But he'd maintained to him, to the office, that he'd flown to Amsterdam on the Wednesday evening. Jess, it seemed, chose her words carefully. Her lovers too?

They'd made it to Quay Road, the Pier Hotel ahead, looking lost in the second decade of the twenty-first century. There were some people out walking, some with small dogs, some with big dogs. Most of them were old and well wrapped up despite the mild sea air – people and dogs.

'Fine,' she said, as they veered past the Pier Hotel, and the concrete shelters further on, facing the beach. The strip of seaside shops and cafés were up on their right across Beach Road, hugging the bottom of the cliff. 'Dunstan Hall, that posh place on the outskirts of Norwich?'

'Yeah?' Frank sighed. 'I know it.'

'I was going to meet Rich there on Thursday, for lunch.'

'Lunch?' Frank laughed.

'Then I was going on to my sister's – honestly.'

Rich had not mentioned this to Frank, meeting Jess at Dunstan Hall, but he could believe it. A gleaming white Hummer with black-tinted windows and bright chrome hubs was taking up two parking spaces beyond the concrete shelters. It was facing out to sea too. Three men were standing by the beefed-up bonnet with its ridiculous shiny chrome grille. They looked too old to be associated with such a vehicle. The vehicle looked too young to be sitting there, like a spoilt teenager that had wandered into the lounge of an old people's home. Shamed into silence.

Frank didn't recognise the men by the Hummer. He should have. 'So what happened?' he asked.

'Rich sent me a text Wednesday evening, said his plans had changed and he couldn't meet on Thursday after all. He had urgent meetings in Yarmouth. It pissed me off, I can tell you. I like Dunstan Hall. It's got a great spa – steam rooms, hot tubs, the lot.'

'Thursday morning then?'

'Thought I'd get an early start as well. It's a hell of a long way. The traffic's always shit, up around Peterborough.'

'And Simon said nothing about Rich?'

'No. Why would he?'

Frank shook his head. 'This is stretching my imagination, Jess, which is not great at the best of times.'

'If you think Simon and Rich rowed on Wednesday, who knows? Perhaps something did snap between them. But it wouldn't have been about me. There's no point you trying to understand Simon.' She shook her head. 'What is this? The Spanish fucking Inquisition? I rang you, Frank. I wanted to see you.'

To say what exactly? 'What time did Simon get in Wednesday evening?'

'I don't know,' she practically screamed. 'I'd already taken some pills, sunk half a bottle of wine – I was pissed off about Rich cancelling Thursday. Simon must have got back from work at some point. I seem to remember him fucking me in the night. He can be very demanding, Frank, before he goes on a trip. Thinks I owe it to him.' She tried to pull a face. But the Botox was not so giving this time. Perhaps she wasn't putting enough effort into it.

'Next I knew for certain it was morning, and there was no sign of him. He's always fucking sneaking in and out – those brothers for you. I didn't speak to him until he was in Amsterdam, and I was halfway to my sister's – when he rang me to tell me about Rich.' She carefully ran a finger under her eye. 'She lives outside Manchester, in Chorlton. I wasn't going to drive straight back here. I needed time to think. I didn't get the sense Simon wanted me to rush back either.'

Frank felt like a drink, not a cup of tea. He didn't think Jess was choosing her words quite so carefully now. 'It's definitely changing round here, isn't it?' he said. There was a new surf-and-turf joint on the lower esplanade. Above it, cut into the soft cliff, sat some sort of outdoor bar and terrace with sun umbrellas and patio heaters, and a low wall of glass to break the breeze. Frank shook his heavy head once more. The bar looked like it had yet to greet its first customer. It wasn't going to be him. Not today.

'Fuck this,' he said, 'let's get a drink in the Harbour Inn. You know where you are there.' There was always a rough prick or two at the bar. But they usually shut up when they saw Frank.

They headed the short way back to Quay Road, and the old pub nestled into the curved terrace of mainly residential houses, some occupied, some not. The redundant lighthouse stood at the end of the row. Thin, towering and redbrick, it had been there for a couple of centuries at least, weathering all storms. Frank wasn't so sure about how he was going to weather the gale blowing around his head. Sex, fucking sex. It was always dirty round here.

He held the door open for Jess, and they stepped into the bar. 'You want me to think that Simon killed Rich?' he said, quietly but insistently, as she grabbed his arm for support. It was dark inside the Harbour Inn, and there was a big step down onto worn flagstones.

'What does it look like to you?' Jess said. 'Rich, committing suicide? I don't think so.'

There was only one prick at the bar. He glanced their way, knew better than to stare and returned to what there was left of his pint.

'I think you're lucky to be alive,' Frank said. 'Or there's more going on in your brain than I thought. What are you having?'

28

Tatty reached over to the bedside table, retrieved her phone. Couldn't believe the time. Couldn't believe she'd missed so many calls. There were some messages too. How come people always rang her now when she was asleep?

She needed reading glasses. She'd needed reading glasses for quite a while. Nathan had left a voicemail message and sent some texts. She deleted the voicemail without playing it. Tried to read his texts. One appeared to say, *I love you*. The other, *I'm coming over*.

'Fuck,' she said aloud, sliding her legs off the bed. Finding her feet. Standing. She was a little dizzy. She walked to the French window. The blinds had not been closed. But darkness was not so far away, sweeping in from the North Sea. The house faced almost due east. She had always thought she was more of a morning person, daylight signalling the end of her torment. She wasn't so sure now.

A few boats sat on the near horizon, fading into the gloom. Down the road, the large Mercedes jeep was still parked up. Now she remembered where else she'd seen it. In Yarmouth, on the Golden Mile, when Frank had stopped to head-butt that waste of space who owed them £40,000.

That would be £10,000 for each of them: Ben, Sam, Zach and herself. A nice bit of pocket money. But what about Frank? What would be his fair share? She didn't know. She needed to know. He was going to some trouble. He wore nice traditional shoes, even if his jackets were out of date.

There was no sign of Nathan's white Audi coming from either direction – and she would have noticed it. She'd never asked him why his car was not grey. She went back to the bed, her phone. Saw that Nathan had sent his last text ten minutes ago. She was meant to meet Megan in twenty minutes for a spritzer in Galleons. No Rich to stop her.

She thought about ringing Frank. Found herself going through the other messages on her phone. Sam had rung. 'Hi, Mum, you OK? London's weird. Nothing feels right. Love you.'

There was another answerphone message, this one from a blocked number. She put the phone to her ear, heard a man saying he was DI Peter Leonard. She hadn't been able to remember his name the last time, and he hadn't offered it. She pictured his hollow cheeks, his pale skin, his skeletal frame with the dark anorak hanging off it. His blinkered vision.

He said he'd been trying to get in touch with her, and asked her to give him a call, as soon as possible, 'please'. He left a landline number, easy to memorise. She looked at Rich's watch. She supposed she'd always think of it as Rich's watch. What time did these coppers get off work? Weekends, evenings, they seemed to be putting in some shifts. But they must have had more than enough to be dealing with now – the two drug murders brutally coming to mind – besides the fact they were surely under-staffed. Round here anyway. That's what Rich always used to say.

She listened to the message again, trying to discern from his tone why exactly he might have called, what news he had now.

She thought about ringing Frank once more. Didn't think too much about why Ben hadn't rung her, as he was never as dutiful as Sam. Except she wanted to hear his voice badly, she realised. Her big boy. Have him near. She rushed over to the French window with the flat North Sea view. No sign of Nathan's silly white car tootling up Marine Parade. So Rich had thought he was gay. Of course he'd thought that. Perhaps Nathan was. But he fucked her hard and long enough. Sex with Rich had always been swift, sweaty, the satisfaction only ever going one way, and announcing itself in a faint tremor.

She went back to the bedside table, what had always been her bedside table. Pulled open the drawer, saw the small gun nestled on a bed of blister packs, some popped clean, others with pills waiting for the taking. She should have shot Rich in the head when he was still alive. But her mind had always been too fuddled. It wasn't now. If Nathan didn't back off, perhaps she'd have to shoot him.

Pushing the gun aside, she grabbed at the pill packets. Something she'd been meaning to do for days. She flung them onto the bed. It took more than a couple of handfuls to get them all out of the drawer.

She went into the bathroom. Opened the cupboard under the double sink. Searched for more mind-numbing medicines, those lurking at the back, in the far corners, half-hidden by Rich's dusty toiletries – more presents he'd never used. She was not amazed at what was here. Diazepam, lorazepam, amitriptyline, the instruction sheets for Zispin and Effexor, an empty packet of Zimovane. Rich could have helped himself to whatever he wanted. Rich had always helped himself to whatever he wanted.

Reaching further, her hand then pulled out a small blue box of Viagra. Viagra? This was amazing. He'd never admitted to having taken Viagra. He could never get much of an erection with her. Certainly not one that lasted long. Shaking her head, she added all these packets and containers to those already dumped on the bed. It took a couple of trips. What she needed now was a large bin bag and Nina. Nina was an expert at getting rid of sensitive waste, while never removing anything of note unless specifically directed. There were places in the house that she knew not to disturb. Rich had made sure of that. Nina would be in tomorrow.

This could wait until tomorrow, she decided. There would be no relapse. She was sleeping like a baby. She went back to the French window. There was no sign of a white sports car. But the black jeep was still there. She looked over her shoulder at her phone. Thought yet again about calling Frank. Thought some more about all three of her children, and her duty as their sole parent now. Took in the mound of unused sleeping pills and antidepressants, anxiolytics, and that poisonous packet of Viagra. Was that what he used when he fucked Jess and the rest of his younger women, who expected more staying power, more athleticism?

But that wasn't the case. She expected just as much. Her satisfaction was what mattered now. Though not if it came in the form of a pathetic, grey-haired old man. *We belong to each other.* No they didn't. She didn't belong to anyone now, except her children.

The pills were glinting at her on the bed. Come and get me, they were saying. There would be no relapse, even though she was nervous, scared. Who was watching her? But she had a gun. And her youngest son was in the house somewhere. He was a big, strong lad. They could protect each other.

Looking back at Marine Parade, the street lights glowing sickly as drizzle began to fall, she saw Nathan's car creep round the corner of Yallop Avenue. Saw the car slow further before it reached the big jeep. Saw the car swerve round the jeep, gathering pace. Nathan's car then accelerated, shooting past Tatty's driveway. She watched it until it disappeared at the top of Marine Parade.

She went for her phone now. Found the contact details. Typed a message. *Megan, sorry love, we'll have to meet tomorrow instead. Coffee first thing?* She wasn't going to bother with an excuse. She had an idea about who might be in the jeep, at least who had sent it – good old Frank. But she had less of an idea about Megan – why Megan had taken so long to get in touch, why Megan had suggested they meet at Galleons on a damp Monday night. Because

Megan had always had to make the calls, the suggestions? It was Tatty's terms now.

She opened her bedroom door, stepped onto the landing. The house seemed too quiet. 'Zach?' she said loudly. 'Pizza?'

29

Frank drove fast along Crab Lane, past the cemetery, heading for Yarmouth. The daylight had gone, yet home would have to wait. He glanced at his phone, urging Britt Hayes to call back. But the device lay where he'd thrown it onto the passenger seat, still and unlit.

The route to the North Beach Holiday Park was largely clear, and he was there within ten minutes. It was still spitting, and he felt like he'd had quite enough exercise for one day. Besides, he wasn't planning on hanging around for long. Which was why he drove straight into the main entrance and parked up by the reception lodge. There were no lights on inside, though Frank knew that Rolly Andrews kept a close eye on the CCTV from his caravan. But the CCTV only covered the entrance, this small patch of the park.

Frank got out, zipped up his jacket, went left when he should have gone the other way. The paths between the caravans and static homes were dimly lit, most of the light coming from the caravans themselves, leaking through flimsy blinds and curtains. Some TVs were playing, the sound drifting outside. Canned laughter, car chases, gunfire. The majority of holiday dwellings were in darkness however, deadly silent, their season having ended prematurely, as every summer season here did.

The further Frank got from the entrance, the greater the darkness and the thicker the drizzle. The most prized sites were near the front, with sea views. The ones to the far sides and rear were forgotten about at the best of times, the hottest of summers. Frank was aware of his shoes crunching on the soft gravel paths, aware too that no one was following him.

He made it to the caravan as the rain decided it had had enough of playing and wanted to get serious. He stepped lightly around the large caravan, twice, listening to the rain beating on the plastic roof, accompanied by the rain beating on the roofs nearby, before putting the key in the lock, gently twisting and pulling the small flimsy door open. He climbed up, and into the caravan, reaching out and shutting the door after him. He couldn't remember how many times he'd forgotten that caravan doors opened outwards, not inwards. But he'd remembered this time.

The caravan stank of damp, Formica, stale air freshener and sweat. There was condensation on the inside of the windows. Someone was in the bedroom, having left that door ajar. They were breathing heavily. Frank knew he wouldn't have time to open up the panel and get the gun. Not if they were here to harm him. Knew too that he wouldn't have time to open the door and get the hell out of there. If they were here to harm him. He didn't run away from trouble in any case.

'OK,' he said, shouldering the door and storming into the bedroom, 'what the fuck do you want?' Weak light was making it into the caravan from the lights hanging over the path outside. There was a large shape on the bed. They hadn't been breathing heavily. They had been snoring lightly. Rain thrummed on the roof. The shape sat up. Frank put on the light.

'Hello, Frankie Boy,' the shape said, groggily.

'Get your feet off my bed, will you?' The man still had on his boots. Redwings, light brown. Well worn.

'It's your bed, is it?' said Howie.

'It is now,' said Frank, taking in his friend. He was wearing a light Puffa jacket and a dark-coloured beanie. He looked like he was dressed for some outdoor, nocturnal adventure, like burglary. Not a snooze in a caravan. But it wasn't his caravan. 'What the fuck are you doing here?'

'Hey,' said Howie, getting up off the bed, and taking a step towards him, rocking the caravan. 'Good to see you.'

Frank put his arms around him – and there was a lot of him – gave him a manly pat on the shoulder. Howie reciprocated, hesitantly. 'Still,' said Frank, letting go of him, 'what are you doing here?'

'Have you got anything to drink?' Howie asked as they moved into the main room.

'Tea?' said Frank. 'That's all. And long-life milk, if you can bear it. I can't.'

'You sleeping here at the moment?' Howie said, tapping the small built-in table.

'I came to get something.'

'I had a feeling you'd turn up sooner rather than later. Thought I'd save myself a trip out to Bradwell.'

As if it was far, Frank thought. 'You been here long?'

'Not so long.'

'Back in Yarmouth?'

Howie shook his head. He hadn't removed his beanie. He rarely removed his beanie.

'Britt said you were away.'

'You know what she's like.'

'She knows what you're like too,' Frank said. 'Why did she tell you I was asking after you?'

'That's the thing,' said Howie. 'You sure you haven't got anything to drink?' He was opening cupboards, drawers.

'No,' said Frank.

'How did Rich entertain his guests?'

'I'm not sure drinking was at the top of his agenda.'

'Uh.' He closed a drawer with something of a bang. Focused on Frank. 'Big mess, what's going on. I'm sorry about Rich.'

'Thanks.'

'Britt thinks they're on to her, the brass.'

'Doesn't she always think that?'

'Those two murders, it seems her boss has been waiting for a chance to get stuck into Yarmouth.'

'You saying the authorities are finally taking notice of this town? They have the manpower?'

'He's a right young prick – wants to make his mark.'

'Don't they always?'

Howie sighed. 'I could do with a drink, Frank.'

'It's Monday night. The club's closed.'

'The casino?'

'I don't know who's running around out there, Howie. I thought I knew. I thought I knew everything.' Frank shook his head, his head feeling like a lead weight. If he went into the river, he'd sink head first, like a shot.

'Britt said to say, don't try to reach her. By any channel. That's why I'm here.'

'Back to being the go-between? If she sent you out, on her behalf, she must be worried.'

'You know how long it took her to get into that position. None of us want that to be jeopardised.'

'No,' said Frank. He turned, tried to look out of the closest window. Saw nothing but a slick of condensation against a faint black night. 'But she'll want to get out of there one day.'

'So I keep telling her,' said Howie. 'I'm transportable.'

'I thought you'd done enough running.'

'Depends what from.' Howie stepped over to the sink. Ran the tap. Splashed some water on his face. Shook the water dry, but still wiped his face on his sleeve. 'Do you need a hand with anything? You know I'm not good at sitting around twiddling my thumbs.'

'I've got Jack keeping an eye on Tatty, the family.'

'In that stupid Mercedes of his? Who'd put silver hubs on a thing like that?'

'That's why I asked him.' Frank moved to another window. Saw no further. 'Hey, you know anyone who drives a white Hummer?'

'A white Hummer?' Howie laughed. 'You've got to be kidding. A white Hummer, round here? No way.'

'Yep,' said Frank. 'Saw it down by the model yacht basin.'

'In Gorleston?'

'Yeah, next to three guys looking out to sea.'

'What's the world coming to? People running around getting ideas above their station?' Howie looked at Frank.

Was that a warning look? Frank looked away. Howie knew him better.

'Owen, how's he behaving?' Howie asked.

'Britt will be taking care of Owen. Did she not tell you?'

'She only tells me what she needs to. You know that.' He sniffed. 'Damp in here, isn't it?' He sniffed again. 'About time that prick was taken out of the picture.'

'Rich was stuck in his ways,' Frank said. 'Besides, he thought it would be nice for his son to have the odd sail on something other than a Broads cruiser.'

'Frank, what sort of a wanker was Rich? Putting his son's freedom at risk?'

'He didn't see it that way.' The rain was hitting the roof of the caravan harder. It was not so comforting being out of the rain tonight. Frank didn't know how Rolly Andrews stood it.

Howie laughed. 'They never do. Do you think someone's trying to move in?'

'Someone's always trying to move in.' Frank reached for the panel above the sink, felt for the loose corner. Gave it a thump. The panel flew open.

'This looks different. And the timing, Frank?'

'OK,' said Frank, pulling out the gun, wrapped in its crusty tea towel. 'There are two people I want to find. Kenny Shawcross, who's been blathering about a female cop being friends with yours truly.'

'You're kidding?' Howie said.

'No, I'm fucking not.'

'Where did he get that idea from?'

Frank shrugged, said, 'Had him in my hands this morning. Should have finished him off then, but I was with someone who needs acclimatising. And then there's an American, according to Kenny – trim, black guy, who's been wandering round town asking questions about Rich.'

'He shouldn't be difficult to find,' said Howie.

'Presuming he's not some figment of Kenny's raddled imagination. Oh, and I relieved a couple of Eastern European kids of this,' Frank said. He'd unwrapped the gun, and was holding it out for Howie to take a good gander.

'The Glock, hey.'

'Someone gave it to those kids, told them to go after me with it.'

'I heard. And when they fucked up, that same person slit their throats?'

'Maybe they were always going to get their throats slit. Britt doesn't know about Kenny, or the American, by the way. At least, I haven't told her. I was waiting for her to call back.'

'That's why I'm here,' said Howie, smiling. 'The go-between. Who first then?'

'Kenny, don't you think? The American might be more useful alive – for the time being.'

'Should he exist,' said Howie.

'Should he exist,' said Frank.

30

'Hi, love,' Tatty said, approaching Megan. She was sitting at a small table at the back of Bread & Bean. 'Sorry I'm late.' She was amazed she wasn't later. She'd slept through the alarm, only to be woken by Nina at the front door. Ringing to be let in. Zach should have told her about the keys. Surely he couldn't have been that forgetful. It was almost like he was trying to hide something. She couldn't fucking believe it. Anyone could let themselves in. At least Zach was at home now, guarding the fort – along with the man in the Mercedes jeep down the road.

'Oh, gosh, Tatty.' Megan struggled to rise from her seat gracefully.

Tatty wondered who was more nervous. They kissed each other, but there wasn't much of an embrace. Megan was as soft and round as Tatty was trim and angular. Tatty slumped into her own chair, exhaling as if she were somehow trying to deflate them both. Bread & Bean was always crammed. 'Well, here I am,' she said, smiling broadly.

'I would have come back straight away,' Megan said. 'If I could have got a flight.'

'I know you would. But there was no need. I'm OK, honestly. The kids have been a great comfort.'

'Poor them, to lose a father at such an age.'

'They're grown up,' said Tatty brightly. 'And they've got me.'

'So they have,' said Megan. 'It's – oh, I don't know – mine get a lot out of Steve, even though we've been separated for like ever.'

'Perhaps because of that,' said Tatty. 'Not sure how Rich would have handled fatherhood if we'd ever split.'

'He was always such a big, strong figure,' said Megan. 'He'd have pulled his weight. But you would never have separated, would you?'

'No, of course not.' Tatty doubted she'd ever be able to remember what she'd told Megan and what she hadn't. But she knew she'd never been that honest with her. She wasn't quite ready, she realised, to change things there. Megan was not family.

'Don't take this the wrong way,' Megan said, 'but you do look rather well.'

'I've been sleeping,' Tatty said. 'Amazingly.'

'Well, that's something.' Megan took a sip of her froth.

Tatty couldn't decide what she wanted to drink. She didn't have long. She looked at her watch.

'I can't believe Rich is dead,' Megan added softly. She wiped at her full lips with a napkin. 'And suicide.' She shook her blubbery face. 'I'm so sorry, Tatty.' She let go of the napkin and reached across the table and took hold of Tatty's hand. 'What a shock – for all of us.'

Megan's hand was hot but papery dry. Tatty didn't want to be touched by Megan this morning. She pulled her hand away and looked over towards the counter, the chalkboard above advertising the various types of coffee. It was a long list. Though whatever you asked for at Bread & Bean, you always got the same amount of coffee and froth.

She looked back at Megan. 'It's going to be bloody difficult accepting that, Megan. But you never know what pressure people can be under – I guess.'

'Were there work problems? I know Rich was always involved in so many schemes.'

Tatty couldn't quite discern Megan's tone here, or what schemes she might have been referring to. 'You know that was something I tried not to get involved in. I'm talking to Simon, of course, and I suppose the accountants and the lawyers will start doing whatever they have to do in such situations. Maybe something will be unearthed.'

'What do the police say?' said Megan, looking at her closely. 'His car was found in the river, wasn't it?'

'Oh, the police,' she huffed, knowing they'd been trying to get hold of her. Knowing she needed to call them. 'They're not the most sensitive souls. But they've got a job to do, haven't they?' Tatty's mouth felt as dry as Megan's hands. Her eyes flicked back to the counter. She signalled to the spotty young boy behind it. He was new here, but he looked familiar. He'd probably gone to school with Zach. Cliff Park. Until Zach had been excluded, and they'd had to send him to the private place up the road. But at least he'd got into uni from there.

'Did Rich leave a note?' Megan asked. 'Because, well . . .'

Tatty was shaking her head. 'No. No note. Look, Megan, Rich was never that good at writing. He was dyslexic. It embarrassed him. There's no way he'd have left a note.'

'The not knowing must be so devastating,' said Megan. 'I'm sorry. So what happens now? The funeral?'

'We're working on it.' They weren't, of course. Tatty needed to get the police off her back first. She would have to call.

'If there's anything I can do,' Megan said, 'I'm here for you.'

Bullshit, was the first word that came to Tatty's mind. But perhaps Megan could be useful. Was she any good at flower arranging? Cake making? There didn't seem to be anything corruptible about her. A straight friend might be necessary going forward. Hadn't Rich carved his path through Yarmouth by having the right connections? 'That's so good to know, Megan.'

'I was thinking,' said Megan, 'Rich's father committed suicide, didn't he? Sorry for mentioning it, but it might explain something.'

Tatty looked back to the counter. She was going to have something silly: a honey blossom mocha. She shouted as much to the spotty youth, without asking Megan whether she wanted anything. Tatty turned to face her friend. Some people, she supposed, went in for comfort eating. She'd always gone for comfort dieting. Megan, it seemed, was not going to elaborate further, however much Tatty looked at her. 'That was what some people thought, at the time,' Tatty eventually said. She'd had enough silence for a lifetime.

'Oh,' said Megan. 'So he didn't?'

'He was found in a beach hut with an empty bottle of vodka by his side. It was winter. Who's to say he didn't doze off and never woke up?'

'I see what you are saying.' Megan was nodding her head like a hungry dog.

'Or, I don't know, maybe he wasn't alone all night.'

'Someone, what, did something to him?'

Tatty was not going to go much further with this. Megan was an innocent, saw the best in people. 'It was a long time ago and he was a local figure, so obviously there was a lot of gossip. Same thing's already happening with Rich's death.'

'How awful,' Megan said. 'That must make things even worse.'

'We need to put the record straight. Remind people of all the good that Rich did. And how, I guess, it's not always possible to meet everyone's expectations, least of all your own. Rich set a pretty high bar for himself.'

'That couldn't have been easy to live with,' said Megan.

'You said it,' said Tatty. Fortunately her drink arrived then. Unfortunately it looked every bit as disgusting as it sounded. She glanced at her watch. She'd spent more than enough time here – for appearances' sake. She wasn't even going to take a sip.

'Poor Rich,' said Megan. 'Boys have it tougher, don't they? Always trying to outdo their fathers.'

Tatty leaned forward, lifting the heavy mug to her mouth, and took a sip of the hot, sweet, creamy liquid. Give her sleeping pills and antidepressants any day. 'I don't think girls have it any easier.' She winked at her friend. 'But you know what, we're so much more resilient, and resourceful. I'm out of here, Megan.' She rose from her spindly chair. 'I've got to get to work.'

'Work?' said Megan.

'Someone's got to look after Rich's interests – our interests now. Business in Yarmouth is fucking tough, I'll tell you that.'

'You've barely touched your drink,' Megan said, blushing.

'You can finish it, love.'

'I'm here for you, Tatty, please don't forget.'

'I won't.'

Tatty stepped out of Bread & Bean and onto the tight pavement at the beginning of the High Street. There was a sharp dampness in the air but the sun was trying to push through the low thin cloud. It was warmer than yesterday. A mobility scooter was trundling her way, on the pavement. The mobility scooter was not going to stop. She was not going to get out of the way. The man at the handlebars could not have been much older than her. 'Get off my pavement,' Tatty said.

His childish face tilted her way. He opened his mouth, but no sound came out as the scooter veered towards the road, its offside wheels dropping over the high kerb as it went. The scooter slowly capsized, with the man firmly trapped behind the controls. There was a soft landing. Too soft. But a bus zooming up behind had to put on its brakes, hard.

Tatty hurried across the road, heading for her car. She didn't look back.

31

Admiralty Steel took up quite some space, Tatty was thinking as she slowed along South Denes. The warehouse and works stretched over two blocks and went all the way back to the river.

Graham Sands was taking up too much space in her mind as well, she realised. How dare he try to frighten them. As for getting control of the Yare Hotel. As for Rich letting him get control of the Yare Hotel. Sands should have stuck to steel fabrication. His car was not in its usual space, otherwise she might have stopped short, paid him a visit.

She continued to her block, pulled across the empty road, and parked in front of Goodwin House. There were no other cars out the front. She reached over, grabbed her bag, climbed out of the car, nudged the door shut with her elbow, beeped the car locked, walked up to the entrance. Pushed the door. It didn't budge. She didn't have a key. Still.

She pressed the buzzer, leaned down to the intercom.

'Hi,' came Sian's thin, local voice. 'Goodwin House. How can I help?'

'It's Tatty,' Tatty said. 'Open the fucking door, will you?'

'Yes, Mrs Goodwin, sorry.'

'It's Tatty. I told you to call me Tatty.'

There was a buzzing sound and Tatty bustled through. She made straight for the stairs, taking them two at a time. Within seconds she was approaching Sian's desk. Sian was not alone. A tall young man was standing by her desk. He looked at Tatty and smiled. He had dyed fair hair, olive skin, and hazel eyes. He looked too immaculate in a tight grey suit. The fabric was shining cheaply, the trousers skinny, the lapels tiny. He was wearing black suede Chelsea boots. He was very pretty, and more than aware of the fact.

'This is Mark,' Sian said. 'He works here.'

Mark held out his hand. Tatty brushed it. 'So what do you do?'

'I prepare the reports and work on the presentations, mostly.'

'He's an intern,' Sian added, somewhat dismissively.

'Simon's promised me a job,' he said.

'What about Rich, what had he promised you?' Tatty asked.

'I work mostly for Simon, on the Prime Poker deal.' He was looking down at Sian's desk.

'Where is Simon?' Tatty asked.

'London,' said Sian. 'He should be in later.'

'Sian, get hold of Frank for me, will you. Tell him I need him here, as soon as.' She turned, heading for her office. But stopped short of the stairs. Swivelled round. 'And you, Mark, get some keys cut for me, will you. Or whatever's used to get in the front door here. I don't want to have to rely on you lot to let me in.' She looked at her watch, looked back at him. 'At eleven, Mark, I'd like you to bring me a coffee. Not some weak, sloppy thing, but a strong shot of espresso, with this much froth' – she held up her hand, pinched an inch – 'like so.' She dropped her hand. 'You can also bring the most recent casino presentation material. I'd like to see how it's shaping up. Oh, and Sian, can you schedule a meeting with Will Keene and Amit Sharma? As soon as possible, please.'

She then headed up the stairs to her floor, walking slowly along the airy second-floor corridor, catching her breath. Her hands were shaking. Daylight was flooding through the internal glass partitions, soaking into the drab, dark grey carpet tiles. The door to Simon's office was shut, and she paused before opening it and stepping inside. The room smelt of him, his cologne. She'd had enough of artificial blossoms for one day already.

She walked straight over to the long bank of windows and peered through the venetian blinds. Simon and Jess's house was taking up too much of the view, of course. While down to her right Admiralty Steel appeared to have crept too close to the edge of her property. The river glimmered darkly. Her brain churned. Some men came out of the back of the main Admiralty Steel building, climbed over the barrier and walked to the water's edge. They were in navy overalls – overalls she recognised. They lit up and stood there smoking by the capstans.

Her hands calm now, she took her phone out of her bag, keyed in the number DI Leonard had left for her, which was still at the front of her mind. Numbers were easy, she reckoned, when you concentrated. She was put straight through to him. He started talking, rapidly.

'What?' she said, after some moments. 'The coroner's releasing the body?'

'Yes,' he said, hoarse. 'Hope you're pleased.'

He didn't have to add that. Tatty felt something tingle on the back of her neck. 'And I'm not required to make a statement?'

'No, not at this stage.'

'Why? What's changed? Do you know any more?' she asked.

'Our department,' Leonard said, 'has done everything it can for the time being. We are under certain directions.'

'That's it?' Tatty said.

'I'm sure you'll be interested in the toxicology report when we have it. But for now, yes, that's it.'

The line went dead. 'Fuck you,' Tatty said, slipping her phone back into her bag. She was both livid and elated. No more police, for the time being, but no nearer the truth. Toxicology, as if that now held some answers. The real question was how those substances got into the body, whose choice, whose addiction. Where was Frank?

She looked out of the window again. The nearest ship was some way upriver, a big orange-and-white thing. The men were still there, slacking. Tatty knew there was a message she wanted to get across. Oh, there were going to be all sorts of messages to all sorts of people. Years ago, before it all went wrong at school, she'd thought about doing media studies. Maybe she'd see if there were any online courses she could take. It would be a completely different discipline now, she guessed. But still revolving around information, communication, no?

She left the window and Simon's office, which wasn't to be Simon's office for much longer if she had her way. Rather than head across the corridor to her office, she went back to the stairs, jogged all the way down to the ground floor, pushed through the fire door and out into the rear car park, her bag hooked in the crook of her arm. A cool breeze was coming off the river and the car park was in shade. The river was in shade. The whole town was in shade. But the air was fresh and she was on a high, seeing everything clearly.

However, as she walked across the empty space, the lack of Frank's car was making its presence felt. She looked down at the oily tarmac, the odd tyre mark. Frank had implied that it was no bad thing if people didn't know quite who she was, quite what she was yet. Maybe she was impatient. Who could blame her after all this time?

There were more important things to establish than how exactly Rich died. She looked up as she approached the barrier, her eyes battered by the breeze. A moment of weakness from Rich? Forget it. That would have made him almost human. She climbed over the barrier, realising how much easier it was wearing trousers. OK, they were fine linen, Isabel Marant, but still, they had way more give than her bloody suede skirt. Perhaps she'd have to rethink her work wardrobe.

Checking the belt of her mac was firmly knotted, she strode along the quayside, straight up to the men, who hadn't finished smoking, talking, slacking. 'Morning,' she said.

'Yeah?' one of the men replied.

He was the oldest, about seven foot tall, with a gut the size of a space hopper and long, straggly grey hair. The other two were much younger, lads. Close up she could see all their overalls were stained with black oily grime, as if they did some work some of the time, and not just threaten people.

'I saw you from my office,' Tatty said, glancing over to Goodwin House. She caught a whiff of rotten fish. It was not clear where it was coming from.

'Yeah?' the man said again.

'You work for Admiralty Steel? Graham Sands?'

'Yeah,' the man said yet again. But this reply was not a question.

'Does he pay you well?'

The two lads both shrugged, looked away. The older man smirked. 'What's it to you?'

'I wondered whether you might need some extra cash.'

The man looked down at his younger colleagues. It would have been impossible for him not to look down on everyone. 'You two, why don't you fuck off and let me handle this,' he said. He'd smoked too much in his impoverished life.

The lads both sloped away, saying nothing, taking their time to climb the quay barrier over into Admiralty Steel.

'Yeah?' the man repeated, a question this time. He was looking at Tatty with hazy eyes.

Tatty held out her hand. 'Tatiana Goodwin,' she said.

He looked at the hand as if he'd never seen such a thing. He wiped his own great, smudged paw on the front of his overalls before holding it out and shaking Tatty's hand. His grip was fierce. 'I know who you are,' he said.

'That's the thing,' she said, looking beyond him and downriver, the Yarmouth docks unfolding like a trip down a crooked memory lane. 'You might have known who my husband was. But you have no idea who I am.'

He looked at her with those hazy eyes, the muscles in his face trying to get purchase on some sort of expression. He hadn't a clue what she was telling him.

'Who are you?' Tatty asked, bored with his stupidity.

He coughed, or perhaps it was a grunt. Like an echo, a ship's horn sounded in the distance. 'Stuart,' he said.

'Why were you hanging around the front of my offices yesterday morning?'

He shook his head.

'The three of you.'

He shook his head again. 'I don't know what you mean.' He was looking over his shoulder now, back towards Admiralty Steel. The rear of the complex was over-exposed to the elements. The giant doors had been rolled open. No sparks were coming from inside, but more than a few camera lenses were perched on the roof corners, glinting.

'You know all right,' Tatty said. 'But let me make it easy for you. I'd like us to move forward in a mutually beneficial way.'

That thick look swept across his face once more. Tatty thought of the tide, the speed with which it ran along this part of the Yare. Faster than a horse could gallop, so the saying went, though she'd never quite believed that.

'Yeah?' he said.

'Whatever Sands is paying you, and your mates, to intimidate me and my staff, I'll double it. And you won't even have to get your hands dirty, not for me.'

'I don't know what you're talking about.'

'I'll put it another way then, but only once, so listen carefully. I want to know exactly what Sands is up to. Who he's doing business with. What territory he's trying to grab. Who else he's threatening. Got it?'

Stuart looked more perplexed than ever. 'I don't know anything.'

'But you will,' said Tatty. 'I'll give you a grand a week for your trouble. Divide it up with your crew how you want.'

The man's hazy eyes lit up at this. Tatty caught the unsettled sky in them.

'A grand a week?' he said. 'Well, for that I might be able to keep my eyes open, ask around.'

Tatty stepped back. She was eager for the comfort of her office and her fresh coffee; it had to be close to eleven. 'There are a couple of conditions. Sands obviously mustn't hear a word about this. Not a fucking word. Oh, and if you feed me any false information, you know where you're going to end up.' She jerked her head towards the river, the fat white gulls outrunning it at least.

32

Her phone started going while she was on the last flight of stairs, struggling for breath and a regular heartbeat. Fuck's sake. This wasn't going to be a job where you sat still for long. How had Rich managed to get so fat?

She had the phone out of her bag before she reached her office. It was Zach. She pressed the green icon with her thumb, put the phone to her ear, her bag still hanging in the crook of her arm, while opening her office door with her left hand. 'Darling, don't tell me you're up. Did Nina wake you with the Hoover?'

'Mum,' said Zach, 'I'm going to Norwich. I need some new trainers.'

'Why are you telling me?' Why the hell was he telling her this?

'I thought you'd like to know where I am.'

'I'm not sure that's been much of an issue for a number of years with you.'

'Look, I'm sorry I didn't tell you about the keys, Nina's keys, having disappeared from her house – OK? I should have done.'

'I'll say. So now you're trying to make up for it by telling me you're going to Norwich to buy some trainers?' She dumped her bag on her desk and walked round to sit in Rich's disgusting chair, putting her phone back to her ear as she did so.

'I'm sorry,' Zach was saying again, but his tone was full of defiance. He didn't sound too sorry.

'Well, I don't suppose there's much we can do about it,' Tatty added, feeling more conciliatory than she had first thing this morning. Feeling more confident and in control too. Zach was her youngest son. She had to set the example. 'Other than get Nina some new ones.'

Her eyes had drifted to Caesars Palace. She should have hit Simon harder. As for Jess, she'd like to break her fucking jaw. 'Hey, that's what you can do in Norwich,' she said, trying to slow her mind. 'Get some keys cut for Nina, will you? You have to go to that Banham place, on St Benedicts, and show some ID, something with our address on it.'

'Sure. But, Mum, shouldn't we change the locks?'

Power had to be about control, she was telling herself. About being considered, rational. 'I guess.' She sat back. Despite the foul fabric, it was quite a comfortable chair. No doubt it was well made, Rich never underspent on himself. Besides, the amount of weight the chair would have had to support, it needed to have been well made. She grimaced. 'Look, I'll talk to Frank about it,' she said.

'He's got all the answers, has he?' Zach said.

'He's helping to protect us,' she said.

'From who exactly?'

'Come on, Zach. I don't think I need to spell it out. You have a better idea of what went on here than I do, probably.'

'So where's the gun, Mum?'

'Not on the phone, Zach, for God's sake. Go to Norwich, have a nice day.'

'Have you noticed that black Mercedes jeep, parked up on Marine Parade? It's been there for days now, Mum.' His voiced had changed, the cockiness completely gone. 'What if it follows me?'

'That's something you don't have to worry about,' Tatty said.

'How do you know?'

'Trust me.'

She ended the call, reminding herself how young Zach was. She looked at her watch. Wondered where her coffee was. Looked at the time on her phone. Saw that her watch was running fast, by some minutes. It wasn't quite as superlative as the brand made out. She tapped the face, knowing she needed to call Ben and Sam, to tell them about their father's body being released. They would have to start planning the funeral. She couldn't think who the hell would come, and who wouldn't. Who'd be there for the right reasons. At least Megan could organise the fucking flowers, if Sam let her. Ben could perhaps start dealing with the probate.

A pain hit her side, low down. She wanted all her children back home now. It was lonely at the top. Hoped she might be able to persuade them to stay a bit longer this time – what did either of them have to occupy them in London, except work? And hopefully that would change soon.

However, she supposed she was pleased they weren't here now. It wasn't totally safe, that much she knew. Where the hell was Frank?

There was a light tap on the door and Tatty looked up expectantly, but it was only Mark with her coffee, in a mug. A mug! He placed it carefully on her desk, well away from the large blank monitor, and smiled sweetly. She was not smiling back.

'There's only a cafetière in the building,' he said. 'There's nothing to froth the milk up properly. I tried whisking it with a fork.'

'Don't worry about it.' She shook her head. 'I'll get a machine when we move offices.'

'We're moving offices?'

'Some of us will be moving,' she said. 'To the Smoke-house – my building round the corner?'

Mark nodded keenly, as if he knew exactly what she was talking about. Perhaps he'd seen some of the plans, those presentation details. She'd had a lot of administrative backup from Goodwin House, however much Rich had let her think she was in charge. He'd paid the fucking bills, but it was all hers now. All of this. How quickly everything had changed. She made a point of looking at her watch, at the time moving faster than it should, as Mark continued to stand in front of her desk, his pretty-boy looks making it difficult for her to tell him to fuck off.

'It's a beautiful building,' she said instead. 'Solid, historic. There are some great views from the top floor, too, out over the beach and the sea.'

'I'm still assembling the casino presentation material for you,' Mark said.

'Oh, yes,' she said. 'I was wondering where that was.'

'It seems Simon has some of it with him – and I don't have access to all the files. But I'll bring you what there is shortly.' He stepped back, stopped, added, 'Sian told me to say that she has a key card for you. She'll run through how the alarm works, when you have a moment.'

Sian could have told her this, Tatty thought, doubting whether the tiny PA had yet managed to organise a meeting with the company accountant and lawyer, probate aside. If she had, she would no doubt have got Mark to relay the message. Tatty could already see that asking this lot to do things for her was not going to save time and energy. But that wasn't why she'd asked them.

Mark finally shot out of the room in his fancy boots and almost immediately Frank wandered in.

'You could have knocked,' Tatty said.

'The door was already open,' Frank said.

'So?' said Tatty.

'Mark was leaving. Didn't seem necessary.'

'Knock in future, OK?'

'Right-oh.'

'You could wipe your fucking feet as well. Where the hell have you come from?' Frank's fine black leather shoes were covered in light grey mud.

'Had a bit of business to attend to, out by Breydon Water.' He was smiling. His eyes were open wide, the whites clear and bright.

'Fresh air suits you,' Tatty said.

'The geese are arriving. Beautiful formations they make.'

'Didn't take you for a twitcher.'

'Gardening's my thing. But you can't help but notice nature round here.'

'When you get out and about, I guess,' said Tatty. She looked down at her desk, at no sign of any paperwork on the hard surface, at the monitor to the side, at the mug of untouched coffee. 'Takes some doing though, doesn't it?'

Frank smiled.

'Are you getting out enough, Frank?'

'With the weather the way it's been?'

'You know what I mean.'

'Perhaps we should go for a drive, Tatty. Have a chat in the car.'

'Sure, but Mark's about to pop across with some plans I want to have a look at, for the super casino, and Sian wants to show me how the alarm works, once she's managed to set up a meeting or two. You need to keep an eye on things here, don't you?'

'You tell me. Not my patch.'

'I reckon you've got quite a talent for office work, Frank. You know your stuff.'

'You want me to wait downstairs?'

Tatty looked at her watch. It was getting quite a habit. 'Stop me if I say the wrong thing, but Graham Sands seems to be expanding his business like there's no tomorrow. Putting out some presence with it. How long has Admiralty Steel been next door?'

'Since before this was Goodwin House. Well, that's not quite true. It used to be Anglia Fabrication. Sands took it over ten years ago or so. He made his money initially through farm equipment – pretty legit, supposedly.'

'What was his problem with Rich?'

'They used to get along fine. When the steel market started to collapse and he looked to alternative ventures, some rivalry kicked in. He saw the light, I guess you could say. Fuck all in farming, even when they had those subsidies.'

'What's he have that Rich didn't? How come he got the Yare Hotel?'

'I used to drive Rich around, Tatty. I wasn't his business adviser.'

'Don't give me that shit.' Tatty took a sip of her coffee. It tasted no better than it looked. Plus it was barely warm. 'How far is he going to take it now, do you reckon?'

'He's proving more of a problem than I thought, that's for sure. But you should ask Simon. Those two have been seen around together.'

'You're kidding.'

'Nope.'

'Did Rich know this?'

'Yeah. I told him as much, more than once. Maybe he didn't realise quite what a problem Sands was becoming. To be honest, I'm not sure how much of a problem he is. Not on his own. He's too straight, if you ask me. But these sorts of people attract others – harder, more experienced.'

267

'Simon?'

Frank laughed, shook his head. 'That's not to say Simon's not troubling me more and more.'

'Do you know a guy who works over there, called Stuart?' Tatty asked. 'Looks like he crawled out of the deep.'

'Smokes a lot?'

'I asked him to keep an eye out for us.'

'Why the fuck would he do that?'

Tatty rubbed her thumb and forefinger together. Frank nodded. 'He doesn't look the loyal type,' she said. 'Maybe he'll pick something up.'

'Fast work. I'm impressed.'

'Well, thanks for keeping an eye on us at home. Zach's in quite a state.'

Frank tilted his great head forward, nodded slightly, but determinedly. He hadn't moved further into the room. Worried about getting mud on the carpet, Tatty hoped.

'Not everyone is so keen on Jack's vehicle,' Frank said.

'At least it's not white.'

'Say the word.' Frank was looking at her hard, his eyes still bright and clear. They were boring into her.

'I appreciate all this, Frank. Everything you are doing. But I guess I need to find my feet too.'

'A lot is going down.'

'Stuff I don't need to know about?' She winked at him, remembering the conversation in the car yesterday. How the boss didn't need to know everything. But she had been in the back seat too fucking long. Besides, she was a single parent, her responsibilities went a long way. She glanced at her watch yet again. 'Where the fuck is Mark with those plans?'

'The only person that boy rushes around for is Simon.'

'Simon's not here.'

'He's still in London? Keeping out of your way?'

'Keeping out of my way? Am I the only person he's avoiding?'

'We need to talk about Jess,' Frank said.

'The police,' Tatty said, standing and pushing the office chair back with her legs, 'are releasing Rich's body. Seems they're easing up on the investigation, for now.'

'What did I say?' Frank smiled broadly.

Tatty slapped the top of the computer monitor. 'This fucking computer – can't get anywhere with it.' She stepped round from the desk. Glanced at the shelves, the files, more order to them now.

'You want to get Zach to have a look at it? Might give him something to get his head around. Keep him off the streets for a while – no bad thing.'

Tatty couldn't fathom the look Frank was giving her. 'He's going to Norwich today,' she said, trying to laugh, 'to buy some new trainers.'

'I hope that's all he's buying.'

'What's that supposed to mean?'

'Kids his age.'

At that moment Mark, carrying a laptop and a fat, long roll of thick white paper under his arm, swung into the office. No attempt to knock this time either. 'Oops,' he said, narrowly avoiding Frank.

Tatty noticed the body language between them. A blind person would have noticed. 'Leave all that on my desk, can you?' Tatty said. 'Frank and I have to be somewhere.'

'Oh,' Mark said. 'The thing is, Simon's particular about the plans. He doesn't like them out of his office. I'd rather not leave them here. I'll bring them back, when you're ready, if that's OK.'

'Leave them on the desk, Mark,' Tatty said, nodding for Frank to go first. She stood by the door, waiting for Mark. Mark eventually placed the roll on her desk, and stepped towards the doorway. 'And the laptop,' Tatty said. 'It's the company's, I presume.'

'Yes, yes,' said Mark, 'but it's what I work on.'

'Put it on the desk, please,' Tatty said, 'or you won't have any work to be doing on it.'

Mark did as he was told and hurried from the office, his face flushing as he passed Frank, who was waiting out in the corridor. Mark rushed for the stairs and Tatty turned to Frank, shrugged her shoulders. She was feeling warm too.

'No, if that's what you're thinking,' Frank said.

'I wasn't thinking anything,' Tatty said. 'He's a good-looking boy, though.' They were heading for the stairs themselves now, while the sound of Mark's suede Chelsea boots slipped away. 'What's Simon see in him?'

In the stairwell, one flight down, Frank paused ahead of Tatty. 'What the fuck does Simon see in Jess, that's what I want to know.'

'What does Jess see in Simon?' Tatty said to Frank's back, as he began walking down the rest of the stairs.

'Money?' Frank said, not looking over his shoulder.

'There's more to it than that,' Tatty said, her mouth tightening.

'Yeah, you're right,' Frank said, pushing the bar on the back door and opening up the stairwell to a flood of cool daylight. 'It's never just about money. We need to watch Jess, closely.'

33

Late Tuesday morning and the main car parks were full. What the fuck was everyone doing? *Shopping, because there were no factories, few functioning businesses, no longer any office blocks of note in the city.* It was as if he could hear his father whispering in his ear.

Zach had driven round the inner ring road once. He was about to go round again, waiting at the Grape's Hill round-about for a green light. *Roundabouts with traffic lights, whose stupid fucking idea was that?* Zach could hear his father so loudly and clearly now that he glanced in the rear-view mirror, expecting to see him sitting in the back. But he would never have been sitting in the back of a Mini Cooper S with sport trim, because he wouldn't have fucking fitted, the fat cunt.

Zach realised he was sounding his horn, as if that would make the lights change quicker. Change something, the way he felt, anyway. Blow, he needed some blow, but had no idea where you bought toot in Norwich. He didn't think it could be too difficult to find. But he did have some idea that the dealers in Norwich had connections to the dealers in Yarmouth. Same shitty corner of the world. He was thinking of the distribution network, economy of scale, risk aversion, and all that. Bump and flat, white and brown, spread like fertiliser across the whole of East fucking Anglia. He could ask Frank, but he wouldn't. Not now.

Instead of sticking to the ring road, Zach found himself drifting across the lanes and taking a one-way road into the city centre. It was all vaguely familiar. He rarely came to Norwich – his parents disliked the place, despite the fact his mum had spent time here growing up.

A row of buildings was covered in scaffolding. People were negotiating the constricted pavements. More stalled traffic lay ahead. At least the place felt like a city. So what if shopping was now the primary function? What the fuck else was there? Bars and restaurants? Clubs? He needed some new trainers. He only hoped there were some decent options. *With all these fucking malls, Primarks, Poundlands?* His master's voice again. Spotting a parking space in the bay on his left, he felt that his luck might be about to turn, if it hadn't already. Hey, he was free, breathing fresh-ish air.

Stepping onto the pavement, fishing into his pocket for some change for the pay-and-display machine, looking up at the patchy sky, and some sort of ancient civic building, he thought about his freedom some more, Frank's connections, and the fact his father had never done any serious business in Norwich, that he knew of. Why the fuck not? Did his mother hate it that much? What the hell happened to her here? He'd never bothered to ask, not that she'd offered.

There was a half-decent club scene at least, on Prince of Wales Road – not that many of the clubs were to his taste, but still. Maybe, if he was given a bit of licence, he could shift some money, product and expertise here. Expansion, adapting to and moving with the times – yeah, that was what his mother expected, wasn't it? His family hadn't strayed far, had they? If anything they'd narrowed their focus. OK, Ben and Sam were in London, for the time being – square as bears. And he was meant to be off to Loughborough soon. But the ops were in Yarmouth. How fucking great was that?

'Zach.' The voice came from behind, as did the shove in the shoulder.

He turned, saw a figure in front of him, but with a sheet of bright white daylight behind, traffic and people shifting in the periphery of his vision, some dark pigeons occupying unlikely ledges, it took Zach some moments to focus on who it was. He opened his mouth but his voice wasn't there.

'Have you been avoiding me?' Owen said.

Zach shook his head. He realised he was still fishing in his pockets for change for the machine.

'You didn't finish the job. When I contract a crew, I expect them to see it through. You didn't sign up for a fucking booze cruise.'

He hadn't actually signed up for anything. His dad had organised it all. Not just when he had to be in Ibiza, but even the taxi to the port. Zach thought back to what Frank had said and hadn't said. Thought again of the distribution channels and connections – East fucking Anglia, with its own ports and quiet road and rail links, the endless backwaters. Bumpety bump. How also his father must have known the risk he was exposing his son to. Frank had spelled out enough. A wave of anger like he'd never felt before swelled through him. 'What the fuck are you doing in Norwich?' Zach asked, finding his voice.

'Getting my hair cut.' Owen smiled, removing his baseball cap. He patted his perfectly bald head, then replaced his hat. 'You think I'd use a barber in Yarmouth? The clowns in that town? They'd as likely cut your fucking throat.'

'Have you got any change?' Zach asked, finding he had only coppers.

Owen looked at him. Laughed. Shook his head.

'You do owe me some money,' Zach added.

'You're your father's son, aren't you? Better-looking, though. I should kick your fucking arse all the way down this fucking street, you cheeky sod.' He reached forward, grabbed a fold of Zach's cheek. Gave it a big fat pinch. 'I'll tell you what,' Owen said. 'Come down to the yard tomorrow and I'll give you what you're owed. Around teatime, the boat will be back by then. There's an evening tide. Oh, and sorry about your dad.'

Owen then winked, walked around Zach, and continued the way he'd been going, away from the ancient flint civic building and the city centre. He was wearing a pair of white-and-gold trainers with combat trousers, and Zach watched him walk off with some jaunt. Zach would have worn such a pair of trainers. Maybe they were just what he was looking for. For an older guy, Zach thought, Owen had a certain style, a certain amount of cred. Unlike Frank, whose dress sense made no sense at all, particularly his footwear.

Zach realised he still didn't have the change for the machine. Realised he didn't care whether he got a ticket or not. What was sixty fucking quid, or was it eighty? He didn't know. He'd never had to know. His dad took care of all that, or his dad's PA more like, the little girl with the big lips.

He kicked the pavement with his old Converse. Once red, they were now a disturbing shit colour. He looked up. He'd drawn level with the ancient building. It was made of flint. Flint bricks, end on. He didn't think he'd ever seen anything so fine and solid, and ancient. Walls like that would be impenetrable. Even now. He would like to have a home made of flint walls, he decided. With slots to fire arrows from. Or guns. Norwich Castle was sitting up on the near horizon, above the shops. But the castle had never seemed that serious to him. It was too castle-like. From a kid's story. Make-believe.

Across the wide pedestrian walkway and a short way down an alleyway was a men's boutique. The window display seemed to denote a store of some street awareness. Hip and urban without being too grimy. There were some cool Adidas in the window, on the feet of the cool blue mannequins, not even trying to be lifelike. The force reawakens, Zach thought, making a beeline for the entrance. The moment he stepped into the shop he wondered whether this had been where Owen had come from. Surely he didn't drive all the way to Norwich to have his head shaved and polished. He hadn't been carrying any designer shopping bags, but maybe his business here wasn't all garment-orientated.

The two guys chatting behind the counter, behind the gentle thud of some lazy drum and bass, were quietly tattooed and pierced. Did these fellas only sell clothes? Zach thought momentarily of Lukas and Dominy, who he supposed would now be in those metal fridges in the morgue where his father was. Though his father was being allowed out, to be buried. Or burnt, rather. You wouldn't want him polluting a landfill.

While the Lithuanians would probably be forgotten about, left in cold storage forever. Who the fuck had killed them? The latest news had nothing. Frank had revealed fuck-all. Zach thought Frank was meant to know about this shit, that he had his ear to the ground. He wondered whether he should tell Frank about Owen offering to pay him what he was owed. Sure Frank had told him not to go anywhere near Rare and Yare, or to contact Owen. But he bumped into Owen. Bumped! A sign. Owen didn't seem so annoyed with him. He was cool, even if he'd pinched his cheek fucking hard.

'Nice shoes in the window,' Zach said walking up to the glass-topped counter. Inside the counter, on the top ledge, were various bits of jewellery. Studs, rings, pendants, brooches, badges and pipes. Pipes! 'Look,' Zach said, trying to be quiet, but loud enough so he could be heard above the drum and bass, 'what I properly could do with is something that will give me a lift – you know what I mean?'

34

'An American,' Frank said, 'that's who we're looking for. Trim black guy. Early forties. Neat dresser. Tough talker. Seems to have been putting ideas into people's heads. Making all sorts of vile suggestions, and ludicrous promises. It's greatly disruptive in the current circumstances – which seems to be the whole fucking point.'

'The person Kenny Shawcross mentioned?' Tatty said.

Frank looked around, for show this time, Tatty was certain. He'd been checking the place out constantly since they'd walked in. It was still empty, except for a couple of half-asleep staff propping themselves up behind the bar. It smelled faintly of beer and salt-and-vinegar crisps, cheap cologne, and bad drains. It was not the smell of a glamorous casino. It was not a glamorous casino, but a no longer loved part of Rich's empire, like a stale affair. Tatty decided then and there that when the super casino opened this would be closed, turned into a luxury boutique hotel. It was a classy building. Regency, so Nathan had told her. In fact, it had been Nathan's idea to turn it into a hotel – not that she would ever give him the credit.

'Yeah,' Frank eventually said. 'Kenny wasn't lying, not about him. Look, I don't want him creeping up on you, or any of your kids.'

'Unlikely. I've been paying attention.'

'These people are clever, canny.'

'What people? Who is he?'

Frank shrugged. 'That's the thing.' He held his large hands up. 'We don't know. We don't know who the hell he's working for. What he's after. But he's making some noise.'

'He's an American,' Tatty said, smiling. 'Is he something to do with the Prime Poker people?'

'Why not be upfront, book a fucking meeting?'

'You just said it, Frank. We don't know who he's working for.' Tatty tried to look round the big, bald man. She couldn't see far through the nearest windows because of the heavy curtains falling across much of the glass, and the way the daylight must have been playing on the tint. But she knew that it was bright and dry out, that the front seemed busier than it had for days. So some holidaymakers were hanging on, mingling with the long-term unemployed, the newer immigrants, some legal, many not, the terminally deprived. An Indian summer it wasn't, though it was mild, and less moist and blowy than usual. Becoming settled, some people might have said.

'Yeah,' said Frank, sitting back. 'That's right.'

He was being slow on the uptake today, Tatty thought. He had heavy bags under his bulging eyes. He didn't look like he'd got a lot of sleep last night. 'Prime Poker is leading a consortium, isn't it?' she said.

Frank nodded.

'Maybe he's working for one of the members,' Tatty said, 'making sure their money will be safe and sound.' She wished she had some idea how safe and sound her own assets were. Sian still hadn't organised the meeting with Amit Sharma and Will Keene. Who was holding who up here?

'That's an idea,' said Frank, tiredly. 'I don't have details of the arrangement. Simon's bag now, I'm afraid. I'm not the businessman.'

Tatty smiled at him. 'Bullshit.'

He fixed her with a look. Tatty wasn't feeling too comfortable in his presence today. If he stood on the periphery, it was as much to stop people getting out as getting in. 'Simon – what does he know about this American sniffing around?'

Frank shook his head. Looked grim. 'He won't listen to me. A hundred grand, Tatty, to clear off, that's what—'

'Get over it.'

Frank exhaled. 'You need to speak to him, when he's back. See what he might know. I'll keep working on Jess.'

'The bitch.'

He nodded. 'Like I said, we need to watch her closely. Something doesn't stack up there.'

'Say that again.'

'I can't figure out whether she's working with Simon or against him. I'd like to get rid of them both.' Smiling slyly, Frank made a gun shape with his hand. Fired it.

Tatty sat back in the uncomfortable chair. It was both hard and soft, but in the wrong places. 'They both fucking deserve it,' she found herself saying.

'It's your call,' Frank said. 'Though if they are playing each other, let them do their own dirty work. But it'd be good to know if there's anyone behind this, pulling strings.' He leaned forward. His chair creaked worryingly.

'Because neither would be capable on their own?'

'What do you think?'

'Jess has always been a fucking mystery.'

'You're sitting on a lot, Tatty. Have a word with Simon, will you?'

'What makes you think he's still talking to me?' Her throat was dry. She looked around the large empty room, reeking of bad bets, missed opportunities. 'Who is talking to you? You said "we", a couple of times. "That's who *we're* looking for." Are you including me here, or someone else? You have quite a few friends who are happy to do what you tell them, even if it means sitting in a car for hours on end. Though, come to think of it, I'm not sure I do always remember to shut my blinds when I get undressed.' She smiled, trying to lighten the atmosphere, leaned forward, picked up her glass of champagne. Took a sip. But she wasn't in the mood for champagne today. Work required a clear head. This sort of work.

'I have a few friends,' he said, nodding. 'Even fewer I can trust. There's Jack, as you know. He's a good boy. You don't need to worry about him when you're getting undressed.' Frank screwed up his eyes like he was trying to see clear through her. 'We need to talk about Zach, Tatty.'

'That's one friend, then,' Tatty said. She didn't want to discuss Zach now. 'Who else?'

Frank smiled, his whole face lighting up. 'There's this other guy – look, you don't need to know his name. But he's the most capable guy I've ever come across. Protection, enforcement, you name it. Yeah, I'd trust him with my life, and yours, if it came to it. It would be hard to do what we do in this town without him, his connections. He's not greedy either. It's taken me a while to understand what motivates him.'

'I should meet him,' Tatty said.

'No, you shouldn't. This is a distance that benefits everyone. It has to stay that way.'

She leaned forward. 'He's that good, is he? That well connected?'

Frank nodded.

'Yet you and him are still not getting anywhere with this American?' Tatty pushed her champagne glass away. 'How does that work?' Frank was having pineapple juice.

'Give us time. We've put a message out – let's see if he bites.' Frank took a sip of his juice.

The juice had come out of a Britvic bottle, which was on the table in front of them, some pale brown sediment sticking to the bottom. Tatty had a feeling it was long past its sell-by date. Even the label looked weathered. *Britvic*. It was coming back to her now. The memory of someone shoving such a bottle inside her, without paying extra for the privilege. Shortly after she met Rich.

Tatty flinched. 'What happens when he does bite?' she said. 'You just use your heads?'

Frank smiled. 'Oh look, here comes my dins.' A club sandwich was slowly placed on the table in front of Frank by an ancient-looking man in a dusty black suit.

Where the hell had he climbed out of, Tatty couldn't help wondering. No time or place that she'd ever known.

'I'm starving. Shouldn't be eating the crisps, but what the hell,' Frank said, his eyes bulging, along with his stomach.

'How long's he been working here?' Tatty said as the man shuffled away, holding out the tray for balance, like a tightrope walker.

'George? George has been here forever. Rich was very fond of George. He's the only one who bothers to bring you a drink. All the others expect you to go to the bar. Fuck knows how old he is. He's not really called George.' Frank took a bite of his sandwich. Grease and some ketchup dripped onto his hands as he did so. He put the sandwich back on the plate, reached for the napkin, wiped his mouth, his hands. 'Fucking thing.' He had another go with the napkin. 'He's been asking questions about Rich, the business, the backend.'

'George?'

'The American.'

She'd always supposed it was difficult to have a dry sense of humour around here. 'Such as?'

'What territory Rich owned, what positions,' Frank continued, still with some food in his mouth. 'He was after the fine details, the trade secrets. Even names of those out on the streets, everything.'

Tatty shrugged. The food seemed to have instantly enlivened Frank. She'd ordered a prawn sandwich, but it hadn't appeared yet. The hot food coming first? She wasn't going to chase George for it.

'Also stuff like where Rich went out to eat, where he drank. Where he played golf. Who he fucked – sorry.'

'Nosy sod.'

'He's been asking about you, the kids, as well. So Kenny said. What you lot get up to. Deeply troubling.'

'He's not armed?'

'Didn't need to be, according to Kenny.'

'What's that mean?' Tatty's heart sank. George was shuffling back along the sticky, dark, swirly carpet, with another tray, loaded this time with a small white plate, propped up on which were four small triangles of sandwich in fawn-coloured bread. With some awkwardness George, or whoever he was, managed to remove the plate of food from the tray and place it on the table between them. The table was getting quite crowded now. He then handed Tatty a napkin, white cloth at least. Tatty studied her sandwiches. They were oozing Marie Rose sauce.

'He'd been trained. Fully professional.'

'Meaning?' Tatty still had plenty to learn.

'There're some new players in town. Feels like they're closing in fast. It's not only this guy, but those Lithuanians who were taken out. They were well equipped. I don't like coincidences.'

'How come they were taken out if they were so well equipped?' She wasn't stupid.

'You can be well equipped, but if you don't know what you're doing even a shiny new Glock's fucking useless. Besides, they'd been relieved of their weapon hours before they were killed.'

'Care to elaborate?'

'They were not our guys. Real amateurs – not the sort we normally bother with. They have a limited shelf-life as it is.' Frank went for his club sandwich again. Took a monstrous bite. More fat spurted out. Tatty watched him chew, felt her stomach sink further. Found she was looking at a bit of prawn falling out of a triangle of the faint brown bread, along with some pale pink sauce. Rich had liked prawns, tiger prawns especially, but he'd preferred bacon, pork.

Frank grabbed his napkin, mopped his mouth while still chewing. There was a smear of grease above his eyebrow. It was catching what daylight was filtering into the room and Tatty wanted him to wipe his brow now too. He didn't. 'So who killed the Lithuanians?' she asked. 'Did Kenny have any idea about that?'

'We didn't talk about the Lithuanians.'

'Did Kenny mention your copper friend again?' Tatty decided it was her turn to fix Frank with a look, stare right through him. 'The person he mistook me for?'

Frank exhaled. His lungs could hold a lot of stale air. 'Are you not having your sandwich?'

'I shouldn't have ordered prawns here. I don't want to think about how long they might have been lying around. Do you want it?'

'Don't mind if I do,' Frank said, reaching for her plate. He popped one of the triangles into his mouth, whole. Clamped down on it.

'Kenny?' she prompted. 'The person he mistook me for?'

Frank motioned to his mouth, indicating he couldn't talk. Or wouldn't, about that.

'So where does this leave us?' Tatty said. Her phone was going. It was not on silent, but it was in her bag, down by her feet, muffled. Tatty could see she was going to have to provide the questions and the answers, given that Frank's mouth was still full. 'I have to talk to Simon. You need to work on Jess.' She looked at Frank, looked away – his eating was a car crash. 'And maybe lean harder on your mate with those connections.' She exhaled, briefly; her lungs were not massive. 'Who knows, perhaps Stuart might come up with something,' she continued, ignoring her phone. 'I'm paying the creep enough. By the way, the back of Admiralty Steel is covered in CCTV cameras. You think they might have picked anything up?'

Her phone had stopped ringing, Frank had popped another triangle into his fat gob. He wasn't going to be joining in the conversation anytime soon. She retrieved her phone from her bag, checked the screen before it died. Nathan, being twelve. Dropped it back. She made a whistling sound again, feeling a slight twinge, not in her empty stomach, but lower down. Be strong, Tatty, she said to herself.

'I need to have a word with Nina, too,' she said. 'Did you hear, Frank, that she thinks she was broken into? Her keys, from the houses she cleans, were stolen. Ours included.' Frank nodded, as if he knew. Had Zach said anything to him?

'Jack'll be out there on Marine Parade for the time being,' Frank said, swallowing. 'He's not as old as some of those other fuckers parked up, looking out to sea. I don't think we need to worry too much about this. If anyone wanted to get in, get at you, keys are not going to be first and foremost on their mind. They'd be more adept. Those that mean business.' Another triangle disappeared.

'Such as the American?'

'More dots need to be joined, Tatty.'

'Shit.' She looked down at the table between her and Frank, the empty plates, the dirty napkins, the Britvic bottle. Three men had walked into the room. Were heading for the table in the corner, where they'd been sitting the last time she was here.

'You know them?' Frank said, food still in his mouth.

Tatty felt something hit her on the cheek. A fleck of sandwich? She flicked it away. 'Yeah, I think so,' she said, glancing up. The men were settling themselves into their seats, taking their time over it, peering their way while they were at it. 'They were here the other day. And from a long time ago, too.' She had a sense of shit flying at her from every angle in the room. She wanted to bury her head, hide under the tiny table.

'I saw them yesterday,' said Frank. 'Down by the basin in Gorleston, taking the air. Recently back from a few years away, wouldn't you say? Enjoying the fresh air, the space?' He was leaning forward, trying to look out of the window. He soon gave up.

'Twenty plus years?' said Tatty. 'No one goes to prison for that long, not even for murder. How long did you get?'

'That was different, Tatty. I was a juvenile.'

Rich should never have told her. But she was pleased she knew now. 'I think we should go.' She got hold of her bag, stood, feeling her trousers come unstuck from the backs of her knees and fall into place. She wished she'd bought the matching jacket. She'd always fancied a proper trouser suit. She'd get one for the funeral. Pinstripe.

Reaching the exit, having not looked back, but feeling some piercing looks striking her from top to toe, ripping through her clothes, her underwear, feeling also that Frank was beside her, she paused, turned his way. 'I haven't paid.'

'I left some notes on the table,' Frank said. 'I ate more than you.'

'As long as you left enough for a tip for George.'

'George does OK,' said Frank.

They went through the grand double doors, emerging into bright, warm, moist air, and the sound of gulls and the sea, and a long blast from a ship's horn. Tatty had driven this time, Frank having said his car was in need of a clean and he didn't want her to get mud on her mac. Her Merc was a short distance away, in the bay reserved for the casino's VIPs. As if. Jammed next to it was a white Hummer, the size of a fucking tank.

'Jesus wept,' she said.

'That fucking thing again,' Frank said.

'You think I can get in? I'm not climbing through from your side,' she said, turning back to look at Frank, the hazy grey-blue sky merging eventually into the sea at the top third of the frame. For a second she thought she was watching a film, that she was in a film. One of those thrillers where everything is beautiful to begin with – lovely house, large happy family, shaggy dog, endless sun, lazy days – which then gets more and more frantic and bloody, until everyone's dead. Same old nightmares.

'No, you're not.' He turned, began walking back towards the entrance of the casino.

'Wait,' Tatty said, eyeing the gap between the two vehicles. 'I'm not that fat.'

'That's not the point,' Frank said.

'I think it is,' she said. 'I know them. Another time.'

35

'What are you on?'

'Hey,' Zach said, trying not to sniff. 'Fucking great to see you.' He stepped forward, got hold of Clara's skinny shoulders, pulled her to him. She was not being as obliging as usual. 'What are you doing at home?'

'The Star's shut.'

'What do you mean shut?'

'It's shut down. Do you want to come in then?'

'Your mum's not here?'

'No, I told you.'

Zach thought it had to be nearly four in the afternoon. He hadn't checked the time on his phone since he left Norwich, since he'd texted Clara. The time in his car was never right, despite the thing being practically brand new. Even he didn't know how the on-board system functioned. He glanced over his shoulder, saw his Mini parked two houses down on Mariner's Compass, its stupid stripes sticking out a mile. He should get a proper car, something bigger, tougher, with off-road capability. He didn't need a Porsche Cayenne. Or an Audi A8. A Range Rover would do, a Sport. He turned back, unable to remember when he'd last been in Clara's house. It smelled strange, like no one had opened a window for days. It should have smelled of cleaning products, as his house did after Nina had been. 'Where is she?' he asked. 'Your mum.'

'You won't fucking believe it, but Mum's got a bloke. And he's got dogs. They go walking, Caister way.'

'She said she wasn't in at the weekend, when the keys went. She even blushed.' Zach whistled. 'So that was it, she'd been strolling with her fella. Nice.' He reached for Clara again, her waist this time, managing to drop his hand over her arse. She was in a black T-shirt and black leggings. He wanted her to get those leggings off, quick.

'Do you want a drink or anything?' She was still trying to step away from him.

He let go of her. 'What's up?'

'Nothing.' Her voice suggested the complete opposite. She walked towards the door at the end of the short dim hallway, pushed through it.

Zach shut the front door behind him and followed her. The kitchen was tiny, with one window above the sink, looking out onto the concrete yard. A washing rotary was set up in the yard with a lot of white things hanging from it. 'What do you reckon happened to the keys then?'

'How do I know? I was out,' Clara said. 'What are you looking at?'

Zach realised the white things were undergarments, not small flags of surrender, some film coming to mind. Nina's knickers and bras, he reckoned, because he'd never seen Clara in any underwear that was white. 'Fucking weather,' he shrugged. 'What's in the fridge then?' He moved towards it.

Clara got there first and opened the door. It was about a quarter of the size of his fridge back home. He looked over her shoulder, at the few things on the few shelves. No wonder Clara was so trim. How the other half lived.

'There's some Coke,' she said, reaching for a can. She straightened, handing it to him.

It was Diet Coke. He hated Diet Coke, but he was incredibly thirsty. He cracked it open, took a long sip. Wiped his mouth. 'Better, man, cheers.' He put the can down on the counter by the sink, felt in his pocket for the wrap. Squeezed it, feeling how thick and lumpy it was. He'd barely touched it. It wasn't bad, for the price. 'What the fuck are you looking at?'

Clara was smiling at last, looking down at his feet.

'New trainers?' she said.

He shrugged again. 'Yeah, suppose.' Suddenly he was conscious of how white they were, with the brightest of gold markings. Whiter than Nina's smalls out on the rotary. *Smalls?* Whose fucking word was that? Not his dad's. His mum's, perhaps, once upon a time. He wished he hadn't seen the washing out in the yard, the cheap wooden fence too close to the kitchen window. Everything here was so cramped. He felt trapped. A half-life, he thought, laughing to himself. 'Look, I've got some stuff. Do you want a line?'

'Now? For fuck's sake, Zach. I know your dad's just died, but it's the middle of the afternoon.'

'So? Have you got to work later or something?'

'I told you, the Star's shut. Shut down, for good. It's gone bust or something.'

'Oh right, yeah, sorry. Didn't hear you properly.'

'Do you ever?'

'We're not fucking married.' She looked great in her leggings, but he was fast going off the idea of helping her out of them. He picked up the Coke can, drained it. 'So like the hotel's shut? What, they make you redundant?'

'Who knows what's happening. We were told to go home.'

'Fucking hell.'

She shook her head, her shoulder-length brunette hair looking like it had recently been washed and conditioned. It was picking up what daylight was managing to get into the kitchen.

'What happened to the guests?'

'There were a couple of big coach parties that left on Sunday. Not sure if anyone else was booked in or they had to leave. Relocated, maybe. There are enough half-empty hotels in Yarmouth. I don't know. I wasn't working yesterday.'

'Got to admire the balls.' He thought she might be tearing up, knew he'd said the wrong thing. 'Hey, look, have some toot. It'll make you feel better.'

She shook her head. 'I'm not in the mood, Zach.' She looked away from him, out of the window, to what view there was.

'Why did you say I could come round then?'

'I don't know. You rang me. Haven't seen you for weeks. Felt bad with what happened to your dad, too.'

Zach got out the bump. 'And you're the one who needs a fucking lift.' He moved over to the far corner of the counter, furthest away from the sink and any water that

293

might have been lying around. He began to unfold the wrap.

'Zach, do you have to? What if Mum comes back?'

'You said she was out.'

'Still.'

'What's wrong with you?' He was tipping some of the coke straight onto the work surface, which was also white. But the coke was slightly yellower, the crystals reflecting the daylight. He could see it well enough. 'Bad summer?'

'Did you see the news about those two guys who were found murdered? Some drug feud, the police are saying.'

'Yeah,' he said. 'So what?' He had his bank card out now, and was working up two fat lines.

'Round here? It's not fucking London.'

'I guess.'

'Where did you get this gear from?'

'Not from here, if that's what you're thinking.'

'No,' she said. 'Course fucking not.'

He stood back, thinking of Owen, whether he might have had something to do with it. How full of himself he'd seemed out on the street in Norwich, getting his head shaved, prancing about in new shoes. More territory for him? But what of Frank's involvement? His dad's? Not in the murders – he could tell Frank had nothing to do with that, was shocked himself – but the whole drug business round here? Who'd controlled Dominy and Lukas?

Zach fished out a note, rolled it up, held the note to her. She didn't come any closer, so he turned back to the counter and took a line. Sniffed it up good and hard. He was in two minds about going by Owen's yard tomorrow to collect his money. Perhaps he could pick up something else. Oh yeah. He turned back to Clara, holding the note for her. 'Sure?' Reputations were at stake, he felt.

'Oh, fuck it,' she said, taking the note from him and snorting the other line, and having a good sniff too after. 'Did you know them?' she said, still clearing her nose.

'Who?'

'Those two who got murdered?'

'Course not.'

'You must have known of them.'

'Clara, give it a break. It's not as if you didn't snort that line like a fucking hoover.' He sniffed too, feeling more burn. 'What do you want to do now?'

She was at the fridge, getting herself a can of Diet Coke. Popping it, taking a long sip. Not offering him any.

'Should we go upstairs?'

'This is a bungalow, you fucking idiot.' She was laughing now though. She stepped over to him. Kissed him lightly on the mouth. Pulled back. 'This stuff's OK. So where does it come from?'

He held his hands up. 'Norwich, if you must fucking know.'

'Where you got your trainers?'

'Yeah.' He was feeling so much better about being here. He didn't care he was in a bungalow that smelt of dog he now realised, with a tiny back yard where Nina's big smalls were busy going nowhere. 'Where did the keys go then?'

'Mum's keys, to where she cleans?'

'Yeah, Clara, those keys, including ours. Who the fuck took them?' But the creeping paranoia was still lurking. Zach felt his bowels shift.

Clara was looking down. 'My room then?' She moved towards the cramped hallway.

'Your mum's new boyfriend, what's he like?' Zach followed her, trying to keep the conversation on track in his mind, the bits that didn't add up.

'It wasn't him, if that's what you're thinking. He's practically crippled. Worked on a supply vessel, until he was injured.'

'I thought all he does is walk his dogs. How's he manage that?'

'Don't ask me. Mum likes him though.' She was talking awfully fast.

Zach had forgotten what had happened to her father, if he'd ever known. He wasn't going to ask now, he wasn't that rude. They'd reached her room already. But Clara stopped by the doorway. Was she going to let him in or not? He thought he needed the toilet first anyway.

'You've been away like all summer,' she said, reaching forward and touching his arm.

'What's that supposed to mean?' he said, clenching.

'It's not like the world stops when you're not around.' She laughed, not kindly.

He'd seen that look in her dark, sly eyes before. Her mum might have been as honest as anything, but Clara probably had more of her father in her – whoever he was. How could he fucking trust her, the slag? 'I get it,' he said, wanting to hurt her – explosions going off in his head, like there was a packet of sparklers in there or something – but needing the toilet more. His muscles weren't up to much right now. Besides, it wasn't like he owned Clara, he thought, turning, making for the toilet. He wasn't a kid.

No voice came from his dad, but one did from Frank: *Calm down, Zach*.

'You OK?' Clara was saying, out in the hall.

'Who the fuck is he?' Zach shouted from the tiny cubicle, through the cheap door.

'You want to know something?' Clara said. 'I took the keys – Mum's keys. She's not getting them back. Neither are you. So what do you fucking think about that, Zachy?'

Her voice was growing quieter as she was walking away. But Zach knew she wouldn't be able to go far in the house, the bungalow. He was smiling, not quite laughing.

'You can't have everything you want, wanker.'

He stopped smiling, looked around for the toilet paper. Couldn't see any.

36

'I don't know,' said Tatty. 'Oak, I guess. Look, darling, can we talk about this later?'

'You rang me, Mum,' Sam said.

Tatty peered through the windscreen, thought she saw movement. 'There's so much to think about. I can't keep track.'

'Of course you can't, Mum. I'm coming home, tomorrow. Soon as I've cleared some shit out of the way here. They'll let me have the time off. They'd better.'

'Are you sure?' Tatty said, too enthusiastically. Would it be safe for Sam here? But there was Jack in his jeep, Frank with his mysterious other friend, the one with the great connections who he'd trust his life with. And she had a gun, after all. It was with her right now. 'That would be wonderful,' she added. Then thought some more. 'Can you come down with Ben?'

'Maybe. I'll ring him.'

'Should I?' Tatty said, leaning forward for a better view, her eyes and her mind elsewhere. 'I need to speak to him. It's . . . ' She didn't know what else to say, and didn't finish the sentence.

'It's OK, I'll ring him,' Sam said. 'You sound busy.'

'He listens to you,' Tatty said. That's what she'd meant to say.

'Mum,' said Sam, 'he listens to you too. He's a bit preoccupied with this girl Avani, that's all.'

'And he's never liked to talk to me about his girlfriends,' Tatty said. 'We know that.'

'He hasn't had a girlfriend for like ever, Mum.'

'I know, which is why I don't want to get in the way.'

'But we've got Dad's funeral to plan, haven't we? Isn't that a priority?'

'Yes, darling, of course.' Though Tatty was already thinking of other priorities. Someone was home. Upstairs. She wouldn't have been able to see what was going on on the ground floor in any case, because of the sheet metal wall rising to head height from the pavement. But then she remembered that the house was the wrong way round. The guest bedrooms and gym were on the ground floor, and the sitting room, kitchen and dining space were on the first floor, with the master bedroom and en-suite on the top floor, with its own wraparound balcony. The late afternoon sun had disappeared once more and a thin low cloud seemed to be descending fast, the metal wall throwing a cold hard stare back at her. She was not about to be intimidated.

'Don't make any decisions until we're there with you, OK?' Sam said, reminding Tatty that she was still holding her phone to her ear. 'I know Dad liked oak, but what about something more environmentally friendly? They make coffins out of recycled cardboard now, you know.'

Tatty laughed nervously. 'Sam! Your father would have fucking hated that.'

'Not sure he'd have liked being dead much. We all need to be part of this, Mum.'

'You are. Of course you are,' Tatty said, knowing she had to get off the phone, get out of the car. Knowing too that someone had killed Rich, and that whatever she might have come to think about her husband, she couldn't let that go unpunished. Revenge was a form of power. People needed to know exactly who was in charge, and how ruthless she could be. 'Tomorrow then, darling?'

'Definitely,' said Sam.

Tatty ended the call, slipped her phone into her bag, into the inside pocket of her beloved Birkin. Was she seeing things? The harder she looked, the more she realised that the stitching on the pocket was coming undone. Surely it wasn't a cheap copy. She picked at the loose stitching, and it began to unravel further. She let go of the thread and allowed her fingers to curl around the pistol that was lying at the bottom. She felt its weight, its solidity. Pulled her hand out of the bag, purposely didn't close and fasten it fully. She then loosely gathered the alligator-skin handles in her left hand, as if she couldn't quite grasp something that might be fake, while opening the car door with her other hand.

She had worried about leaving her car on the street, but didn't like the idea of finding it stuck behind a metal barrier if she needed to get away fast. Besides, she wasn't sure Simon would be too happy about opening the gate and letting her drive in. At least not until he'd heard what she had to say.

The pavement was narrow on this part of Ferry Hill, but empty of pedestrians and mobility scooters. She looked ahead, through the rapidly thickening air, seeing the old brick-and-flint wall that lined the sloping park that led down to Riverside Road. On the far side of the road was an old merchant's house with a fine round lookout protruding from the roof. She knew you'd be able to see not only across the river from up there, but across the thinning spit of Yarmouth, to where the Goodwin super casino would one day tower and gleam.

The place was currently run by some sort of charity, showing all the outward signs of an institutional lack of resource. It was yet another restoration project that would have suited Nathan to a T. She was still squinting at the building, and she wasn't mistaken about this either, there was an estate agent's sign attached to the low wall that enclosed the forecourt, which would once have been a carriageway, she reckoned. She knew that Zach, especially of her children, craved newness, the sharp angles and smart, hi-tech materials of the twenty-first century. She wasn't quite sure where she stood on that, but it was a grand building, with a commanding view.

At least, it could be a grand building, if a certain concrete box wasn't half in the way. Who did she know on the council, the planning department? Perhaps she wasn't quite done with Nathan – of course she wasn't. Perhaps she was more of a traditionalist, after all, or was that a conservationist with a healthy sex drive?

She drew level with the sleek metal gate and pressed the intercom that even in daylight was glowing an evil blue. Simon would know it was her, he could see her car.

'You've got a fucking nerve,' came his voice, loud but crackly, from the small square all-weather speaker grille. A car shot past Tatty's other ear.

'We need to talk, Simon, urgently.' She could hear him clearing his throat. There was a lot of crackling, not all of it electronic.

'You need to control your temper.'

'Me?' said Tatty. 'Are you kidding?' She glanced over her shoulder, feeling stupid talking to a metal wall. Saw, thankfully, that no one was sweeping up on her. Another car went past, this time going the other way.

'Now's not a good time,' Simon said.

'It's important,' Tatty said. Her bag was tugging her hand closer to the slimy-looking tarmac. It was all cheap tarmac pavements here, not even concrete slabs. Gone were the days when this street would have been cobbled, the pavements proper stone. She glanced over her shoulder once more, at the fine merchant's house. Yeah, she could live there, watch her business grow. She wasn't going to live in Yarmouth, across the River Yare – far too fucking dangerous. 'There's something you need to know.' She could feel herself smiling, vengefully, power-fully.

'Can't it wait until tomorrow?'

'You were meant to come into the office this afternoon. Sian said you were coming in when you got back from London. I waited specially.'

While she was waiting, Stuart with the straggly hair popped by. Amazing what a few quid could do. Said he had some CCTV footage she might like to see, from an evening last week when a certain Merc left the back of Goodwin House then drove up the wrong side of the barrier. There was more than one person in it. But it would cost her another grand if she wanted to get her hands on it. Amazing how fucking greedy the seedy could be. She told him if he didn't return with the footage within twenty-four hours, she'd gouge his fucking eyes out before he was flung in the drink. She'd be asking Graham Sands if he wanted to watch as well.

'Tomorrow, Tatty. Now's not a good time,' Simon said. 'We'll meet in the office, first thing if you like.'

'It's about Rich,' she added. 'New information.' She thought she heard some more cross, crackly mumbling, followed by a sharp, echoey snap, but Ferry Hill had got busy, as if Gorleston had a rush hour after all. She looked at her watch, not sure where the afternoon had gone, the days since Rich had died, the years, the decades, before then. She looked back at the gate to see that it was slowly drifting open.

The path to the front door appeared even slimier than the pavement outside the fortress. It seemed to be made of some sort of buffed, pebbled concrete. Tatty couldn't remember the last time she'd been here. But she couldn't have been paying much attention to the architecture, the finishes. She'd have been with Rich, who she knew definitely wouldn't have been paying much attention to his surroundings. Just how long had he been fucking Jess? It didn't matter. How long had Jess been fucking with him, with all of them? That's what mattered.

37

Simon was in the doorway by the time she reached it. He didn't look well. Aside from the reddish lump on the side of his face, erupting from his careful hairline, it looked as if quite some years had crept up on him overnight. 'What about Rich?' he said. 'What information?'

'Is Jess in?'

'No,' he said far too stridently, shaking his head.

For some reason, Tatty thought of a giraffe. A tall, thin, long-necked, small-headed animal. No, not a giraffe, an ostrich. 'Where is she?'

'Look, what's this about? Rich, you said.'

'Can I come in?' She was comforted by the weight of her bag. Realised too that Simon wasn't half as frightening as his elder brother had been. She couldn't see him murdering Rich, being the other occupant of the car. He'd slunk away fast enough when she'd thwacked him the other day.

'Tell me here,' Simon said. He had a smear of blood on the left sleeve of his shirt.

'What do you think Jess has been up to?' she said, staring at it.

'Apart from fucking your husband?' He suddenly tried

to hide his arm behind his body, noticing where her eyes were focusing.

'That never bothered you, did it?'

Simon pulled his small head on its long neck back too. He was looking uglier by the minute. What was he hiding now?

'All right, you better come in.' He turned and stepped to the side.

Tatty entered an oddly dim, faintly remembered reception area. Raw grey concrete lined the walls, making her think of Nathan. But despite Nathan's love of the colour, he was a restoration man, not much of a modernist – perfect for the two projects she now had in mind. She felt the weight of her bag, knowing she couldn't be weak, but having an idea too that real progression came through compromise as well as exploitation. Not wasting opportunities.

The thin, solid steel door closed firmly behind her. Tatty couldn't immediately see where the door handle was, how you opened the damn thing. 'Can I have a drink?' she asked, something catching in the back of her throat now.

Simon cleared his throat. The concrete did nothing to dampen the sound. 'We've got a problem,' he said.

'You think I don't know that?' She was watching his every move but still couldn't read him.

'Let's just say Jess and I had an agreement. At least, that's what I thought. You don't want to know the specifics, believe me.' He'd folded his arms in front of him and was hugging himself tightly. 'There are certain things in my life I'm not proud of. But we all have to move forward, don't we?'

Tatty could have said as much herself. She almost felt sorry for him.

'She played me, Tatty.'

'I thought I was coming here to tell you that,' Tatty said.

'So you know who she's been working with? There are others?' He said this too keenly.

Tatty was shaking her head. She needed to think clearly, stick with what she knew, what she suspected. 'Can I have that drink?' She lifted her left hand, her eyes catching hold of the gold watch face in the cool grey space. What was it with grey? Nathan, Simon, men of a certain age, and disposition, perhaps. There was never anything grey about Rich.

'You'll have to come upstairs,' said Simon, doing that thing with the back of his throat. It must have driven Jess nuts. 'There's been a complication. Follow me.'

There was a spiral staircase in a corner of the hallway, all steel. Tatty knew there was a lift as well, at the side of the building, by the service entrance. Simon led the way up the stairs, the soft soles of his designer trainers creaking and squeaking, with Tatty again feeling that things were moving faster than she could keep up with. At the top, on the first floor, the building opened out to a large living room, with both a dining area and a kitchen. The views were all one way, over the Yare and across vast tracts of industrial Yarmouth. Mist and the oncoming night were clogging the detail, however. The bank of windows must have faced due east. Everywhere that was anywhere around here faced east.

She turned back to the room. Simon was in the kitchen bit, going from the sink to the fridge. It wasn't as big as theirs, but it was sleek and steel-faced. Her eyes moved over to the sitting room, the massive L-shaped settee. 'She is here,' Tatty said, spotting Jess half on the wide cushions, half on the floor. She was dressed – in jeans and a blouse – but the blouse was missing some buttons, and some blood had come out of Jess's nose, while foam had settled around her mouth. 'Oh,' Tatty gasped. 'Is she dead? What the fuck happened?' Tatty stepped closer. Jess was dead all right. Her bright blue eyes were wide open, but taking in nothing. Even the space around her was deadly still.

'I said we had a problem,' Simon said, moving rapidly across the large room. He had something in his hand, something gleaming. It wasn't a glass. It was a small paring knife.

'Don't be an idiot,' Tatty said, her hand delving into her bag, her fingers managing to free the gun from its cloth cover. She pulled it out, dropping her bag onto the polished steel floor at the same time. The soft clatter seemed to distract Simon, and she had the gun pointed at him before he could get closer. She knew it was a Smith & Wesson, in a revolting matt black polymer. But she wasn't sure whether the safety catch was on, or how many bullets were actually inside it – she hadn't managed to get it open to check. She thought she was prepared to find out now though. Squeezing a trigger didn't require much practice, surely.

'That's Rich's, isn't it?' Simon finally said.

'What might have been Rich's is mine now, you know that.' Rich shouldn't have tried to keep it from her, hidden in the old Rolex box in his desk. He could have shown her how it worked, out on the North Beach dunes. Did he not want her to be able to defend herself? Who ever knew what was round the corner? Or was he worried about what she might actually do with it?

Simon let his arm drop to his side. The knife was resting against his black jeans. 'We had a fight.'

'And you killed her?'

'I didn't mean to kill her.' He cleared his throat in a way that was almost too painful to hear.

'What happened – her neck got in the way? Look at her – poor fucking swan.' Tatty knew she should feel more upset for her sister-in-law, but she couldn't.

'She wanted me dead,' Simon said. 'She went for me.'

Tatty moved closer to the body. It was the second dead body she'd seen in under a week. Two more than she'd seen over the last couple of decades. She hadn't realised quite how blue Jess's eyes were. They were neon. Or quite how slight she was. 'Why? How? Look at her. There's nothing to her.'

'She blamed me for Rich's death. She thought I was responsible. That I'd killed him somehow,' Simon garbled. 'She said she loved him, that they had plans. And that she was going to tell everyone what I'd done, what sort of a person I was.'

'Put that knife away,' Tatty said.

Simon looked down at the knife. 'I thought you'd want lemon. I was going to make you a gin and tonic.'

'For fuck's sake.' She was still holding the gun, though not exactly pointing it at him.

Simon stamped over to the kitchen area, threw the knife onto the nearest counter. It skidded along the surface, though stopping before the far edge. 'I didn't mean to kill her,' he said once more, turning back, and wiping his hands on his jeans.

'Why did she think you killed Rich, your own brother?'

'Because I wanted to control the business. All of it. And I was sick of her sleeping with him,' he huffed, as if that were obvious. 'But we had our arrangement. Why would I go back on that?'

Tatty was shaking her head; it was like listening to a guilty child dredging up excuses from the shallowest of streams. Except her children were never so pathetic, so stupid, even when they'd been particularly naughty. They'd always had more imagination too.

'You want to know the truth, she killed him,' he said. 'Not me.'

'That's what I thought,' said Tatty. 'But she was accusing you? I don't get it.'

'She was working herself up into a fine state. Practice, I'm telling you. You know what she wanted to be before she realised she had no talent? An actress. She couldn't even get onto one of those stupid reality TV shows – not for lack of trying, mind. She found fucking a lot easier.'

Simon was looking at Tatty in a way that he shouldn't have been. He knew about her past, for sure. 'You want to bet?' she said, with as much venom as she could muster. She'd spat at men before for less – and paid the price.

Simon held up his hands in surrender. 'For her, Tatty, for her.' He needed to clear his throat. Thankfully he didn't.

Tatty was prepared to let this go for now, but not forever. 'So what's happened to your line about Rich having taken his own life?' she said, not convinced by Simon, by anything she'd heard today. She glanced out of the massive windows, no longer sure quite how attractive the view was. For a split second her mind shifted to Ibiza, the view from the terrace, over the pool and towards the San Antonio hills.

'That's what I'd hoped. Can you believe that? But I was the one who wasn't paying enough attention,' Simon said, his voice growing steadier. 'The thing is, Rich wouldn't leave you for Jess. Nor would he leave me to get on with the business and take full control. Who knows what Jess's longer term plans were. Either way, Tatty, Jess thought she was losing out. She was greedy and impatient – like Rich, in a way. But she was obsessed with status too. Couldn't fucking stand it when she didn't get what she wanted, what she felt she deserved.'

'So she lashed out? First at Rich, then you? She must have had some bottle, some head on her.'

Rich was far less of a fool than Simon, wasn't he? Yet he hadn't seen it coming. None of them had. Not even Simon?

'She was used to getting her way, Tatty. She had expensive tastes. And . . . I don't know, perhaps there's more to it. Other people involved. People after our business. We'll see.'

Excuses? From the shallow stream, or the fast-flowing mouth of a river where the truth was always out of reach? Tatty looked at Jess's pathetic, crumpled body once more. She couldn't have been dead long. Knocked unconscious with an almighty blow to the head, then strangled? 'How did she kill Rich?'

'I don't know, I wasn't here. I was in Amsterdam.' This came out too fast and clear. 'But I found these in the bathroom.' Simon hurriedly reached into his jeans pocket. It was a tight fit and it took him a moment or two to pull his hand free, which he then held towards her.

Tatty immediately recognised the twisted, half-popped blister pack. Lorazepam, clear as day.

'Jess didn't always sleep well. Could be anxious as hell. But I didn't know she was taking these,' Simon said. 'I guess you know what they are?'

'This doesn't prove anything.'

'No,' said Simon, 'but it would be good to know exactly where Jess was last Wednesday night when I was on my way to Schiphol. In Rich's office, bouncing around on his lap? He liked his brandy. It would have been easy enough to slip in a pill or two. You think Jess wouldn't have been capable? She could have made him swallow anything.'

Tatty thought of previous conversations, with Simon, Frank and Sian, looked once more at Jess's body. She wished she could feel some pity for Jess, and Rich, but she didn't. If Simon really was out of town on Wednesday night, she didn't think it would be too hard to check. 'Why shouldn't I go to the police?'

Simon all but laughed. 'You're a Goodwin. We can work something out, you and me. There's too much money at stake. Think of your children, their inheritance. OK, maybe I should never have come back to this part of the world, got involved, but it's in my blood too. Rich and I were born down the road. We grew up here. I can help you, Tatty, you and your kids. We can make this thing work.

The Americans love me. I can pull the Prime Poker deal off. Give me that chance, at least.'

She looked at him, wanting a gin and tonic more than ever. Fuck that. Wanting her amitriptyline, her lorazepam. Who could have blamed her for shutting all this out? But not any more. Her eyes were wide open. Wider than Jess's. Bright and alive, and every bit as calculating. 'You want me to give you a chance?' Tatty had raised her gun again, she realised. It was pointing in the rough direction of Simon's trim chest. She wouldn't have missed, had it been Rich. There was always so much more of him.

'It's your business, Tatty,' Simon said. 'I'll accept that. Use me.'

She could have screamed: Finally! Instead, she said quietly, 'What are we going to do with Jess's body?'

'Frank?' said Simon.

'You need him now then?' Tatty said.

'We all misjudge people.'

38

Frank was not as quick as Howie. He was wearing the wrong shoes, and the wrong jacket. And now he could feel his phone vibrating in his chest pocket. But Howie was looking over his shoulder, clearly wondering why he wasn't right behind him. Frank raised a hand as if to indicate, I'm doing my best here. There was no way he was going to stop and answer his phone. He increased his pace, feeling his shoes sinking further into the soft sand with each step. Feeling, also, the far heavier weight in his other chest pocket swaying into his ribs.

The light was dimming almost as fast as they were running, though Frank was certain Howie was gaining on the man.

They'd found him in the car park, on the badly tended patch of sea-frontage scrub, the block beyond the pleasure beach. He'd been sitting in a light brown Lexus, waiting for Kenny. Except Kenny was under a metre and a half of thick, clayey mud on the edge of Breydon Water. Frank had made sure he'd relieved Kenny of his phone before he and Howie had buried him last night. But it had still taken the American some time to reply to the last message Kenny had ever sent. Frank was beginning to think he'd left town.

As it was, he'd been early, but parked facing the wrong way for an easy exit. A professional? Frank and Howie had got out of the Range Rover, which they'd used to block the saloon in, walked up, each of them covering the front doors. But Frank hadn't thought that the car could take off so suddenly, not having heard the engine idle. It was a fucking hybrid, and had shot forward, but it hadn't got any further than a clumpy dune just before the beach began. The long Lexus, with something of a wide turning circle and low clearance, had lost traction in the fine sand as it had accelerated. The athletically built driver must have thought he'd have no problem outrunning them on foot. He hadn't reckoned on Howie.

Frank was gasping, slowing, realising there was no way he was going to catch anyone. He was almost beyond firing range already. He wasn't a crack shot anyway, not with a pistol he hadn't handled before. All the same, he pulled the Glock from his jacket pocket, sick of it banging against his side, doubting anyone out on the beach in the evening gloom would be able to discern what he now had in his hand.

Howie wasn't armed. It didn't look like he needed to be. He'd already tripped the guy, fallen on him. Started landing punches. Frank broke into a jog once more, conscious of waves tumbling fiercely onto the shore, or maybe that was the sound of his heart thumping, Howie's knuckles hitting flesh and bone. His phone was ringing once more too.

'Hey,' Frank said, with what breath he had left, 'make sure he can still talk, will you?'

Howie looked over his shoulder, getting to his feet while leaving the man coughing into the sand. 'Oh, he'll talk,'

Howie said, taking the opportunity, now he was standing, to boot the fellow in the ribs, which had the effect of rolling him over so his bloody face came into full view.

Despite the blood and the lack of daylight, Frank could see it was a fine, strong face, the man's colouring gleaming against the greying sand. Frank worried for a moment, however, about him choking on his own blood, the damage that Howie might have done already. There was some more coughing and spluttering. But then came some words.

'You're picking on the wrong man,' he said in a choked American accent.

'That's what they always say,' Frank replied. Howie was standing back. It was Frank's business, after all. 'If you ask me, mate, you're picking on the wrong town.'

The man was shaking his head slowly, trying to sit up.

'What the fuck are you doing here?' Frank said, some anger coming back. The man's looks were so distracting.

'You ever been to Vegas?' The American was sitting up now, brushing sand off his jacket. It was a navy suit jacket, to go with his navy suit trousers, and black Oxfords.

Frank found he was admiring his shoes. Who wore shoes like that, for a run on the beach? His shirt seemed to be a pale blue, where there was no blood on it. Frank shook his head. 'No,' he said. Frank didn't think he'd like Vegas. It would be far too straight. Fat American men imposing themselves on super-skinny women. His mind flashed to Jess. Her sort of town.

'This deal Goodwin Enterprises is working on with Prime Poker,' the man said. 'He's cool?' He indicated Howie, who was looking away.

315

'Yes,' said Frank. 'He's cool.'

'People who put up that sort of money like to know what they're getting.' The man was trying to stand.

Frank held out his hand, helped him up. He felt light, sprightly. Had he been wearing more appropriate shoes, Frank reckoned Howie wouldn't have caught him. Or maybe he wanted to be caught. 'What are you saying?' Frank said.

'You think lawyers, accountants are capable of doing the sort of background checks that these people require? They like to know everything, and I mean everything.'

Frank looked inland, towards the block of dark vacant land that was to be the super casino, and further south, to the outer harbour, where one day cruise ships from across the North Sea would moor up. 'Fuck you talking about? These people would be as keen to get a bargain as anyone else,' Frank said. 'A few local difficulties, and prices could plummet. And I'm not just talking about supposedly contaminated land. Drug feuds, a couple of brutal stabbings – not the sort of town for a hundred mill investment. Know what I mean? But half that, for the same stake? A quarter?'

'I was meant to be meeting a local snitch called Kenny Shawcross. Instead I get the late Richard Goodwin's right-hand man, and his friend, who, if I'm not mistaken, has some history of working for law enforcement. I'm honoured, guys, that you've taken the trouble.'

Frank didn't even have to look. He could feel Howie bristling. 'You need to watch what you say,' Frank said, 'if you ever want to get out of here.' A bad debt was one thing, snitching another – but Kenny had paid the price for knowing too much about Frank's association with a certain female copper, and letting on. If this guy was implying anything similar, God help him.

'Come on, guys,' the American said, sensing the danger. 'Moves like that? Someone's been trained professionally. How do you think I can tell?'

Was he backtracking, or ignorant? Frank wasn't sure he, or Howie, could risk it anyway. But they needed to know who he was working for, what exactly he was doing here. How far he was taking this. 'Why would you meet Kenny?'

'Information. He wanted to meet me, guys. But you know that. You set this up, didn't you? Where is Kenny, by the way?'

'Last time I saw him,' Frank said, raising the Glock, 'he was stuck in some mud.'

'There's a lot of it around here,' Howie said, behind Frank.

Frank glanced over his shoulder. It was dark now, the night breaking across the shore with the waves. Further out to sea, a sprinkling of lights, some white and flashing, some red and static, announced the presence of the wind turbines.

'Look, guys,' the American said, 'I was sent over here by an old family business to check you out. No big deal. They just want to know what they're getting for their money, who they're getting involved with. It's the way they do business, always have.'

'What's your name?' Howie said.

'Dennis. Do you have to keep pointing that thing at me?'

He stopped pointing it at Dennis, turned it on its side. It wasn't so heavy for something that could do so much damage – when loaded. 'I'm confused, Dennis,' Frank said, 'about the questions you've been asking and why you expect people to answer them.'

'I've not been carrying, if that's what you're thinking. In the UK? I'm not stupid. Doesn't seem much need, round here. Plenty of people will do and say anything for some extra cash. They don't need to be threatened.'

'But the tone of these questions, Dennis? They've been a little too personal, haven't they? Disgusting, from the sounds of it.'

'Not my fault what people want to tell me,' Dennis said. 'I asked simple enough questions. All very politely, even if my time here was running out.'

'You can say that again,' Howie mumbled. He was now standing between Dennis and the car park, a big solid shape. He looked like he'd be happy to stand there all night.

'Look, if you don't mind, I've got a plane to catch,' Dennis said.

'We haven't finished,' said Frank.

'Can we get off this beach, at least? Have a civilised conversation out of the wind?' Dennis wiped his mouth on the sleeve of his fine jacket.

Frank looked to Howie. Howie looked the other way.

'I might be able to help you guys with something,' Dennis then offered.

Frank could feel great clumps of sand in his shoes. His phone was going yet again. Fuck's sake. 'Yeah?' he said. He was sick of the beach as well.

'Those street dealers who wound up dead?' Dennis said. 'What I heard was they hooked themselves up with a new supplier, keen on exclusive distribution rights, fast.'

'What they always want,' came Howie's voice, louder this time.

'Yarmouth, Lowestoft, Norwich,' continued Dennis, 'the whole region is what they're after. They're happy to equip their operatives as well. Not so happy when some of that equipment goes missing. Who would be? The price of those things, round here.'

Dennis was looking straight at Frank. Straight at the Glock still in Frank's hand.

'Old school, I'd say,' continued Dennis. 'They can be brutal. Not sure my employers want to be investing in an environment where this sort of thing goes on, out of their control. Not quite sure what they see in the region in any case. Atlantic City in the winter's warmer.'

'You wouldn't happen to know how I can get hold of these lovely fellows, would you?' Frank said.

'You haven't met them already?' Dennis said. 'They're driving around town as if they already own the place.'

'Don't tell me,' said Frank. 'Three guys in a stupid white Hummer.'

Dennis nodded. 'You got it.'

Frank tried to catch Howie's eye, but it was too dark. Howie would have taken note, however. He always watched, listened – Britt's eyes and ears, as much as she looked out for him. What people did for love, Frank thought. Because they weren't in it just for the money, that was for sure. They'd been offered enough over the years.

'Are you going to get that?' Dennis said.

Frank realised his phone was going for about the fifth time straight. He turned seaward, pulling it from his jacket pocket. Saw that it was Tatty. He stepped further away, pressed the answer button. 'I'm busy,' he said.

'It can't fucking wait, Frank,' came Tatty's breathless reply. 'Where are you? We've got a problem, lying on Simon's couch.'

39

'Fuck,' said Zach, opening the front door. 'Don't tell me someone's taken your keys.'

'Sorry, darling, I'm tired and filthy, and my house keys are at the bottom of my bag somewhere, and I saw the lights on down here.' His mum pushed past him, bringing a cloud of thick night air seasoned with salt and something he couldn't place. A perfume perhaps, but not his mother's normal scent. She dropped her bag so it clattered loudly on the shiny hardwood flooring – too loudly. 'I wanted to get inside without touching anything.' She looked at her hands. 'Yuk.'

'Where the hell have you been?' Zach closed the front door firmly, turned towards her. He was going to make sure they got the locks changed. Didn't like the idea of what Clara might do with the keys. It had gone eleven.

His mum was kicking off her shoes now, which were smothered with light grey mud. She picked them up carefully, walked over to the hall closet, threw them inside. Came back for her bag. What did she have in there? Oh, he suddenly had an idea. She rushed for the stairs, still wearing her mac. Mud was caked on the bottom of her trousers, and all over the back of her mac as well.

'Mum,' Zach said, 'where the fuck have you been? I've been sitting here, getting anxious, man.'

She stopped before the first step. 'That's not like you. There's no need to worry, darling. I need to take a shower, wash this muck off, then I'll be fine. We're all fine.'

'Fine?' said Zach. He'd had a miserable evening, taking the rest of the gear on his own. Playing *Call of Duty*. Waiting for Clara to text – to say sorry. Which she hadn't. Having to answer the front door, more than once. 'Someone came round for you.'

'Who?' She turned to face him.

'Some old creep. Tall guy, but with a massive gut. You know what I mean? Horrible long greasy hair.'

'What did he want?'

'You.'

'You said.'

'He had something for you, an envelope.'

'Where is it?'

'I put it in the kitchen, I think.'

'What's in it?'

Zach shrugged. 'A disk?'

'You opened the envelope?'

'I didn't need to. I could tell. What's on it?' he asked.

Tatty sighed. 'I'm exhausted, Zach. It's been a very long day.'

'So, what's on it?'

'You sure you didn't check?'

'I don't have a computer that plays disks. Mine are too modern, Mum.'

'It's work-related,' she said. 'A bit of corporate spying.' She winked. 'I'll deal with it in the morning.'

'What happened to the jeep?' Zach said. 'It disappeared about eight. They were there to protect us, no? And this guy, looking like a zombie, can just walk up?'

'More important things for it to do, I guess. Frank thinks we're safe enough for now,' she said. 'Various problems have been taken care of.'

'Not all of them. You want to know about the keys? Nina's keys?'

'Shit, I almost forgot.'

'They were stolen, by her fucking daughter.'

'That sweet girl?'

'Yeah, right.'

'Nothing to worry about there then either.'

'Don't fucking believe it.'

'What's going on here, Zach? I can't even get up the stairs. I'm tired and filthy. Let me just have a shower.'

'It's going to be like this, is it, Mum?'

She'd climbed a couple of steps, swung back his way, her bag hitting her leg. 'What's that supposed to mean?'

'You sneaking around, coming in at all hours, covered in shit.'

'I am your mother.'

'Maybe you should behave like one.'

'I'm going to try and ignore that, Zach.'

'Have you got that gun in your bag?'

'Zach, I've said this before: whatever I do, now Dad's not around, with the business and everything connected to it, is for you lot – you, Sam and Ben. I'm not saying it's always going to be easy, but you're going to have to trust me.'

'Fuck's sake!'

'What's up with you? I thought you went to Norwich, shopping.'

'You been there recently?' All he could taste was tobacco, and the burn from the bump. His throat was so dry. He wanted a drink, and not fucking Diet Coke. What had he been thinking? But he could do with some more bump. Perhaps he would score some from Owen, when he saw him tomorrow. Get it direct from the source. Uncut. He'd played his part in bringing it over here, after all. Zach still couldn't fucking believe that. The risk, the fucking risk, his dad had put him in. His own son. He had to have some dividend.

But Frank had warned him more than once to stay away from Rare and Yare. Zach sniffed, trying to dredge some moisture from somewhere, the last molecules of toot too. Did Frank know everything? Wasn't Frank now telling his mum that they were safe? Various problems having been taken care of. No jeep, no danger. There. Zombies were easy enough to knock out of the way, weren't they?

'Who is she?' his mother said, hesitating on the stairs with purpose this time.

'What do you mean?'

'Clara? Is that who?'

'No, it's fucking not.'

'Let's have a drink, Zach, when I get out of the shower,' she said. 'Champagne? I think there's a bottle left.'

'Sure,' he said.

'Then we can have a talk. Not that I'm the world's best expert on relationships.' She laughed, weakly.

'It's not Clara.'

'Whoever she is — she's a lucky girl,' his mother said, finally making some headway up the stairs.

'How come there was all that champagne in the fridge anyway?'

'It wasn't for your father's fucking birthday, I can tell you that,' she said, without looking over her shoulder. 'Sometimes you just need a lift, don't you? Who knows what's round the corner.'

Who the fuck was she? Where the fuck had she been? Maybe he was liking his mum more and more.

40

Tatty pulled on her jeans, an old V-neck sweater, fawn, cashmere, that had been lying on the bench at the foot of her bed. Yes, it had once been Rich's, but it had shrunk, or had never fitted him, or it was the wrong colour. She couldn't remember. She looked about for some mules, the flats. Couldn't immediately see them, so she walked over to the French window in bare feet. Sun was streaming onto the balcony. She opened the doors to the smell of sea and warmth. It was warm today, already.

She glanced at her watch. It was nearly noon. She shook her head, not believing how well she'd slept. But she didn't want to think about what time she finally got to bed, after her heart-to-heart over the last bottle of champagne with her youngest. She couldn't believe she'd missed the fact that he'd met someone in Ibiza, a local. He was all over the place, even talking about rushing back there, poor kid.

At least the other two would be here soon. Sam had persuaded her big brother to come straight back with her. They'd be able to help cheer up Zach. He'd have to wait until after the funeral before he flew off to the Balearics, though, and then he'd have to return sharpish if he were to hit freshers' week. Loughborough still seemed a world away.

She wasn't going into the office today; she'd decided that before she'd opened her eyes. She needed to let Sian know, and she wondered whether Simon would be in, keeping up appearances. 'Jess has gone back to her sister's,' would be his story, for the time being. At some point he'd have to declare her missing. But Frank reckoned that, without a body, without any evidence, the police would struggle to make a case. Besides, he had connections, didn't he. Knew how to get attention diverted. As it was, they'd buried her under a ton of mud, on a lonely corner of Breydon Water, beyond a thick, wide stretch of tall reeds – Frank and Simon doing the digging and the lifting. She'd stayed on the bank, keeping an eye out, not believing how quick and easy it was to make someone disappear, and cover tracks, round here. But they were lucky the tide was out. Lucky too that Frank knew what he was doing. Local knowledge for you.

Marine Parade was stark under the piercing early autumn sun. She was not surprised to discover the Mercedes jeep was gone, nor that the car park at the end of the clifftop was filling up. A variety of saloons and small, blobby hatchbacks had jostled their way to the key spots on the front row. They were facing out to a sea that had gone the colour of cold steel under the warm white glare. A few ships were hugging the horizon. Gulls, fat as pigs, swooped inland. Mobility scooters were trundling, toy-like, along the upper esplanade. What a position this would make for a sniper. She was going to take shooting lessons, as well as business management classes. It wasn't all about media, communication, getting your message across. The phrase 'leadership through experience and expertise' came to her. One of Rich's? She wasn't so sure.

Tatty reached for her phone, which was on the bedside table. There were a number of missed calls, some voicemails, some texts. What did she have a PA for? She tapped the screen, put the device to her ear, was halfway to her bedroom door when Sian answered.

'Sorry to bother you, Mrs Goodwin,' Sian said. 'I've been trying to get hold of you.'

'So I see,' Tatty said.

'Are you coming in today, Mrs Goodwin?'

'It's Tatty,' Tatty sighed.

'I've arranged the meeting with Amit Sharma and Will Keene. It's for this afternoon, at two. It's the only time they could both do this week.'

'You'll have to cancel it,' Tatty said. 'Family matters. Tell them I'll see them tomorrow.' The company lawyer and an accountant? She was paying them. Her terms.

'I don't think that will be possible.'

'Tell them I'll see them tomorrow at two.'

'OK. I'll do my best.'

'Is Simon in?'

'He was in earlier, rushing around preparing. He's off to the States this afternoon, via Amsterdam.'

'He's rearranged that already, has he?' He hadn't mentioned anything about going to the States last thing yesterday. 'Yes. The flights were no problem to book. It's only the early morning flights from Schiphol that are usually full.' There was a pause and Tatty imagined Sian making a big O with her heavily made-up lips. 'Will you be going to Athens in place of your husband?' she asked. 'Simon said that you'd be the person to talk to about that. There have been some emails. Do you need me to arrange anything for you?'

'That's going to have to wait,' Tatty said. Maybe forever. She thought of Sam and Ben's imminent arrival. Perhaps they'd all walk down to the basin in the sunshine, get some chips, wander to the end of Gorleston Pier, watch the giant ships sail in, the way they used to. Zach was looking quite pale yesterday, his tan having faded even faster than hers. She looked down at her old sweater, her jeans, her bare white feet. She felt so comfortable at home this morning. Necessary. Hungry also. She hadn't even had breakfast. 'Have you seen Frank today?' she asked, staring at her closed bedroom door. It was such an insipid colour, such a bland door. But the statements she'd made with it. And Rich. He was forever slamming doors. He once caught Zach's finger – on purpose, she had always suspected. The tip went purple, the nail eventually coming off.

'No. Is he meant to be coming in?'

'Only asking.' She ended the call and opened her bedroom door, feeling claustrophobic, not at all relaxed and comfortable. Or hungry. She ran down the stairs, calling for Zach once she was at the bottom. She wasn't expecting a reply and she didn't get one.

She headed into the kitchen, seeing the sun swamping the back garden, though the dining table was still in shadow. She'd tidied away the empty bottle and glasses last night, but the envelope was still there, its contents no longer seeming particularly urgent, or necessary. She didn't want to touch it. Jess was dead. She was pleased Stuart had come to his senses. He could be handy, going forward. Pleased too that Zach had not been able to watch his father's last moments. No one should have to see that.

The floor was cool on her bare feet, the coffee machine in need of warming up. She was still desperate for a shot of caffeine. A call to Frank couldn't wait, however. Why had Simon rushed off without telling her?

'Hi,' she said, as Frank answered on the second ring. 'Where are you?'

'In the garden,' he said, 'doing some clearing. Beautiful day.'

'Simon's on his way to the States. Did you know that?'

'No, but I'm not surprised.'

'Shouldn't I have been told?'

'Where are you?'

'At home.'

'I could ask you why you are not in the office, but that might sound cheeky.'

'It might,' Tatty said, not sure she could get the coffee machine loaded one-handed. 'The truth is Sam and Ben will be here shortly.'

'That's nice,' Frank said.

'It would have been Rich's birthday today,' Tatty said.

'I know,' Frank said. 'But he never made a big deal out of birthdays, did he?'

'Stuart – you know, the guy from Admiralty Steel, who works for Graham Sands?'

'Your mole?' Frank chuckled.

'Yeah, him. He came round here last night – left a disk.'

'Well, you've offered to pay him more than a few quid, haven't you? He was going to come up with something.'

'The thing is, we can't play it. Our computers are too modern.' She laughed.

'Technology for you. Might not be suitable for family viewing in any case.'

'That's what I thought. You know what's on it?'

'I'd ask you over, Tatty, I've an old machine somewhere, but there's something else I want to watch this afternoon.'

'You certain you know what's on the disk?' she said.

'The number of cameras plastered to the back of Admiralty Steel – you saw them yourself. I've a good idea what one of them must have picked up.'

'Yeah?' Tatty scrunched her bare toes on the smooth stone floor.

'We need to meet,' said Frank, 'and I'll explain. This evening? Bring the disk, if you want.'

'I don't know where you live, Frank.' She could hear birdsong and a faint breeze. He was in his garden.

'I'll text you. By the way, keep a close eye on Zach today, will you?'

'Sure. Why?' She thought she heard a car thump onto the forecourt and pull up outside the front of her house.

'He's stubborn.'

'Like his father was.'

'Yeah, but Rich wasn't always stupid.'

'Could have fooled me.'

331

'Look, something'll be going down at Rare and Yare. Zach still thinks Owen owes him money. Zach likes his gear, too, Tatty, sorry to have to tell you.'

'How the hell do you know all this?'

'Call it a trade, one of many that we have to make, and a bit of intuition. Knowing a Goodwin.'

'Fuck you, Frank.'

'Rich used to say that.'

Tatty threw her phone onto the counter next to the coffee machine, stepped towards the kitchen door and out into the blinding hall, just as Sam and Ben came through the opened front door, along with direct sunlight and fresh sea air – the best things this part of the world had to offer. She had her arms around Sam first, pulling her into a tight hug. She couldn't believe it had only been a couple of days.

Ben was hovering awkwardly to the side, in his long-limbed, emotionally stilted way. Tatty let go of Sam and willed Ben to give her a hug. 'Come here, darling,' she said, impatient. He put his arms around her then. He didn't pull her in tight, but his lips brushed her cheek, before he straightened up, backed away.

'Hi, Mum,' he said.

'Thanks for coming home,' Tatty said. 'It was tough without you two. Tougher than I thought. Zach and I made do, but it wasn't the same. The four of us together, this feels complete.'

'Where is Zach, Mum?' Sam asked. 'My poor baby brother – love-torn.'

'Still in bed,' Tatty said.

'Did he tell you about this person in Ibiza?' Sam said.

'He did,' Tatty sighed.

'Why didn't he mention her when he first got back?' Sam said.

'Maybe he didn't realise he was going to miss her,' Tatty said, her mind flicking to Nathan. Zach couldn't have fallen in love with this girl, whoever she was, at his age. It had to be a sex thing. But she had fallen in love with Rich at that sort of age. Almost instantly. It took her years to fall out of love with him, long after the sex died.

'I'm going to get him up,' Sam said, heading for the stairs, taking them two at a time. 'We've got stuff to organise, haven't we?'

Tatty was left in the wide, empty hall with Ben, feeling an awkwardness almost immediately descended. 'You got off work OK, darling?' she asked. He was still standing stiffly. Even as a kid he didn't like to be cuddled. Maybe he'd start to thaw, now his bullying bastard of a father was where he belonged.

'Yes, of course,' he said. 'They understand. To be honest, I had other things I needed to do in London anyway.'

'I know you did,' Tatty said, smiling. 'I hope she works out.'

'We'll see.' He looked away, at the still wide-open front door. He walked over, shut it gently. The hall went dim. 'Sam said you were thinking of oak?'

Tatty looked at her eldest, striding back towards her. She wasn't sure about the chinos he was wearing, or his shirt. Seemed a bit too corporate for a man so young. But Rich at his age looked no more casual. 'Oak?'

'Dad's coffin.'

'Yes. He loved oak, didn't he? Look at this stupid hall.'

'Seems a waste,' said Ben, 'for a coffin. What's wrong with cardboard?'

'That's what Sam wants.'

'Better for the environment.'

'And you know what your father thought about that.' She laughed, loud and true.

'What about Zach, what's he say?'

'I haven't asked him yet,' Tatty said, calmer now.

'Mum?' Sam was coming down the stairs as fast as she had gone up them. 'Zach's not in his room.'

'His car, is that here?' Tatty thought of Frank, telling her to keep a close eye on Zach today. Some operation going on at Rare and Yare. She couldn't fail as a mother any more.

Ben had flung open the front door, disappeared outside. He soon came swooping back. 'No, the Mini's gone.'

'Frank,' Tatty said, 'we need Frank. Zach has to be stopped.'

'Have you ever managed to stop him doing anything you didn't want him to do?' said Sam.

'This is serious, Sam,' Tatty said. 'Things are different now.'

'About fucking time,' said Ben.

41

'Let me tell you this first,' Frank said. 'Simon wasn't on his way to Amsterdam last Wednesday evening. He took a flight in the morning, the six ten. He was booked on the eight ten the previous day, but he didn't make it. I'm not sure he ever intended to take it. Jess left early the Thursday morning also – she was heading for her sister's, earlier than she'd been planning, so she told me. What I'm saying is, they were both in Yarmouth that evening.'

'You sure?' Tatty hadn't touched her tea, even though it was in a nice china cup, with saucer. Everything in Frank's house was immaculate, tasteful, well considered. Bradwell was a conservative, peaceful suburb of Yarmouth. But it wasn't homely. It was all far too ordered, bare almost. Even the garden.

'Simon's behaviour yesterday?' Frank was saying. 'There were always going to be questions. I'd like to see her phone – not that we ever will. What messages she received, and when. Was anyone else involved? Or did Jess and Simon cook this up together?' Frank was drinking his own tea happily enough. He'd loaded it with sugar.

'You think Jess could have played both Simon and Rich?'

'Simon had issues that someone like Jess was always going to manipulate,' Frank said, before taking another slurp. 'But if he had nothing to do with Rich's death, why was he so keen to get rid of Jess?' He was shaking his massive head.

Tatty shook her own head. Relief and anger were bubbling away. Some disbelief too. The police round here. But there were also Frank's connections, not to mention his guile and guts? Boy, was she going to stick close. Give him a pay rise too, if he'd accept it.

'Should we have a look at that disk then?' Frank eventually said.

He got up, went over to the old laptop on the glass coffee table in front of them. As he was inserting the disk, tapping at the keyboard, Tatty glanced out of the cramped window at the three vehicles on the wide expanse of gravel. She wasn't sure where she'd been meant to park, as there appeared to be a number of plants poking through the stones. Not exactly weeds either. Frank's Range Rover was the only vehicle that seemed to be in the correct place, over by the fence. Zach's Mini, like her Merc, was on the wonk, crushing rare flora no doubt.

At least Zach hadn't yet zoomed off. She could see him in the driver's seat, on his phone, smoking – smoking! – waiting for her to finish with Frank. Would he follow her straight home? 'Do what you have to do, kids,' he'd said, stepping outside, shortly after she'd arrived. 'I've been enough fucking trouble for one day. Cheers, Frank, for saving my bacon. Should have listened.'

'OK, Tatty?' Frank said. 'Not too much glare on the screen? It's grainy, black and white. Grey all over, more like.'

'I can see,' she said, watching closely.

The quay was empty, except for swirls of heavy rain. Electric light crept across the tarmac and out onto the river.

Some seconds went by. Frank was breathing heavily. Tatty was trying not to breathe at all.

A car appeared, driving slowly on the wrong side of the barrier. A series of stilted manoeuvres followed, as the car shifted round, between two capstans, so it faced the river. More rain came down, plenty of it horizontal. There was some movement inside the vehicle, but it was impossible to tell what exactly was happening.

'The thing I hate,' said Tatty, thinking of Zach, thinking of everything, not bearing the peace and quiet, 'is the lying.'

'You not used to that?'

'From your kids?'

'Like I said.'

A car door opened, and another. One in the front, one in the back. Two figures got out. One person then walked round to the other side, the driver's side. Opened that door, bent inside. The other figure was close by, standing upright. Tatty could see shoulder-length hair catching the wind and the rain. It looked like Jess was carrying a compact umbrella, not opening it. With that wind? The other person stood back, straightening. He was trim, Simon's height. Almost instantly the car started to crawl forward. Simon shut the driver's door as it did so.

The screen went blank before the front wheels were over the edge.

'What?' screamed Tatty.

'Even if the police were to get hold of this, I'm not sure there's enough,' said Frank. 'They knew exactly what they were doing. Seems someone at Admiralty Steel had a hand as well.'

'Fuck,' said Tatty. 'Sands? Is he involved?'

'It could have been any number of people,' said Frank, 'not just out on that quay.'

'I'm getting it,' said Tatty.

'It's a shady place,' he said, 'for—'

'Is that meant to be funny?' she interrupted. 'What if Simon never comes back from Las Vegas?'

'He'll come back. People like him wouldn't survive long there, from what I've heard. Besides, I've got a new friend who I'm sure will help us out if Simon doesn't return of his own free will.'

'And when he does return, then what?'

'You tell me.'

Red Hot Front
Harry Brett

Tatiana Goodwin has finally begun to piece her life back together after the events of the past year. Having taken over her late husband Rich's empire, Tatty has put together a massive deal to capitalise on his dirty dealings – and hopefully extricate herself from a life of crime she'd been unwillingly drawn into.

But following a suspicious fire in the firm's new HQ, and a number of unexplained deaths in the town, it soon becomes clear that there's more than one person who's after the Goodwin family assets. With her daughter in a rocky relationship and her teenage son Zach beginning to follow in the footsteps of his gangster father, everything is getting a little too close to home for Tatty's liking . . .

As the family is pulled further into the criminal underworld she sought to protect them from, Tatty has some difficult decisions to make – before her enemies make them for her.

corsair